Ko-Foe

The Story of a Nigerian, Muslim, Family in the New York Diaspora

A Novel by Lande Yoosuf

"In Ko-foe, Lande Yoosuf masterfully explores what happens when a prodigal daughter of the Nigerian diaspora grows up on her terms in Brooklyn. Ko-foe is a brilliant debut from a novelist as multidimensional as the characters she creates. Fans of fast-paced television and reality show drama will adore this book. Watch out for the fire that emits from Yoosuf's mighty pen. Her words will undermine even your most steadfast assumptions about success, womanhood, and what it means to be one in a family."

Melanie Beth Curran
Writer, Musician, Professor
Montclair State University

"Once you pick up "Ko-Foe" you won't want to put it down. Lande creates dynamic characters that you are bound to resonate with. She uses a Nigerian lens to tell a relatable story regardless of your background!"

Alesa Andrew-Breuer
Senior Director of Operations, Digital Video
People TV! (A People Magazine Platform)

"I was featured on the short film that led to this book & I'm ecstatic that more people get to enjoy the full length of this fantastic story. Read, enjoy, and thank you, Lande!"

Gina Yashere,
Comedian, Actor, Television Showrunner
"Bob Loves Abishola" on CBS

"'Ko-Foe is an insightfully funny and informative look into the lives of different family upbringings, traditions, and cultures. This is a book for the new generation of Black readers!"

Lesley Martin-Nunnery
Producer
"Red Table Talk" on Facebook Watch

ISBN: 979-8-218-10624-9

ACKNOWLEDGMENTS

I knew I always wanted to write a novel and here I am! This experience has been gratifying, humbling, and nerve wrecking at the same time. My personal dedication and the will of Olodumare, my ancestors and spirit guides pushed me past the finish line of completing "Ko-Foe", but I also wouldn't have gotten here without the help of some very dear friends, colleagues, and family members, some of whom I have listed below:

- **Oladimeji Alabi** – Also known as my beloved fiancé. You were my very first cheerleader and made me believe I could write a novel. Thank you for always pushing me towards greatness and reminding me that I am amazing. You are the best thing that happened to me, and I love you.

- **My Immediate Family: Mommy, Daddy, Yemisi** – I know you don't entirely understand all that I do professionally but thank you for always giving me the space to figure it out. You have contributed to my self expression in varying ways, and I wouldn't be who I am without you. I promise that all the sacrifices you've made for me won't be in vain. This book is evidence of that. I love you and thank you.

- **My Extended Family: The Core Families and Beyond** – You are the first to show up, last to leave. You've donated to my projects and offered support, resources, connections, prayers, and other grand gestures towards aiding in my success. My experiences with you all shaped my development as a Nigerian American woman. This story wouldn't have materialized without your existence. I love you and thank you.

- **Alesa Andrew** – My business sister. We are kindred spirits, and our experiences repeatedly confirm this truth. You are an amazing colleague, an amazing friend, and a beautiful person inside and out. I love you dearly.

- **Anoor Ajala** – I am *so proud* of you. You are blossoming into an A-grade professional. The "Ko-Foe" book tour wouldn't exist if it wasn't for your hard work. You're doing an outstanding job!

- **Jasu Sims** – My trusted publicist and friend. We have come a long way from our origins in the early 2000s. Thank you for working with me and being flexible with all that I had going on. You are thorough, professional and on point with all that you do.

- **Abbesi Akhamie** – What did I do to deserve a friend like you?! Your commitment to our friendship is forcing me to show up in ways that make me uncomfortable but continue to pave the road to my success. You've been nothing short of an angel.

- **Lesley Martin** – When I called, you picked up and didn't hesitate to help me when you didn't have to. I truly am grateful for your friendship, your support, and your kindness. I can't wait for us to make the next hit series or film soon! Thank you.

- **Gina Yashere** – You are such a powerhouse and an inspiration. Thank goodness I casted you in "Second Generation Wedding." I knew you were a big deal and would continue to become a bigger deal. Congratulations on all your accomplishments! I can't wait for us to work on the long form motion picture version of "Ko-Foe" with you involved!

- **Melanin Magic** – Adeola, Del-Ann, Lauren, Modinat, Del-Ann, Brandi, and Tanya. You all have made a big impact on my life in varying ways. When I was going insane and trying to rub pennies together to make this novel, you stepped up without hesitation. You show up at every event; you help set up, clean up, you donate money and resources when needed… thank you so much ladies for being there for me throughout the years.

- **Jennifer Small** – My play cousin! Thank you for your out-pour of resources, support, introductions, and connections. The "Ko-Foe" book tour was elevated because of you. I know you don't think it's a big deal to give so freely, but your generosity means a lot to me.
- **Professor Melanie Curran** – My very first book editor. Your feedback convinced me I had something worth pursuing. You are an amazing human being, and I am beyond grateful for your support.
- **Jessica Ambres** – My second beta reader. I know you have discerning taste. Your response to my material fueled my desire to complete this book that was taking so much out of me. You are a wonderful friend and supporter of all that I do. I appreciate you.
- **My Therapist Ms. Lola** – Our sessions forced me to believe that I am indeed talented when many in the world attempted to prove otherwise. Working on myself with your help has been a game changer.
- **Katrice Boland** – I didn't realize how much I needed a professional coach. Thank you for reminding me I am indeed on track, and complications along the way always have solutions. You are a wonderful soul and I'm so glad that you continue to assist me in gaining perspective on how I can truly achieve my goals.
- **Mama Lynette and Baba Bill** – Your guidance has been life changing. This book wouldn't have happened without your advice.

I'm clear on how to move forward because I met you both. I am grateful to have you as elders advising me on my path to actualizing the life of my dreams.

- **Black Film Space Screenwriting Accountability Group** – Our group is designated for screenwriters, and when I declared that "Ko-Foe" is an adaption from a short film, my group cheered me on when I showed up for myself daily. Black Film Space means everything to me and has changed my life. I don't know where I would be on my artistic journey if it didn't exist.

- **Cast, Crew, Supporters, Screeners and Distributors of "Second Generation Wedding"**– The short film was the starting point, and I wouldn't be here without the existence of "Second Generation Wedding". Thank you for seeing the vision of my project and being a part of my origin story.

- **My Beloved Family, Friends, Supporters, Followers and Colleagues** – Thank you for every call, text, email, like, repost, RSVP, event booking… I am overcome with gratitude from your encouragement. You constantly confirm the strong promise of my artistic path. I love and appreciate you all!!!

Ko-Foe

The Story of a Nigerian, Muslim, Family in the New York Diaspora

A Novel by Lande Yoosuf

This novel is dedicated to the children of Black, African immigrants all over the world. I wrote this because I see you. Thank you.

CHAPTER 1

"If I decide to marry you, will you learn how to make jollof the way I like it?"

Kofo Adebayo curves her lips into a tight smile, sipping her vodka tonic while leaning on the bar. She glances down at the almost empty glass, realizing that she needs another one to get through this conversation with yet another nameless West African banker, doctor, engineer or lawyer.

Kofo's oval, chocolate colored, perfectly beat face scans the room while he rambles on and she finally spots her saving grace walking into the Holiday African Professionals Happy Hour—her childhood friend Janelle. They make eye contact, happy to recognize each other.

"Thank you so much for the drink." Kofo gently touches his hand and puts her drink down at the bar before making a quick move to her Jamaican play cousin near the venue entrance.

"He was cute." Janelle grins and nudges Kofo's shoulder, waiting to hear another excuse to reject what seems to be a good catch.

Kofo rolls her eyes. "He was as flat as my drink. I'm hungry. Let's get out of here."

"Not until you find someone to get me a drink first." Janelle peels off her dark brown fur coat and lands it on a bar stool, revealing a perfectly tailored burgundy pantsuit with chunky gold jewelry. She looks expensive, which makes Kofo the better candidate for getting more spirits for the night.

Kofo marvels at her gorgeous friend as she straightens out the feminine curls framing her face. Everyone always asks her "what are you?" when they are together. While insulting, Kofo knows that her Indo-African features mean more than just a racial quandary. Her beauty was indeed different and Kofo willingly shrank herself in her company to avoid resenting something they both couldn't control.

Janelle picks a piece of lime pulp off of Kofo's full lips. Kofo loves when her friend shows interest in making her look just as good. She feels seen.

"You need a red lip, boo. Use those perfect lips and Nigerian cheekbones. That'll make the bar busy for us."

Kofo applies red lipstick that contrasts her smooth dark skin with ease, using her Chanel compact mirror. She straightens out her mid-sized afro, white silk button-down shirt, and camel-colored wool pleated skirt through a bar mirror. Her feet lit up a painful fire since changing into her brown knee-high boots in the Dunkin Donuts bathroom down the block, but it's doing the job of getting male attention and adding inches to her slender, petite, frame. Kofo may not be stunning, but she definitely is a cutie. A sexy cutie at that.

Before Kofo goes off to mingle, she feels a body hovering behind her.

"Hi ladies," her sister Eniola greets them, about to topple over with a heavy Louis Vuitton tote in one hand, and a Tumi computer bag in another. She drops her belongings on the floor next to Janelle's coat and exhales loudly after taking off her black floor-length Ralph Lauren coat with gold hardware.

Kofo turns around, raising her eyebrows. "Ennie?! What are you doing out on a school night? Does Cedric know you're here?"

Eniola laughs and shrugs off the question. "He's occupied with long hours. And shouldn't you be studying for your exams, Ms. Business school?", she quips.

"Already did that earlier today," Kofo shot back in a high pitched, sarcastic tone.

Kofo notices her sister is sweaty and studies her face long enough for Eniola to feel self-conscious. Eniola notes Kofo's stare, and smooths out her worn out weave, gliding her palm along the greasy strands. Eniola is better looking than both her sister and Janelle with smooth, warm chocolate skin, feminine dainty features, and a perfectly proportioned body that most Black women in her orbit envy—they called her a "dime piece" on her block as teenagers. Kofo encourages her to wear form fitting outfits that will turn heads, and bring attention to her beauty. But Eniola hides behind a modest wardrobe and the conservative grooming style of her peer group that skews a few years older than Kofo.

Janelle grabs Eniola's hand, spotting a thick diamond tennis bracelet. The stones blare off of Eniola's wrist, bordering into tacky territory.

"Oh my God!!! Did Cedric get that for you?!", Janelle squeals.

Eniola blushes out of embarrassment as the event-goers turn to the three ladies to discover the commotion. Eniola hides her hand, uncomfortable with all eyes on her.

"Shh! I want to surprise my friends with my new gift." Eniola gives them a pompous grin before searching for said party.

Kofo side-eyes her sister's unnecessary bragging. She hates her personality in this environment and remains quiet before her feelings become apparent.

Eniola swivels her head to a group of young African women in a far corner, feigning complete confidence in her new trinket before grabbing her things and walking off.

"So, when are we finally going to Nigeria for Ennie's wedding? Cedric sounds like a keeper," Janelle asks Kofo.

"Let's complete our mission for drinks first. I spotted someone." Kofo sees a guy on the other side of the bar with a fitted, dark grey sports coat. He looks away once Kofo signals mutual eye contact. He glances again and her almond-shaped eyes pierce his with intensity. Kofo walks in his direction, seducing him with her smile and slender legs encased by her stylish footwear.

***

"These fries hit every single time, yo." Kofo stuffs a Five Guys fry in her mouth as her Brooklyn accent peaks through a more relaxed atmosphere.

Janelle belches in response and they break out into laughter, ignoring the scores of drunk, young, professionals swarming them who also left Thursday night mixers in nearby West Village bars.

"I feel you're looking for your Nigerian husband at these events. When are you going to really start networking, Kofo?" Janelle twists her mouth to form a playful grin.

"Isn't that covered by the high cost of business school?" She sucks her teeth at Janelle's question.

"I know, but you should make solid contacts, just in case. It's always good to get connects for a future pivot."

Janelle gets sloppy and takes off her red bottoms, crossing her feet in the bright red booth. Drunk Janelle amuses Kofo. She is a Brooklyn girl to the core—a fast talker, has a thick accent, is confident, swagged out, a hustler, and committed to a luxury lifestyle with a slight Caribbean flair. They met during the first semester of freshmen year shortly after joining the Black Students Association in undergrad at Stonybrook University. Janelle was the "it girl", drawing the attention of horny, eager upperclassmen that fought over the new, cute face on campus. Her instant popularity made the women on campus jealous, but not with Kofo. They bonded over their indifference towards community peen, and their friendship sped up quickly. Janelle saw beyond Kofo's jittery, inexperienced eyes. She inspired Kofo to bring out her inner vixen after many nights of them discussing their relief from overbearing, strict Black mothers who emphasized academic achievement at the expense of social skills or forming an identity beyond the voices of parental authority that took up much space in their heads. Janelle's hooptie or The Long Island Railroad was their transportation of choice to shop at high end shopping outlets with their work study money, each buying mostly skirts, crop tops, short dresses and fashionable shorts to make sure they could borrow each other's clothes despite their significant height difference. They were on a mission to upgrade their lives after being on lockdown as teens, longing for the lifestyles they worshipped on shows like Sex in the City or Girlfriends. If there wasn't a party to attend, they spent time in their dorm rooms braiding or styling each other's hair every other night.

Kofo and Janelle extended their friendship, built on blossoming into women after graduation, but life is impeding their ability to spend as much time as they used to over the years. They made good use of the mixer for a much-needed outing, picking up where they last left off. Kofo longs for their college days on nights like this. She doesn't have to choose her persona and can just be; other times, Kofo dabbles in and out of her Brooklynese and inner-city energy depending on the setting to avoid judgement of being seen as "ghetto". Hanging out with Janelle feels like a reunion, a reminder of what made her who she is.

An obnoxious group of white 20-somethings barge in, yelling about any and everything. A fighting, drunk couple trails them, and Kofo looks away in discomfort.

"Fuck him, Kofo," Janelle responds before taking another bite out of her burger.

Lande Yoosuf

"Fuck who?" a male voice joins their conversation and slides into the booth next to Janelle as Kofo eats another fry.

"Her fuckbio ex." Janelle looks at the guy, signaling to Kofo her assessment of him potentially being one as well.

Kofo inspects him and knows right away that he isn't. He is just as fine, just as charming, just as good of a dresser, and smells just as good. But his earnest expression says differently. They convey what Kofo has been looking for what she couldn't find in her twenty-eight years. He's making her back tingle.

"We shouldn't speak ill of the dead ladies." He reveals a megawatt smile with straight, white teeth that contrast his brown complexion.

Wow, Kofo thinks, ogling at his perfect jawline that peeks out from a well-trimmed goatee. His broad nose aligns with his face, highlighting his perfect, symmetrical features.

"This is Janelle." Kofo gestures her hand to her friend, counting herself out. She's used to it and typically meets guys when she is alone.

"It's nice to meet Janelle, but who are you?" Kofo expects him to steal a peek at her breasts or any other body part that will inspire the pursuit of a one-night stand, but he maintains focus on her face. It gives her an opportunity to stare longer into his inviting, almond-shaped eyes that glisten with tranquility across the table. She is connecting with what she is interpreting as kindness looking back at her. This form of seduction is unfamiliar to Kofo, intriguing her to know more.

"Kofo. My name is Kofo."

"Do you mean Kofoworola?"

7

Janelle frowns. "Kofo-what?"

"Yes. That's my full name, but everyone calls me Kofo."

They stare at each other for a few moments because Kofo cannot believe this man is also Nigerian. And British.

"Do you want me to get you more fries, Kofo? We can share them."

"Yes, please."

He gets up from the booth, joining the long line to grant Kofo's wish for more fries.

"What's your name?" she shouts.

He turns around to look at her and grins. "Tunde. Babatunde," then focuses again on his task.

Kofo smiles, staring at Janelle with wide eyed, composed, excitement.

Tunde returns, sitting next to Kofo this time. He looks at her, smiles again, lays napkins on the table, and uses his groomed, masculine hands to open the brown paper bag filled with fries. He does it with extreme caution and precision, as though he's performing surgery.

"Let me tear that up for you." Kofo reaches her arm out to assist but he stops her with a with a certain head nod.

"Oh, no... the grease hits better this way. Once you lay all the fries out, the oil to fry ratio is perfect."

"They have Five Guys in London?"

"How do you know I'm from London? I could be from somewhere else in the UK."

"Really? We're doing this? You have a thick ass accent." Kofo grabs a fry. "Don't worry. I think you sound sophisticated." As she chews, something feels off. "Where's the salt?"

8

Tunde grabs three packets of salt from his pocket, aligns them symmetrically, and tears off the top of each at the same time. He salts the fries in a circular motion.

"I feel like I'm watching a magic show."

Tunde chuckles. "My dad has high blood pressure, so I'm conscious of how I consume sodium."

Kofo raises her eyebrows, impressed.

"So, what are you? Scientist or something?"

"Finance."

Janelle gives off a "humph", throwing off their banter.

Tunde stares back and forth at them both. "What?"

Kofo telepathically interprets her reaction. "African men in finance are often Yoruba demons." His outfit is a bit demon-esque. He has on a black calf-length fitted wool coat with a fine gold link chain resting on a black turtleneck sweater, skinny black creased trousers and black suede Gucci loafers. The logo for his shoes is visible, but tastefully small. His attention to detail is apparent because it leaves people with the right impression he wants to express—that Tunde is a fly and he knows it.

"Yoruba demons are everywhere." Tunde maintains composure, giving a naughty grin on one side of his mouth, clarifying that he's familiar with this kind of interrogation.

Janelle leans into the table in his direction. "How can my friend know you won't lead her to the pits of hellfire?" She and Kofo look into the pile of fries as though something is going to jump out, then tell them everything they need to know about Tunde.

Kofo giggles at Janelle.

Tunde cocks his head to the side, still grinning. "I make no guarantees about how someone will experience me."

Kofo blushes, realizing that she wants to find out for herself.

***

The seats in the theater are hard and stiff, but Kofo tolerates the discomfort because it means she will get to know more about this new guy from London. What she's learning so far is that he's not as by-the-book as she thought. He's twenty minutes late for the play he invited her to and now they won't have much time to talk until the intermission. She isn't excited to see a performance about a failed marriage during colonial West Africa, although they had several discussions about history during their long phone calls. She figured he assumed it would interest her because of their shared backgrounds, which she appreciates. As her mind continues racing on his whereabouts, hoping that she didn't get stood up—Tunde slides right into the seat next to her.

"Hey."

"Hey…"

"I'm so sorry for being late. I'm still trying to figure out these trains, even a year later."

Bizarre. He lives in Harlem near the 2 train at 125th street. The same train line as the theater in Times Square. It's a straight shot with no transfers, and Kofo knows this. She says nothing, though.

She feels Tunde studying her face as she attempts to hide her irritation.

"You look cold. Do you want my jacket?"

"Sure. Thanks."

Tunde removes his coat, then stops and pauses. "Let's leave and just take a walk around the city."

"What?!"

The lights go dim and an announcement goes off via the theater speakers. Ladies and gentlemen, the show will begin in two minutes. Please head to your seats.

"You paid for these tickets, Tunde. Let's stay."

Tunde touches her hand. "I don't give a shit about this play. I want to talk to you and I was late. We can go."

"Are you sure?"

"Yes. Very."

Kofo rises, following his lead out of the theater.

***

Kofo and Tunde walk twenty blocks from Times Square while Kofo points out more specific details about New York City outside of cliched facts regarding her hometown.

"That's Madison Square Park." Kofo points at the entrance on 23rd street and Broadway. "Never walk through there at night unless you want a troupe of rats to follow you home."

Tunde laughs, grimacing at the thought.

Kofo stops strolling and turns to Tunde, pushing them to have an intimate moment.

"Why did you move to New York and to America?"

"Well… I honestly always wanted to live here."

"Really? I thought Europeans hate Americans."

"I'm not European though."

"You know what I mean…"

"No matter what, I'm still a Yoruba demon." He grins at Kofo and starts walking again. She follows suit because the movement is keeping her warm. She is relieved that most of the snow from the storm a few weeks ago has melted, avoiding any damage to the boots she wore the night they met. Nothing but good luck has unfolded since breaking them in that evening.

Kofo rolls her eyes, smirking at his comment.

She hesitates for a few moments and then goes for it. "I have to tell you something."

"Are you married?"

Kofo lets out a hearty laugh. "Of course not."

"Kids? Diseases? Criminal background? Are you a psychopath—"

"Come on, seriously."

Tunde stops again and looks at her, more gently this time. "What is it?"

"I'm in the middle of a breakup right now. Like literally."

"Ok…? So?"

"We lived together and I'm moving out in a few days. We dated off and on for 7 years, and I'm newly single."

"You checked out before you ended it, basically. Probably a year or two ago, right?"

Kofo didn't want to admit it, but damn. He's right.

"About three years, actually."

"Savage. You kept a body you didn't want around for three years?! How many times did you cheat?" Tunde's ambivalence is stumping Kofo, but she does her best to keep up.

"Uh... I don't do that. But I masturbated a lot whenever he wasn't home."

"Was he small?"

"Oh my God, you're insane." She playfully pushes him, and he grabs her hand to pull her in. They are now facing each other.

"I don't care, Kofo. You're single, so I'm fine with it."

"Aren't you worried that I may have a lot of baggage?"

"We'll move slow. I'm not even 35 yet."

"Are you sure?"

"For Christ's sake..."

She giggles, and he leans all the way to kiss her on the corner of Broadway and 18th street.

***

Kofo pours a glass of sweet white wine in her Long Island City walk-up apartment kitchen with Afropop playing in the background. She chuckles at a selfie her father sent earlier while taking a morning power walk from her phone on the counter. He's been out of shape for a while and his growing belly concerns Kofo. Hopefully she can slowly convince him to become a pescatarian with her sweet pleas of grave concern for his health. Apparently, his doctor's stern warnings aren't getting through.

Kofo hears dangling keys right outside of the apartment door, interrupting her thoughts. She downs her glass of wine and her phone, then turns her back to the kitchen sink to wash the glass while avoiding eye contact with the person coming inside.

"Salaam, Kofo."

It's the fuckbio, and his name is Fahad. He's tall, cinnamon-colored, with dark hair and dark eyes. His skin is a few shades darker than a Bollywood archetype. Fahad often hunches over or stares downward, giving the appearance that he's shorter than 6'3" and it annoys the shit out of Kofo. His height is part of what makes everyone turn their heads when he walks into a room. But Fahad focuses on many things that take away from his ability to see what makes him special.

After walking in, Fahad watches her, hoping she'll turn back around so they can connect.

"Hi." She places the wine glass upside down on a dish rack, with her back still facing him.

He reaches into a reusable plastic bag and places containers of food on the counter while peeling off a pair of Air Max Nike sneakers. Fahad's feet always stink and Kofo has begged him to get a new pair. He has the money to buy whatever he wants with his high civil engineer salary, but insists on wearing the same type of clothes he's worn since they met in high school, committing to a lifestyle of "modesty."

"My mom said to give you some paratha stuffed with chicken, your favorite. There's also curry lentil with rice."

Kofo finishes drying her manicured hands, still backing him. She finally turns around and looks down at the containers. The familiar aroma from home-cooked food tempts her to fully dive in, but she restrains herself and looks away.

"Thanks," she says while staring past him, facing nowhere in particular.

Fahad makes his way around labeled boxes piled up everywhere before plopping onto the couch. Kofo watches him but doesn't move from the kitchen. When he's fully seated, he removes his soiled North Face puffer coat, taking in his apartment with fresh eyes. She observes him looking at the now empty walls and shelves, savoring the last moments of Kofo's good taste in home decor.

"Kofo… please sit next to me."

Kofo sighs and walks over, watching him bury his face in his hands before sitting down.

"Sweetie…"

"Don't call me that." Kofo is ready to spar with him, staring through the corner of her eyes with rage.

Fahad puts his hands down and faces her. "My father said sorry. Don't you think this is a dramatic response?"

Kofo looks away for a few moments before she finally lets it out.

"I can't be with you, Fahad. Your family will never accept me."

"That's not true. They love you!"

"No. They thought I would work because I am Muslim, but they forgot I am also Black."

"Sometimes they can be ignorant, that's their old school thinking. It has nothing to do with how they feel about you."

"Why do they refuse to call me by my Nigerian name, even when I ask them to? Why won't they ever call my dad back when he reaches out? I traveled all the way to California to nurse your sick sister, and not one of your family members called me to say thank you."

Kofo gets back up to the kitchen and grabs the bottle of wine from the counter to fill up the same glass she just washed.

"You shouldn't be drinking during Ramadan," Fahad watches her sip the glass as Kofo creates distance between them during a critical argument. He barely had a grip on her while they were together, but he holds nothing now. This conversation is a waste of time, but as usual he persists on a dead issue—this time it is their relationship.

"You shouldn't be having an affair with women from your parents' mosque. Not during any time of the year."

Fahad gets up to face Kofo across the counter.

"I've apologized, I cut her off, I've gone to counseling, I even went to Hajj to prove to you I am ready for change."

Kofo looks down at the kitchen island counter that was recently replaced. The only reason it got done was that she insisted Fahad call 311 to report the lazy property manager. He behaves like he doesn't know his rights as a tenant and they fought over that too. She hates the cheap quality faux granite the contractors used. It's heavily stained and worn, just like this conversation.

"I'm moving tomorrow morning. I can't do this anymore."

"Did you meet someone else?" Fahad's intuition is often on target, which made him great at manipulating Kofo to stay with him longer than she should've over the years. She shuffles, nervous to give him any hint of Tunde's existence.

Kofo looks up, staring at his face for a few moments to figure out how he sensed it. "No. I am just sure of what I want now."

"I hope you know I love you and will always love you. Even if a life with me isn't what you want."

That comment hits her hard with guilt. Too bad it's not enough to make her stay.

"I think it's best for you to marry someone from your culture. You and your family will be happier."

"You are my culture. You're Muslim, Kofo."

"I'm Nigerian first."

"He's also Yoruba, isn't he?"

"It's pronounced Yor-ru-baa." Kofo takes the bottle and the glass, then walks away towards the bedroom while slamming the door on her way in.

Fahad takes the plastic containers of food off of the counter and puts them in the fridge.

***

"I love this piece. It reminds me of my family house in Ogun State on my dad's side." Tunde holds a painting that he picked out of a box in Kofo's new apartment. It's a newly renovated, very large, two-bedroom unit. She loves the size of prewar spaces, the detailed crown molding, waxed wood floors and the echo that rings through the spacious units. It warrants the high rent prices, as opposed to the tiny places she lived during her years after college. Kofo balked at the rent being $3,000, but at least she has a fifth-floor view of Prospect Park via Ocean Avenue from her living room window.

Kofo walks over to Tunde's examination of the painting. It is an acrylic piece of a house built during the 1800s in Lagos. The color scheme inspiration is similar to the red clay grounds found throughout Nigeria. "I got it in Lagos, but Ogun state is where the actual painter was from."

"Score!" Tunde smiles and pecks Kofo on the lips. He's always smiling. It lifts her spirits.

Tunde continues to rummage through the box and pulls out a prayer rug.

"As Salaam Alaykum." He opens it, revealing a beautiful blue velvet material embossed with shiny gold threads that outline a mosque building structure in the center.

Kofo snatches the rug from him playfully. "I'll take that from your pork-infested hands, thank you."

"You should hang that up though, for real. It's beautiful and can go with your color scheme."

Kofo looks down at it, studying the rug's details. "I'm more of a neutral tones kind of lady, but that's not a bad idea."

Tunde continues unpacking items in her decor and accessories box, placing picture frames of family members on a wooden side table. He studies everyone in the images, including the portraits of Kofo with her father throughout the years in the larger frames compared to the others. He collects photos of her dad holding Kofo as an infant, her first day of school, high school graduation and a recent photo in front of a mosque. Kofo is wearing an elaborate jalabiya with a matching hijab. A banner with the words "EID Mubarak" is in the background, and she's leaning deep into her father's torso with a huge grin on her face.

Tunde finishes arranging the pictures and looks up to face Kofo.

"Do you pray five times a day?"

Kofo hates talking about religion, it reminds her of Fahad. "Sometimes. I follow certain things, but not everything." She avoids eye contact with Tunde and keeps her head down, rummaging through a box. Kofo doesn't want to make him feel bad for unintentionally triggering her.

"Do you want to continue being Muslim?"

"Yea, I do. But I want to practice it my way."

"What if it's against the doctrine?"

Her box is now empty, forcing Kofo to look up. She stares at the wall, hoping Tunde assumes she is brainstorming home decor ideas.

"I know a lot of religious people. And I don't think it has much of an impact on their character. I decided that my relationship with God will be informed by Islam, but ultimately in pursuit of being a better person regardless of what that looks like." Kofo turns around to look at him. "Do you like being Christian?"

"I never really thought about it, honestly. It's just something I do, a tradition that I follow because I assume it makes sense if my family's been doing it for so many generations, you know?"

Kofo nods. She totally gets it.

***

"How much did you put him to work?" Janelle asks, FaceTiming Kofo while lying in bed.

"He unpacked almost everything."

"He's winning me over a bit. I might just drop the demon from his title."

Kofo shakes her head, humored by her friend's assumption of authority over her love life.

"Don't forget about me, boo." Janelle smiles.

"Come on Janelle, don't say that."

"I just want you to be sure of what you want before Tunde whisks you away into his British castle."

"We're moving slow. Promise."

"Did you fuck him?"

Kofo hesitates.

"Oh God, what happened to your new ninety-day rule?!"

"We only did oral."

Janelle gives a disapproving look. "And???"

"It's perfect. Size, shape… it's even curved…"

"Hallelujah!" Janelle exclaims.

Kofo laughs, but is as worried as Janelle. Tunde consumes her thoughts, and she hates that he is not in her place, lying beside her.

"Listen. Call me if you need anything. I know Tunde is fresh, but you are still going through a major transition with Fahad out of the picture. I can even come through tonight if you need a shoulder to bitch on."

"I'm done with Fahad."

"I'm clear. But he's not done with you, so you need to process how you're gonna keep boundaries with him."

"I'm not a patient, Janelle."

"Yes, the fuck you are right now. I don't want my friend dealing with unnecessary wahala. Is that how you say it?"

"Yes. And okay."

"Tunde is very sexy. Take your time."

Kofo groans. "Can't I just immerse myself, though? It's addictive."

"No."

Kofo leans her head against her headboard. "I'm going to bed. Pray that I don't have a wet dream."

"Bye. Love you."

"Love you too."

They hang up. Kofo's self-control is at an all-time low. Deprivation is not her strong suit, and she hates that Janelle always reminds her of it.

***

"Can I have two croissants and egg sandwiches with English Breakfast tea for each? You can add bacon to one," Kofo requests from the barista at a brand-new coffee shop in Lefferts Gardens, which is really Flatbush as far as Kofo is concerned.

While the employee works on her order, a few Black teen males walk in as they cat-call a young adult woman walking past their huddle before the storefront. She ignores them in typical Flatbush fashion, jerking away when one guy tries to break from the group for a more direct pursuit.

The inside of the cafe is littered with clusters of hipsters drinking variations of lattes while munching on various pastries. A Rastafarian mother with three chocolate babies is occupying a table. Kofo smiles at the mother and the mother smiles back, happy to spot a nostalgic scene of her typical childhood neighbor. Kofo misses Brooklyn deeply. This coffee shop is an updated version of the delicious takeout restaurants that occupied these same streets ten years prior. The uptick in new types of businesses makes the neighborhood appear nicer, but the ethnic identity of her childhood stomping grounds feels different and not in a good way. She struggles with patronizing this business and would rather order a fish patty with coco bread from one of her favorite spots that survived gentrification. But Tunde fell in love with the croissants here, so she compromised.

"I got it," Tunde whispers in her ear while grabbing her waist from behind and kissing her on the cheek.

"You better." They both chuckle at Kofo's humorous reply to his offer, although she is dead serious. She makes her way to the condiments table behind them to grab covers for the cups and napkins while he takes over.

"Thanks mate." Tunde grabs the tray of drinks and a brown bag with their sandwiches from the barista with authority. He does everything with such confidence. His steady, deep tone of voice, broad shoulders, the glide in his steps, the way he smiles at Kofo. He is everything, and it turns her on. A lot.

They plop on a bench right outside the perimeter of Prospect Park and dive into their sandwiches. It's the first day of spring, and the blaring sun fools them into thinking that eating outdoors is a good idea. Tunde is a messy eater which grosses Kofo out. But she does like that he has some unflattering traits. Otherwise, he would intimidate her. Tunde takes a bite and the flakes from the croissant are all over his leather jacket. Kofo brushes it off while he licks a piece of bacon off of his lip. He winks at her while taking another bite, rendering her cleanup useless.

"I'll wait till you're done."

He chuckles, inhaling his favorite breakfast sandwich. He devours everything like that, including her.

"My dad used to take me on walks around the park. A little under three and a half miles. If I didn't complain, he would treat me to a fresh, plain, fluffy Jewish bagel that's toasted with butter. Brooklyn Bagels are heavenly," Kofo says in between bites.

Like many Nigerian daddies, Kofo's father is knowledgeable about history. He knows about all the European historical figures in Lefferts Gardens dating from the 1700s and told her stories of how they colonized the area from its indigenous habitants. She then debated her fourth-grade social studies teacher during an inaccurate lesson about "settlers", and her teacher promptly sent her to the principal's office. Kofo specifically requested that they bring her father. When he arrived, he argued with them on her behalf with references he knew from memory. Kofo longed to be as brilliant but the moment never arrived for her. She relied solely on her father's genius for input on most of her decisions since that day.

Tunde responds with a reluctant smile. "Looks like I need to outdo a lot of fond memories with him."

Kofo blushes and gives him a nudge. "You're doing great."

Tunde looks down at the sidewalk, chuckling to himself. "I hope he agrees. He's not hiding in the bushes behind us, right?"

"No, silly," Kofo says before giggling.

Kofo gathers their sandwich wrappers and napkins, stuffing them into the paper bag. After several moments of awkward silence pass, Tunde puts his arm around Kofo to keep them both toasty and she leans in on his shoulder.

Kofo sits upright, and Tunde loosens his grip. She sighs and lets more silence pass. "Well… I wouldn't tell him I'm dreading entering the workforce. That's why I went to business school."

Tunde widens his eyes in between chews. "But you're about to graduate, so now what?"

"I don't even know. I'm so bored."

"Well, what do you want to do?"

"I think I want to take time off and figure it out. I feel like I'm bored because I'm boring."

"If you were boring, I wouldn't be fucking you."

They both laugh.

"You're an excellent cook. You are impeccably stylish. And you're very good at being beautiful."

"So basically, I have zero employable talents that are unrelated to you dating me."

"I think you do. You just haven't figured it out yet."

Kofo grows silent.

"I'm good at getting my way. I need to turn that into a job."

"That's a hard skill to hone and a great place to start. I'm sure it'll help you discover your passion."

She loves it when he pours into her. It feels so thoughtful.

"Do you enjoy working in finance?"

Tunde reflects on the question and is more honest than usual. "I enjoy the life that it gives me. And the way it makes me feel."

Kofo nods in agreement. She can see his feelings projecting outward in his suave, measured and charming persona.

***

A bright May morning fills Kofo's bedroom, forcing her eyes to open on her queen-sized bed. She lies longer than she should, annoyed that it's her last day of stalling the pursuit of her life's purpose under the guise of being in business school. She grabs her iPhone on her nightstand and it's flooded with messages from Janelle and her dad, wishing her good luck because two out of three of her tests are likely to be difficult. Kofo smiles to herself, happy that they remembered, but a ring interrupts her thoughts at her door.

Kofo lifts her peephole to find an unrecognizable man holding a basket wrapped in clear plastic.

"Gift delivery," he mumbles.

Kofo smiles, opening the door to receive a bouquet sandwiched in between dark chocolates, yogurt covered strawberries, and sweet white wine.

"Thank you so much." Kofo grabs her purse on a rack next to the door and hands him a five-dollar bill.

After closing the door, Kofo detaches the note to the bouquet that reads,

You're going to ace every test now that you got the Midas touch through these flowers. Congratulations, I'm so proud of you for pulling through! With Love from your man (?), Tunde.

Kofo rolls her eyes, laughing. Of course, Tunde would ask to be in a relationship in this manner.

***

Kofo walks through the doors of her last final exam at 5:30pm, and she finds Tunde leaning against a car holding a "Congratulations!" helium balloon straight out of Party City, coupled with a small gift bag. All the students pouring out of the building are checking him out, assuming he is a celebrity that is wooing Kofo. He has on a stylish textured jacket, skinny jeans and suede shoes. His hair is freshly cut, and he smells like money. She feels prosperous and notable standing next to him, although they both technically are nobodies, moving as though they are worthy of public recognition.

"Tunde, you are killing me with all these gifts. Thank you so much." She pecks him on the lips.

"Babe, you deserve it. You have an MBA!" He gives her the gift bag. Kofo opens a velvet jewelry box, revealing a pair of green peridot and diamond stud earrings cased in 14-carat gold. They are not of the highest quality, but they are beautiful and authentic. Her eyes water, then she makes eye contact with Tunde. She is an August Leo and peridot is her birth stone—her favorite stone. He remembered. Without hesitation, Kofo gives him a long hug, and he kisses her forehead while they embrace. All gifts throughout her life have been about what's in fashion, or what the giver assumes she needs. As she closes the velvet box with her gift, Kofo reflects on the measly dinner she took him out to on his birthday in early February. It was during a terrible snowstorm and she insisted they still go out. She was tired of them ordering delivery and it was not birthday worthy. The dinner was at a quaint Mediterranean establishment where the food wasn't fresh and the service could've been better, but he loved it. He said that women barely take him out or give him anything. He loved their night cap too, but the lingerie she ordered arrived later than expected because of the snowstorm. It was a mess as far as she was concerned, yet he didn't care—he was happy to be with her on his 33rd birthday, his Jesus year. They prayed together that morning Islamic and Christian style because he wanted Kofo's blessing on his new life and a new chapter in the United States. While they were building memories over the past six months, their relationship status never came up. The lack of pressure from Tunde made Kofo suspect perhaps he didn't want to make their relations more than what it was. Deep down, Kofo knew she wanted Tunde all to herself, and that's why she didn't protest when they started seeing each other five days a week after their third date. This gift is finally her answer on what to do with him now that school is done. Kofo must do better with all gifts moving forward.

"So, you love me, huh?" She still couldn't believe it. "And you want us to officially be boyfriend and girlfriend?"

Tunde smiles, flashing his flawless teeth. "You were already my girlfriend months ago."

"You never asked."

"I did everything a boyfriend does for you since then, right?"

Kofo knows he's just testing her threshold for jokes, as usual. She kisses him as confirmation that she agrees to all of his terms.

"I love you too, boyfriend."

Tunde is cheesing from ear to ear. They are official in union and in feelings. The past couple of seasons have been a whirlwind of romantic highs between these two and she didn't want it to end. Tunde puts his arm around her and they walk off.

"Daylight savings has been over for a while. Let's go to the rat park and chill for a bit before we meet our dinner reservations at Gramercy Tavern." Again, another point for Tunde. Kofo tried to make reservations there for months with no luck. He really listens when she rambles about any and everything.

Kofo chuckles for the umpteenth time around him. "Aw… thanks babe." Kofo can't stop blushing. She was supposed to call Janelle right after class to meet up for drinks, but she'll text her later to reschedule for another day. Tunde is now her biggest priority.

CHAPTER 2

Busy doesn't describe Friday nights at Al Ahmed Mosque in Canarsie, Brooklyn. Mommies and Daddies file into the mid-sized building by the minute and their children, ranging from infants to late teens, follow. The building is not run down, but improvements are needed in the bathroom where wudhu is performed and the floors could stand a good wax to spruce up the place. Those aesthetic flaws are inconsequential, as this mosque is one of the few lifelines for Nigerian Muslims in New York City to stay connected during the night of their Sabbath.

There are four floors in the walk-up—the basement that holds the kitchen, the ground floor for general congregation and classes, the second floor for the men's prayer room, and the third floor for the ladies' prayer room. It's one of the few structures buzzing with activity on the often-quiet block of mid-century houses that line up the street. Some of the

Caribbean families with empty nester baby boomers called 311 for noise disturbances, but after the ladies in the mosque offered tasty containers of Nigerian food left over from their cook, those complaints swiftly subsided.

Morenike Adebayo—a woman in her early sixties, wraps up her prayer led by the Imam whom she can view on the monitor and hear through the speakers. Toddlers run in circles around her on the carpeted floor while their mothers also finish Salat, but that doesn't sway her commitment or devotion to prayer.

Once she's done, she grabs her test beads and whispers Islamic incantations as she pulls each bead along the long thread, holding them all together. Her phone pings, alerting her of a text from her daughter, Kofo. She grabs it from her purse with her free hand.

Hi Mommy, did you already arrive at the mosque? I want to talk to you about something.

Morenike grows with worry, a lump forming in her throat. *As Salaam Alaykum. Yes, I'm already here. What's wrong? Is Fahad okay?*

Yes Mommy, he's fine. No worries, I'll talk to you tomorrow.

Ok. Have a good night.

You too Mommy.

Morenike puts her phone away, wondering what trouble Kofo got into this time. She is disappointed that her daughter failed to insist that Fahad marry her years ago. He comes from a good, devout Muslim family that shares similar values of immigration-inspired achievement. Fahad is tall and handsome, indicating that their genes would combine well. Their mixed-race children were likely to be attractive with nice hair. Morenike hates kinky afros, even when people complimented her massive wig during the 1970s. She and Kofo would raise children with a bias towards Nigerian culture, combining their efforts of maternal influence. Fathers are sperm donors and a financial resource as far as Morenike is concerned.

Or maybe Kofo flunked out of business school during her last semester—she begrudgingly attended business school after her father's convincing argument of using her advanced degree to add more pedigree to her educational background. Their daughter spent her first five years out of undergrad roaming the streets of New York in the latest clubs, Fashion Week, and Naija or Caribbean parties, to no avail. Once she got that out of her system, Morenike settled for anything her daughter came up with after accepting that medical and law school would never interest Kofo. She has more soft skills, but soft skills don't pay bills. They collectively decided that the best way to monetize her innate gift of persuasion would be through business school. Morenike hopes her daughter didn't screw up her only security blanket. That decision would be a devastating reminder of her own life.

"Alhaja, it's time for your speech." Her good friend, Abidemi Falade, interrupts her running thoughts in Yoruba.

"Oh, yes Mommy Bola, thank you." Instead of referring to her by her first name, Morenike calls her Mommy Bola, a formal display of Yoruba courtesy that references the eldest child.

Morenike snatches off her sheer scarf that exposes her head wrap before rising, lifting her floor length Ankara dress from the floor to make her way downstairs to the Imam.

***

"As Salaam Alaykum," Morenike jitters at the front of the carpet second-floor prayer room, watching all the men in the congregation stare her down while she clutches the microphone. She prepared for this moment, but it was not going the way she imagined. Her nerves deviate from the composed persona associated with her brand of mosque leadership. She looks further to the back and sees Mommy Bola nodding her head, standing by to offer any needed backup along with a few other women. Their friendship dates back to Morenike's earlier days in New York City when they met at a naming ceremony for a child of a mutual friend. Mommy Bola invited Morenike during Al-Ahmed's earlier days when she occupied the first lady seat and is now campaigning to pass the torch to her junior friend. She is a pain in the ass and constantly needs Morenike for favors, errands or other menial tasks she really could do. Yoruba elders often flex the impunity of their authority through errands—it was done to them, so it must be done to the next generation. Aside from that, Mommy Bola is a genuine friend. She's trustworthy, reliable and will show up even if she's judging you.

The room responds, "Wa Alaykum Salaam," right on cue.

Morenike shifts to continue releasing her nerves. She catches her favorite Islamic prayer—Surah Al-Fatiha—on the wall above the ladies. She donated it to the mosque when her family moved and requested it as decor on the ladies' floor, but it looks like several usual suspects that shut all of her ideas down vetoed her ask.

"Thank you for allowing me to speak tonight. The ladies at Al Ahmed want to thank you for your donations to our new initiative to bring Nigerian Muslim women from all over New York City together. We plan on raising money in the following areas and are accepting donations." Morenike clears her throat. "We want to offer Quranic class scholarships to young Muslimah from ages 8 to 21. We also want to use the money to renovate a few ladies' bathrooms at different mosques, including our own, and we insist on flushable seat covers. The ladies at Al Ahmed would also like to arrange an annual gala to get us the money this mosque needs to continue running. We tried several fundraising approaches and I think this would be most effective because of my legal background and the event planning experience of some of our ladies at Al Ahmed."

The Imam interrupts her speech. "We haven't exhausted all efforts to raise money and would prefer to finish those before moving forward with you."

Morenike is over this guy. He shuts everything down but barely knows how to type his name on a computer. "Yes Alhaji, I understand, sir. But with our added skill sets, it can really expedite our needed improvements faster—"

"Are you a practicing attorney?" He interjects in a room of about 75 people.

"If you have a law degree, you are always a practicing attorney," Morenike says.

Another male member chimes in. This time, it's the Imam's second in command, Salim.

"What of your husband? Does he have resources we can use to make improvements?"

"We can, of course, leverage his connections for the initiatives I mentioned, but I think it's best to trust us to take the lead on this."

They respond with silence. Morenike continues.

"While your agreement is preferred, it is not how we will complete our next steps. We will move forward with everything I mentioned. I will review all legal matters such as contracts, establishing any company or non-profit paperwork for our programs and will ensure our accountant has all needed tax documents."

The Imam picks back up, inspired by Morenike's boldness. "Now sister, you know we must agree for all decisions like this—"

"So, what is your feedback?"

"We think it's best for us to hire an actual lawyer and have you work with Akeem to offer any connections."

"I can be better utilized. And I am a real lawyer. I read several documents for free for Masjid El Ahmed for years when we couldn't afford counsel. If you don't want to use me in another capacity, fine. But the ladies at this mosque have seen my potential and they want me to take charge of anything pertaining to the sisters. My husband Akeem is supportive of our strategy."

The Imam blinks in rapid flurries. "Well… I guess if your husband is also in agreement, we should be too, sister."

"Thank you. I will keep everyone updated monthly with our progress during our Friday night announcements."

Morenike hands him the microphone and walks off. When she reaches the back of the room, Mommy Bola along with some of the other ladies huddle around Morenike, hugging her and patting her on the back. Morenike is excited to inspire change in Al-Ahmed—Mommy Bola lost her influence over the years when new crops of members became resistant to her tenured position. It's about time someone shook things up around here and Morenike is ready to play that role. She doesn't need Akeem guiding her every step. He's seldom around for Friday prayers because of his recent business trips.

***

Morenike pulls up into the driveway of her Long Island mini-mansion hours close to midnight, turning off the engine to her four-door Mercedes. Her husband parked his Audi SUV in front of the garage door, signaling his return from his latest travels. She hates when he doesn't put his car into the garage. It negates the point of having a big house if they will not use all of its amenities. He leaves his car in the driveway when he plans on roaming the streets, which is a frequent occurrence.

Morenike walks through the front door and finds her husband Akeem slouched over, deep in sleep, while the television plays MSNBC.

She turns off the TV and watches him for a few moments with disgust. He's snoring and drooling while leaning forward. The smell of liquor is in the air and she notices empty bottles of Guinness on the coffee table. Twenty years ago, she would chuckle at this, humored by her husband's physical response to an occasional drink. His large, tall, authoritative frame oozed of power, and the vulnerability of intoxication was amusing. It's now clear that he hasn't found another outlet for self-soothing despite her urging to lean more into Islam.

Akeem's cell phone pings with a text on the couch next to his thigh. Morenike double checks if he's deep in sleep by waving her hand in his face, and he doesn't flinch. She's figured out his security code over time by watching his fat thumbs whenever they were in close quarters, and by experimenting with the numbers for important dates. It is a combination of his mother's and Kofo's birthday. Never hers.

She puts his phone on silent and then jumps right into his texts from Funmi. Her contact profile includes a recent photo of a woman in her mid-30s. They all look the same—slimmer, younger versions of herself. Morenike contemplated shaving off some weight to regain her husband's attention, but why bother? He never shows gratitude for her commitment to caring for their daughters, or her cooking, cleaning and general homemaking, which is what makes weight loss difficult. Dealing with him drains her enough.

How far, big daddy? I'm still waiting for you to come over. Funmi texts him a photo of her in a sheer lace teddy, showing off her breasts. She sends another photo from behind with her butt prominently placed, leaving Morenike unimpressed. She was sexier than this girl in her prime—she was what they call "slim thick" in present day. Morenike scrolls further up, and there is another photo of Funmi and Akeem together in what appears to be a social club. Wives are rarely, if ever, present because these social clubs also present opportunities for women like Funmi to find their next sugar daddy. Apparently, Akeem is on her roster.

Morenike is numb to the infidelity, but not to the humiliation. Why couldn't Akeem cheat with another Muslim woman from a neighboring African country? Or a woman of another race that isn't this low class? Why one of their own? What if Morenike knows her family, or is related to her? He knows that both of their families are massive and their names spread throughout Nigeria and the diaspora. Akeem is incredibly reckless with the way he steps out.

Morenike grabs her phone from her purse and calls Funmi. She drops her husband's phone back on the couch and walks upstairs to her room while the phone rings. Funmi picks up as soon as Morenike enters the owner's suite.

"Hello?"

"Hi. Is this Funmi?"

"Yes, who is this?"

"I am Akeem Adebayo's wife."

Silence. Funmi hangs up the phone. Morenike chuckles and shakes her head. She sends her a text.

PLEASE CEASE ALL CONTACT WITH MY HUSBAND. Did he tell you he's been married for almost forty years and has two daughters?

Morenike sees the indication of Funmi texting a response on her iPhone.

I'm sorry ma, but I don't know what you're talking about.

Morenike has text exchanges like this every couple of months. It's playing out exactly the way it always does. She would bet on her being a recent immigrant within the past five years or less. They are the most pliable.

Yes, you do. I have connections and authorities that will take care of you. I know that you have been seeing him at social clubs in East New York due to people informing me of your interactions with Akeem. So again… cease all communication with my husband and block his number immediately. Have a good night.

Morenike blocks her number. She doesn't want to give this anymore of her time. Her control over the outcome is limited. Morenike heads to her bathroom and locks the door behind her.

***

The delicious smell of egg omelet and boiled yams for breakfast fill the kitchen and dining room the next morning. Morenike is a fast cook, preparing most meals in under an hour. She enjoys preparing Nigerian food the most, but her doctor told her to slow down on the spices, especially in her older years, which expanded her palate. Thankfully, this meal is one of the few Nigerian meals she can still eat that won't jeopardize her fluctuating blood pressure levels.

Eniola sits on a stool on the kitchen island, marveling at her mother's preparation of another delicious meal. Ironically, Kofo ended up being a better cook considering that Eniola is more exposed to Nigerian customs. The wires crossed on this matter, but at least one of her daughters caught on to being able to feed their future families.

"Mommy, are you okay? Do you need help?"

"No… I'm fine dear. Just prepare the plates in the dining room."

The exchange with Funmi still bothers Morenike, but she pretends as though she's tired. She

38

swore she would never make her daughters hold contempt for their father. She hated her own father because he physically abused her mother and her family, and harboring those feelings torments her life daily. Having her daughter a few blocks away is a treat—she enjoys Eniola's company. Morenike loves hearing her friends brag about the impeccable manners of her eldest daughter. It gives her an opportunity to show off her mothering skills.

Akeem and Cedric are in the living room and she can hear them talking about an election, but she can't make out which one. Of course, CNN is on in the background. Morenike wonders if her husband can talk about anything other than politics. Maybe his feelings, some memories, concern for the people he actually interfaces with. His need to discuss subjects out of reach irritates Morenike.

She gave Cedric a hard time when he started dating Eniola because she wanted Eniola to marry a Muslim. But her daughter assured her of Cedric's father's practice of Islam, so she backed down. Over time, she realized Eniola lied about that to get her to come around on the supposed love of her life. Her daughter dumped her Nigerian, Muslim, boyfriend at the time once Cedric "enhanced" her life with a new wardrobe, new attitude and alleged increase of confidence. Morenike saw slight evidence of Eniola's claims and hoped for her daughter to return the favor by inspiring a conversion from Cedric that never came. What ultimately won Morenike over is Cedric's willingness to be with Eniola, despite a lot of resistance from his future mother-in-law. Morenike also secretly loves his mom, Yvonne. Her warm personality puts Morenike at ease and she's learning southern recipes by watching her cooking from the corner of her eye whenever they spend time together. She noticed Yvonne started making Nigerian dishes as of late, and its proximity to traditional cooking is credible.

***

"Where's Kofo?" Akeem asks while gorging on his food in the dining room at the head of the table. Morenike wonders the same, but she doesn't discuss their family issues around Cedric for fear of scaring him off, considering his experience with their family.

Morenike answers to cut the tension. "She's probably on her way or is busy studying for final exams."

"No, her exams are over. I spoke to her about it the other day."

"Well, I don't know." She wishes her husband would read the room. Eniola and Cedric appear uncomfortable as they look down at their plates. She assumes they know where Kofo is, but won't say anything. Morenike stuffs a piece of yam into her mouth.

Akeem lifts his head in between gulps. "Maybe we should call Fahad. Ennie, call him and see where they are. They haven't showed up to breakfast in a while." Akeem speaks to Kofo more than anyone at the table. Morenike interpreted this command as a flex to reestablish his position as "head" of the family after being away for so long.

"I'll just call Kofo and see." Eniola calls her sister on speaker phone and she doesn't pick up. Kofo sends her straight to voicemail, followed by a text.

Eniola's eyes pop out in surprise. "She's coming in a few minutes."

Akeem huffs, satisfied with this win. "Great!"

Morenike doesn't have a good feeling about Kofo's arrival, and remembers the cryptic message she received the night prior. Hopefully she's not pregnant or moving far away. Everyone else at the table is chatting about current events and Morenike remains quiet, preparing for what awaits them.

Minutes later, she overhears Kofo coming into her house and taking off her shoes. She identifies a male voice speaking in a hushed tone that doesn't sound like Fahad. It then dawns on Morenike that she hasn't seen or heard from Fahad in months, which is odd. He calls regularly and so does his mother. Morenike's current schedule is consumed with her mosque duties and she chalked up their reduced contact to them being equally busy.

Kofo enters the dining area with a Black guy who is not Fahad. Morenike sizes him up—he is wearing freshly pressed button-down top, blazer and slim-cut trousers. This is an upgrade from Fahad—that's if he is a romantic prospect, but who is he and why didn't Kofo prepare them for his arrival? Morenike is wearing a colorful kaftan she purchased during a trip to Dubai, but she isn't wearing any makeup, her jewelry isn't her best and she didn't bring out her China for new guests.

"Good morning, Daddy and Mommy. This is my new boyfriend, Tunde."

Morenike sighs while staring at the couple.

"It's a pleasure to meet you all," Tunde says in a smooth, deep voice.

He's a British Nigerian. Interesting. Morenike knows that his accent is considered ghetto, and he's doing a desperate attempt to hide it. She wonders if Kofo knows; she's sheltered and hasn't traveled overseas much outside of a few trips to Nigeria during her teen years.

"Hi Tunde. It's nice to meet you as well. Help yourself." Morenike gestures to the table and he takes a seat while Kofo formally greets her parents with hugs and cheek kisses.

Tunde waits for Kofo to sit down and he puts food on her plate first, which she approves. Morenike observes Eniola and Cedric's greeting of Tunde and it's obvious they've already met him or are at least aware he exists. She both her daughters are terrible liars. Thank goodness, because her efforts to reign Kofo in as a teenager would've been disastrous.

There is an awkward silence as Kofo and Tunde prepare to eat.

"Did you two wash your hands?" Morenike hates unsanitary practices.

"Oh! Yes, let me lead Tunde to the powder room and I'll go to the kitchen." Kofo giggles after staring in Tunde's direction, downplaying the disruption of their weekly routine.

Morenike sips a cup of her English Breakfast tea with condensed milk. "The kitchen sink is full of dishes. Tunde, the powder room is behind you, down the hall on your left side."

"Thank you, Mrs. Adebayo." Tunde rises to make his way to the first-floor restroom while Morenike nods. Once Tunde is out of earshot, she lowers the projection of her voice.

"I hope you're not moving to London, Kofo."

Kofo smirks at her mother's assumptions. "No, Mommy. I broke up with Fahad a while ago and we haven't had time to really talk about it so—"

Morenike turns to her husband, glaring at him. "Did you know about this?"

Akeem pauses. "About Fahad, yes. Tunde… no."

Tunde walks back to the dining room while Morenike takes another sip of her tea. Kofo heads to the bathroom after he sits down.

"So, what do you do, Tunde?" Morenike might as well see if he's worth her daughter's time since he's already here.

"I work in finance," Tunde says in between bites. Eniola and Cedric try to remain quiet with slow, deliberate movements of their utensils.

"Doing what?" Morenike isn't satisfied.

"I'm an investment banker."

"How long have you been in America? And on a work visa, I'm assuming?"

Akeem leans into the table and uses his palm to cover his mouth. Morenike is crass when she senses danger.

"Yes Mrs. Adebayo, I've been here for about a year. I'm actually a citizen. I was born here and then my family moved to London to meet my dad when I was three."

"Are you planning on going back home after a while? Or do you need a reason to permanently live in the United States?" Morenike doesn't trust this guy. He's too put together for her daughter who is all over the place. Kofo is messy and forgetful. She's emotional, and deep down, a free spirit. Her daughter forms close bonds with dominant personality types, but it never works out because Kofo refuses to be caged in after her resentment kicks in. Morenike is waiting for the shoe to drop with Janelle—she never liked her overbearing personality. She had high hopes for Fahad because he forces Kofo to be decisive. He puts her in the driver's seat.

"Well… I didn't have plans to stay in America indefinitely, just for a few years because I always wanted to experience life here. When my job had an opening in the United States, I went for it. My plans for a temporary stay might change depending on how everything turns out." He looks at Kofo and she blushes, putting her hand on his leg as she returns from the bathroom.

Morenike hasn't seen her daughter smile like this in several years.

Tunde eats. "Wow. This is delicious. I love fried egg and yam. Kofo always makes it and adds some dodo on the side. I see where she gets her culinary skills from."

"Yea. He likes his dodo somewhat burned, the same way I do," Kofo gushes.

"Where do you live, Tunde?" Akeem asks.

"I'm in Harlem near 125th street but I'm soon heading to Brooklyn to move in with Kofo."

Morenike frowns. "Brooklyn?! When did you move to Brooklyn, Kofo?"

Akeem assists her, his expression equally surprised. "And how long have you two been dating?"

Kofo puts her fork down and swallows her food. "Tunde and I have been together for about seven months, right after I broke up with Fahad and moved out of Queens."

Morenike chuckles and shakes her head, staring at the couple with wide, heated eyes. "Tunde—while I'm sure there's a lot more to learn about you, we need to talk to our daughter Kofo about all of this. Alone."

"Mommy—"

"Kofo, stop speaking. Tunde, would you like a plate to go?"

Akeem steps in, leaning into the table towards Kofo and Tunde. "Tunde, you can stay. I just think my wife is very upset that Kofo didn't discuss any of this beforehand."

Morenike remains stoic and sits upright. "When is the next train leaving? We can order an Uber for you."

Kofo shakes her head in protest. "The next train doesn't arrive until an hour from now. It's cloudy outside and rain is in the forecast. He can't wait out in the cold, Mommy."

"Yes, he can."

Cedric looks at Eniola, and she responds with a slight nod. "Tunde, I can drive you home if that's alright with you?"

Eniola jumps in. "Cedric and I were already going to a baby shower in Brooklyn, so it's perfect. Kofo, you can take the next train back."

Kofo sighs before responding. "Okay." She says in a shaky tone.

"Are you sure, babe?" Tunde whispers to her, feeling Morenike's eyes burning a hole through his soul.

"Yea. I'll call you when I'm done." Kofo says with a quivering voice.

"Mr. and Mrs. Adebayo, thank you so much for an amazing meal and it was a pleasure to meet you."

Akeem nods through a tight-lipped smile and Morenike takes one more good look at Tunde while Eniola and Cedric rise from their seats.

"Bye, Tunde," Morenike says dryly.

Morenike, Akeem and Kofo continue eating, the silence of the room filling with the silverware scraping the last remains of breakfast on everyone's plate.

Tunde, Cedric and Eniola leave, and Morenike awaits Kofo's explanation, confronting Kofo's sullen face. Morenike looks at Akeem for assurance, and he doesn't contribute with words or body language.

"Why would you not prepare us for this, Kofo?" Morenike grows impatient.

Kofo stuffs the last piece of Yam and egg into her mouth. "I tried to call you, Mommy."

"No, you texted me. You said nothing about Fahad or this new guy."

Kofo leans back in her chair. Morenike watches her daughter weave her hands together like a nervous schoolchild, unsure of what to say next. "Well... to be honest, I thought you would try to make me get back with Fahad, and I have been unhappy with him for a while."

"What if I called Fahad, unaware of this news?"

"You never call him. He always called you because you were too busy."

"That is not true."

"Yes, it is, he always complained—"

Akeem cuts them off. "Okay, let's focus. You like this guy. Why does he have to move in right this second, Kofo?"

"We're in love."

Morenike does her chuckling again, her predictable form of containing an impending explosion. "Have you even met his family? And what do you really know about love, anyway?"

Kofo purses her mouth into a flat line. "We love each other. He listens to me. Tunde acknowledges my thoughts, my preferences, and my desires. He's supportive—I feel accepted for all of my quirks. I feel like I have the space to be myself. He wants to marry me. We're going to live together to see if we can make it." Kofo's voice cracks and she sips water. "Fahad is boring and doesn't want to change unless I force him to, which is usually after he messes up. Plus, his father is always making racist jokes and he never, ever tells him to stop. Why would I want to marry into that kind of family and raise Black, African children with them?"

Morenike won't let up. "Are you marrying Fahad's father? You have invested almost 10 years into the relationship! He's a good Muslim boy from a nice family. Who cares if his father is ignorant?!"

Kofo's face crushes in disappointment. "I thought you would be happy that I found a Nigerian. A Yoruba at that."

Morenike noticed that Tunde was wearing gold, which means he is Christian or not a devout Muslim. "I want you to marry someone who is committed to Islam."

"I want to marry someone who respects and honors God, someone who is a good person. Why can't that be enough for you?"

Akeem leans in his daughter's direction. "Maybe we should have a family meeting with Fahad's family to see—"

"No! He's already with a Pakistani girl, which I knew he would run to. I don't want him, I'm done."

Morenike hoped Fahad was wallowing in the years he wasted with Kofo, but apparently not with this news. Maybe there's a way to talk to his mother? But it might offend her if Morenike calls so long after the breakup. Although she doesn't want to admit it, she doesn't like Fahad's father either, but their family owns a lot of businesses in Queens and they have money. Fahad is resourceful, often fixing things around her house and her community is familiar with his congeniality that led to him leading a Quranic class at Al Ahmed. What is she going to tell everyone now?

Morenike rises to clean the table.

"Mommy, can you please say something?" Kofo pleads.

"What do you want me to say, Kofo? All I can tell you is good luck." Morenike takes a few plates and walks out to the kitchen, leaving her daughter and husband.

CHAPTER 3

Akeem drives Kofo to the Long Island Railroad train station in his Audi. A radio station blares with the crisp voice of a reporter announcing international news.

"Yesterday, rebel groups in Mali executed a coup—"

Kofo turns off the radio.

"Daddy, I don't want to hear about Africa's instability right now."

Akeem doesn't respond and continues driving with an unreadable expression. Several moments pass before he speaks.

"Tunde seems like a nice guy."

"He is. He's very nice, actually."

Akeem pulls up to the station parking lot.

"I have ten minutes before the train arrives." Kofo undoes her seatbelt in the passenger seat but doesn't get out. "Have you ever truly been in love, Daddy?"

Akeem takes a deep breath, thinking about his daughter's question. He's staring at the ring on his left hand that isn't a wedding band. "Let's just say I used to believe that love would make everything easy, but I was mistaken."

Kofo pauses.

"Is mommy sick or something? Her reaction to Tunde felt like it was about more than just him."

"No. She's under a lot of stress regarding mosque issues and things like that. She'll eventually be okay again." Akeem wishes he could tell Kofo more, but that wouldn't be wise.

"She's always been a part of mosque activities, though."

"She's taking more of a leadership role these days and there are a lot of politics involved. You know your mother likes to do things her way, which many people won't like."

"Right."

A longstanding silence divides their thoughts.

"Kofo—make sure you use your head more than your heart with Tunde. Nigerian men aren't easy."

Kofo smirks, looking down at the dashboard. "I'm familiar enough. I think I'll be okay. Thank you."

Kofo pecks her dad on the cheek and gets out of the car towards the train station platform. Akeem turns back on the radio before pulling out of the station parking lot.

Akeem's phone rings. He presses a button on his steering wheel to answer. It's his good friend Dayo.

"Hello?"

"Ah—Daddy Ennie, bawoni?"

"Mo dupe! Hope you're having a good weekend so far?"

"Yes, sir."

"Are we still heading to Chief Lounge this evening?"

"Yes sir, and Chike is coming."

"Of course." Akeem laughs.

"Ok sir. I'll see you later. O dabo."

"Later." Akeem drops his call.

***

It's 9:00pm at Chief Lounge and Akeem walks in with a nicely pressed shirt, a blazer, crisp, straight leg jeans and leather loafers. A platinum chain necklace adorns his neck. Dayo and Chike sit at a table with large silver bowls filled with water in front of them. Akeem already ate half of the ogbono soup Morenike gave him for dinner, but he likes to eat the food here too, so his friends feel comfortable. Other patrons greet him either by head nods, or younger elders in training with prostrations. The energy shifts with his entry through the tinted store front. He acknowledges everyone with smiles, happy to see his nighttime friends.

Big Auntie, the owner and chef, grants her patrons a makeshift fraternity that allows them to feel at home as African men without the world watching. The smell of fried goat meat is in the air, the televisions play sports and news on rotation, plastic chairs sprawled throughout that are identical to the ones in Nigerian social clubs, floral plastic table covers, and native juju music playing after 11:00pm.

Kemi, Big Auntie's daughter, is the restaurant's only server that dodges creepy advances from several men who lack boundaries. She heads over to Akeem's table with Dayo and Chike, carrying two huge servings of efo—meat spinach stew, paired with eba, also known as boiled cassava.

"Always on time. Ose." Dayo smiles at Kemi.

"You're welcome, Uncle." Kemi smiles back, soft-spoken and agreeable—just the way the "Uncles" like women in her role. Her generous tips are a clear sign. Before she fully walks off, Akeem hisses at her. She turns around, almost at the kitchen.

"What about my plate and our Guinness?"

"Oh! Ma binu Uncle, I'll bring it." Kemi moves quicker with Akeem's arrival. He's one of the biggest tippers and is thus the most demanding.

"Look at my wife and twins." Dayo uploads photos in WhatsApp of his stunning wife and twin daughters who are back home in Nigeria. Every time Akeem comes to Chief Lounge, Dayo subjects him to forced viewing of his family photos. He doesn't know how to tell Dayo he doesn't care and would prefer to avoid discussions about wives and children; it reminds him of his own burdens. Dayo's days at Chief Lounge are numbered once his family steps foot on American soil; he's been counting down their arrivals the last couple of months. "This was my junior brother's wedding she went to on my behalf. My fine lady. We just finished the visa interview a few weeks ago."

Dayo rolls up his sweater sleeves, revealing his chubby arms and puts his hands in one of the silver bowls to wash them off. He scoops a piece of eba, rolls it into a ball, dips it in the stew, and stuffs it in his mouth. Chike follows suit.

"You eat like the food is running," Chike jokes to Dayo. He's the Igbo guy out of their crew, but he is very fluent in Yoruba and his own native tongue. His family moved to Lagos from Igboland in the 1990s and there was no way they could run a functional business without relating to the locals in their language. His family warns him about the duplicitous nature of Yorubas, especially after his father's experience fighting in the Biafran war and some of his own experiences of bullying as a child when his family moved from the east to the southwest region of Nigeria. He's torn on the subject, but he doesn't feel like there's a point to holding contempt for his fellow countrymen while in New York. He's benefitted from his relations with Yorubas as an immigrant.

"I'm fat, but more charming than you. Eat now." Dayo snaps back. Dayo keeps them both on their toes with his quips. His ability to entrance people with jokes is his unique advantage, and he commits to using it at the perfect moments. He explained to Akeem on a slow night how he won his wife over by constantly making her laugh on their first date. She is out of his league, but his sense of humor is unmatched.

Akeem laughs at them both. They're misfits here, but he likes them. They are twenty years his junior and in their mid-40s. Akeem is collecting romantic prospects after they shared difficulties in relating to women in the United States. The expectations of American women demand too much. They want to provide, protect, eat well, have good sex, and be dads—both men would be more content with a Nigerian-bred woman. Many presume they are well off upon finding out their Nigerian nationality, but Dayo is awaiting his mechanic license and drives Ubers to make ends meet. Chike just finished school, and he's been looking for a healthcare administrator position for years. All of his interviews go well and he's secured two positions that were short-lived. Relating to the neurosis of white American workplace demands drains him and he's gotten fired twice for not bending to the will of his supervisors. He's focusing more on working with Jews or Eastern Europeans that may understand the nuances of his immigrant background, but he's competing against thousands of applicants. Time is running out on his visa and his family needs some capital for their business that is struggling in Lagos because of inflation.

Akeem wants to help them financially, but he suspects they both keep him close out of envy, causing him to move with caution. Akeem could ignore these guys and spend more time talking to the older gentlemen in the club, but they are too stuck in the past. He would rather learn about the thoughts of younger Nigerians to help his business affairs back in Lagos.

Kemi brings their Guinness beers and Akeem's food.

"What did I tell you about not bringing me a fork? And I want wipes with my bowl now. Come on." Kemi goes to the kitchen to address his demands. Dayo smirks, amused at Akeem's insistence on the finest dining experiences despite their surroundings.

Chike sips from one bottle after sucking on a piece of meat bone. "Uncle, how's Naija business?"

"It is well. I'm bored of petroleum. I want to get into solar power." Akeem stares at a television screen playing MSNBC with updates regarding Mali while Kemi comes with his wipes. He then dips his hand into his own bowl.

Dayo chimes in. "Ah—solar is expensive o. You can get customers on the island, but what of mainland people? They need light."

Chike swallows, preparing his next thought. "Not if he mass-produces it and makes it more affordable."

"Do you hear yourself? Our government will run him mad before they give him resources to mass-produce solar power for mainland Nigerians."

This is what Akeem comes here for; he loves their banter. "I'm going to produce it affordably, probably with the Chinese."

Dayo looks at him with concern. "Those people will cheat you, Uncle. They did that with your container home ideas."

"It's worth it to try, abi?" Akeem looks away from the television in their direction for feedback. Dayo and Chike shrug at Akeem's whimsical desires and continue eating.

***

Kemi turns down the televisions, dims the lights, and raises the volume of the Sunny Ade blasting through the speakers while all the Uncles and Daddies debate about any and everything they watched earlier. Akeem drags Dayo and Chike to a table with a group of older Uncles.

"My nephew marched from Surulere to Lekki at the massacre! The SARS protests brought international attention. We can't ignore that," Akeem tells the entire table, impassioned after a few drinks.

All the men groan and suck their teeth loudly.

"See this one. Akeem—you think you are the Bill Gates of Africa now?" one of the older Uncles named Tope dares to challenge him.

Akeem frowns. "How can we expect change with your mindset?"

"So why aren't you back home then, Mr. Bigshot? You people know how to say all the right things, but your blood money can't change anything!" Uncle Tope slams the table, drunk. Conversations often get tense, but never enough to prevent them from returning for another heated discussion the following week.

Akeem never grows tired of going back and forth with Tope, who is the mouthpiece for how most lounge members view him. "I run a tight business. Not everyone that's wealthy in Nigeria is corrupt."

The men on Tope's side burst into laughter at Akeem's claims. Chike and Dayo remain silent, watching future versions of themselves on a Friday night, intrigued.

"You all think I'm a crook, so I won't bother explaining how I operate with full integrity."

Tope reassures him. "Akeem, I want you to make your money work for Naija. That's all I'm saying to you. You know me now, right?"

"Yes, sir. I understand you."

Akeem's phone pings with a text and he applies his jacket.

"Ah—you want to leave us now?" Tope's tone grows anxious while the object of his weekly entertainment prepares to leave.

"I have a longer ride than most of you in my gated house. Sorry Sir." Akeem shakes Tope's hand and they laugh, knowing he's not *that* wealthy.

"Let me join you." Tope gets up with bulging, bloodshot eyes.

Akeem walks out of Chief Lounge to his car with Tope trailing him. Tope's body language is eager in a way that makes him uncomfortable.

"Uncle, are you alright?"

"I need your help." Akeem stops, concerned. "My son is about to enter his last year for his pre-medical degree, but my wife and I are running out of money to pay for his tuition."

Akeem sighs before he figures out a way to get out of this request. "I'm sorry to hear that. How much?"

"Twenty thousand."

Akeem continues his walk to his car. "Ah… Uncle, I don't have that kind of money now."

"Akeem, you know I wouldn't be begging you like this as an elder if I didn't know for certain that you have it."

"I put a lot of my savings towards investments. And my daughter needs my help right now."

Akeem arrives at his car and Funmi is leaning on the passenger side window. Tope stares her up and down, then offers a greeting. "Ka a le, Tope. Bawoni?"

She prostrates for him and smiles on cue. "Ka al e, Uncle, I'm fine. Thank you."

Tope grabs Akeem's forearm, moving him away from Funmi to avoid her hearing more than necessary.

"Akeem, what can you do for me? Please."

Akeem shakes his head, shrugging. "Uncle, if I run into any extra money, I'll let you know right away."

"Okay, okay. Thank you. I'll call you." Tope pats him on the back and walks away. Akeem and Funmi enter the car and drive off.

***

Akeem and Funmi occupy a room in one of the affordable hotels lined up on Atlantic Avenue over the past recent years. The staff is acquainted with the pair and knows exactly what they want—a single room with a queen or king-sized bed. These establishments might not meet Akeem's standards, but it's comfortable enough.

Akeem and Funmi are naked, finishing a round of passionate sex. Funmi is on top, riding him like a stallion while he caresses her large breasts. He used to be more of an ass man, but he likes to watch the body parts that turn him on during his favorite position—having the woman hover over him.

She moans loudly during her orgasm, in the same way, every week. Akeem questions if they are real, but it doesn't matter since he's getting his needs met either way. Funmi is one of his most expressive lovers at the moment. Her freeness during sex is a reprieve from most of the repressed Nigerian women he's been intimate with.

Once they are done, Funmi removes his penis from her body and lies next to him, rubbing his chest. Akeem is sweaty and out of breath. Funmi is in her mid-thirties and is a workout for his aging limbs.

"You lasted for almost 15 minutes this time. Good job Big Daddy." She kisses his neck, disregarding his musty senior citizen body.

Akeem chuckles, knowing she's full of shit, but his ego can't get enough of it. He puts his arm around her.

"What did Uncle Tope want?"

Akeem sucks his teeth, irritated. "Nothing. He needs school fee money for his son."

"Are you going to give it to him?"

"Of course not!"

"Ok, good."

Akeem grabs the television remote to turn on the news, but she reaches his hand to stop him.

"Akeem."

When she calls him by his first name—which is a rare occurrence, it's serious. He would never allow it in mixed company, but they have a private understanding.

"Your wife called me last night."

Akeem sits up, wide-eyed. "How? How did she get your number?"

"I don't know."

"Did you contact her?"

"No, she found my information somehow."

Akeem takes a deep breath to calm his nerves. "Shit."

"She threatened to call authorities on me. Is she involved with the government here?"

Akeem shakes his head, humored by his wife's empty threats. "No, she has a law degree and likes to show off. My wife can't do anything to you. You won't get deported, don't worry."

Funmi sighs, relieved.

"Did you block her number?"

"Yes, and I didn't confirm our affair or anything like that."

"Perfect." Akeem turns the television on after lying down and eases into the comfort of the hotel bed. Funmi leans into his body and thankfully his chest hairs are drying up.

***

After washing up and eating breakfast the next afternoon, Akeem drives back to Brooklyn. He's struggling to find a parking space in Kofo's neighborhood, reminding him of the main reason he moved his family out of this area right before Kofo went to high school—it's too congested. He also didn't enjoy having predatory neighbors his age catcalling at his daughters when Morenike sent them out on errands. Long Island shielded them from a lot of things, including social stimulation. While it's full of adventure, dipping in and out of Brooklyn is best for his mental clarity. He doesn't get Kofo's obsession with living here when she can stretch her dollars in the outskirts of the five boroughs.

He won a parking spot over a couple that took too long to reverse their Toyota a few steps away from Kofo's building. Akeem approached the intercom of the Ocean Avenue prewar building he spent much time in when he and Morenike lived in the neighborhood. The management repaired the front door, replaced the terrible lighting and installed a new elevator. It is nowhere near its former glory when Jews lived in the neighborhood post World War II, but it is a vast improvement from the hard knocks of ghetto living during the 1970s to the early 2000s. His friend Oluwasegun used to live in this building and he was terrified whenever he paid him a visit.

***

Akeem sits on Kofo's couch in her well-designed apartment. The early June sun fills her sunken living room, and plants crowd the two window sills. Her plush furniture is in tones of greys, whites, and blues. He admires the creativity of the room, but it doesn't resemble her usual style of earth tones and nature-based materials. Akeem notices the blue and gold prayer rug adorning the wall next to the television.

Akeem gets up to look at papers on a desk that he initially passed before sitting on the couch. He sees a welcome packet from Palette Cosmetics and inside is an employee handbook along with start paperwork. Kofo walks in on him and he heads back to the couch.

"Here you go, Daddy." Kofo gives him a bottle of chilled Guinness she grabbed from the fridge.

"No, thank you." Akeem shakes his head, wanting to focus on his daughter for this visit. She plops on a chair opposite his position after placing the bottle of beer on the table in between them.

"I'm happy for you. You secured employment already."

Kofo grins. "Thank you, Daddy. Tunde's colleague helped me get the interview. I'm an Ecommerce Coordinator."

Akeem nods and looks around for a few moments. "How much is this place?"

"$3,000."

"That's a lot."

"Look how big it is, though? This living room can fit two of my old bedrooms."

It is big, but Akeem believes Brooklyn isn't worth the money. This apartment would've been one thousand dollars around the time they moved away. "Okay," he says, in the interest of keeping the peace.

Kofo is staring at his face, waiting for him to start what he came over to discuss, but he doesn't. "So, what's up, Daddy?"

"I want you to take your time with Tunde."

"Daddy, I told you I'm going to."

"Make me the leaseholder, so there's less pressure on you both."

"Why wouldn't I want him to prove his ability to take care of me?"

"He can do that in other ways."

Kofo sighs. "I thought you wanted to come here to get to know him."

Akeem rubs his bald head, anxious. "Eniola is pregnant."

"Wow." Kofo responds, breathless.

Akeem breaks Kofo's thoughts. "Let me handle your rent, Kofo."

"Daddy, no."

"I'll send you enough to cover your expenses and let Tunde contribute whatever he can. Don't tell your mother and she doesn't know about the pregnancy yet either."

"Both Tunde and I have jobs. We can figure this out. Besides, won't she know about the money? Y'all don't have a joint account?"

"I do my thing for now. I'll send you a little something. Don't fight me on this. You need it, and I don't want you to sign up for anything with this guy too soon."

Kofo looks at the bottle of Guinness at the table, frowning.

"Save anything that you don't spend from me. Don't tell him. I want you to be absolutely sure." Akeem turns Kofo's television on to MSNBC. "When is Tunde coming to eat with us?"

"He's getting some stuff for the house at Target downtown. He'll be back in like an hour."

"Great." Akeem leans back on the sofa and puts his feet on the coffee table.

CHAPTER 4

Jackie Robinson Park is abuzz with Black families that are reunited after another rainy New York City spring and snowy, cold winter. Cedric helps Eniola as she struggles to walk another high, inclined, hilly Harlem block before they get to the park's entrance. The Upper Manhattan neighborhood of Sugar Hill is breathtaking with various shades of brownstone townhouses, walkups made of the finest stones and massive prewar buildings that offer stunning views of the Harlem River, but moving around the elevated streets is exhausting for Eniola. They parked their BMW right next to this same entrance the year prior, but it got broken into and they used a garage before making their way over to the park. Eniola prefers ordering an Uber to avoid traveling long distances on foot, but Cedric wants them to save for a house and watch their expenses. Enola grabs the metal railing before they walk three flights of stairs up another hill inside the park.

"Come on babe, you got it." Cedric takes out a handkerchief and wipes it down her drenched face.

Eniola needs another break when they finally make it to the top. Her makeup melts in the 90-degree, humid heat. They walk a few more steps before seeing a massive sign that reads "Welcome to the Annual Mathis Family Cookout" in bright blue letters.

Before they make it to the crowd, Cedric's mom Yvonne spots her son with Eniola wobbling next to him.

"Ahh!" She's thrilled to see them both and walks in their direction.

Cedric embraces his mom while Eniola catches her breath.

"Hi Ms. Mathis." Yvonne reaches in to hug Eniola, but she steps back. "I'm feeling really gross and sweaty, I don't want to ruin your attire."

Yvonne studies Eniola, who looks ridiculous in a caftan and velvet turban toppling her old weave during this weather. She added a belt and some nice accessories, but no wonder she's swimming in perspiration.

"Do you have pants under that thing?"

"No, just biker shorts."

"Let me get you one of our T-shirts."

Cedric jumps in. "Ma, that's okay—"

"No, Ennie is uncomfortable. Come with me sweetie." She grabs Eniola's wrist, grabs a T-shirt from a box and they go to an area with less visibility.

"Take the gown off, relax."

"I'm not supposed to expose my legs Ms. Mathis."

"You're either menopausal or pregnant. You're too young for the latter, so when were y'all gonna tell me?"

Eniola is still out of breath, wishing she could soothe her overfilled lungs. This moment isn't helping and she stares at Yvonne for a long time, trembling. A tear runs down her cheek.

"It wasn't planned at all."

"I bet. When are you due?"

"September."

"Has Cedric mentioned marriage to you?"

Eniola bursts out crying, shaking her head no. Yvonne rolls her eyes, sighing.

"Take that curtain off and keep your baby safe. Next time, wear cotton leggings and a linen tunic in this weather." Yvonne stuffs the T-shirt in Eniola's face and she takes it. She starts to change. "And Ennie, you know I do hair. What's going on up there?"

Eniola sniffles at her question, self-conscious about exposing her torso and her bra that is too small for her growing breasts. "Here." Yvonne gives her a handkerchief.

Yvonne stares at Eniola, admiring her beautiful oval face while in distress. She has a V-shaped, petite nose with even toned lips and bright almond eyes. Her milky, chocolate tone glistens under her sweat, showing off a long, feminine neck. Eniola is one of few women who doesn't need foundation to have a smooth skin tone. Her body is a younger expression of her mother's perfectly proportioned shape, including a perky, muscular backside.

Eniola folds in Yvonne's presence, afraid that her forward questioning will expose the fragility of her relationship with Cedric. Not much needs to be said when comparing the couple side by side; Eniola's appearance is never aligned with Cedric's clean-shaven grooming and precise wardrobe combinations. When they were initially dating, Cedric used to tell her what to wear, but when they got comfortable, Eniola fell off and has lost sight of her personal style.

Yvonne and Eniola walk back to the growing crowd of Mathis family members. Yvonne gives Eniola one of the parting gifts—a canvas bag—and Eniola stuffs the caftan inside. Cedric glances at his girlfriend while chatting with another guest, failing to move an inch. Eniola makes her way to the buffet to grab food, her head hanging down to avoid eye contact from everyone. Yvonne heads to a lawn chair with the other aunties and plops a fashionable straw hat on her head, covering a very stylish relaxed bobbed haircut. She picks up her cocktail drink from a red cup that matches her nail color and nude lipstick that compliments her caramel skin. Yvonne soaks up any opportunity to offer a large dose of Harlem glamor.

Eniola scours the heated foil pans of fried whiting, catfish, barbeque chicken, mac n cheese, potato salad, candied yams, collard greens, cornbread and more Black American delicacies. She puts everything on her plate, gorging on it all while Alicia Meyer's "I Wanna Thank You" plays from the DJ speakers with other back-to-back soul hits from the 1970s and 80s. Cedric's uncle Shane—Yvonne's brother, grills a massive cut of brisket and waves at Eniola, and she returns his greeting with a quick rise of her palm. He's become a grill master since buying a home in Atlanta years ago. The Mathis family is dedicated to this cookout and they travel all over the country to reunite yearly.

Yvonne watches her son neglect his girlfriend, questioning where the hell she went wrong. Cedric went to the best schools in Harlem that led to an admission into Hampton University. She never pressured him to be a lawyer. She only demanded that he find financial security to avoid ending up like his father, who got caught up with excessive partying and drugs after leaving the Nation of Islam because Yvonne changed her mind about joining. Yvonne believes that her ex-husband is somehow still alive and strung out somewhere near Penn Station—family members spotted him panhandling near the escalator entrance on seventh avenue. Yvonne left Cedric's father after their son's fifth birthday and met her new husband Reginald, an amazing man from Jersey that owns a few chain restaurants and vending machines in grocery stores across the country. His relationship with Cedric started off great until rumors of his biological dad surfaced while Cedric was in undergrad. Yvonne struggled to reconnect Cedric with Reginald and Cedric maintains a persistent distance. She noticed the effects of his biological father's resurgence and encouraged him to go to therapy but he declined. Years later, he still struggles with brooding mood swings and periods of intense coldness that he takes out on Eniola. His childhood wasn't perfect, but there were enough cautionary tales to warn Cedric about the pitfalls of keeping a woman unhappy. Yvonne heard him years before meeting Eniola say that he wants a "submissive" woman because he grew up around women who were too overbearing.

Yvonne sends Cedric a text saying *Congratulations*. He looks up at his mom and she raises her eyebrows with a knowing glance. He joins a growing huddle of attendees that are deep in discussion. Curtis turns away from Yvonne's stare and observes Eniola occupied with a heaping pile of mac and cheese. He peels from the group and makes his way over to Eniola.

"Ennie, they brought Jollof rice from that lady your mom uses. There's a cooler behind the table."

"Oh! Great."

"Do you want some?" Cedric notices dark tracks of dried mascara on her cheeks where her tears rolled moments earlier.

"Sure, thanks so much babe." Cedric goes to get her a plate.

***

Dusk falls upon the Mathis family gathering, and the crowd reaches its peak of attendees. Cedric compromises his task of driving a very pregnant Eniola home due to downing ten bottles of beer. Yvonne breezes past her son to catch her breath—she just finished leading an Electric Slide ensemble of 100 family members while the DJ
played Shaun Escoffery's "Days Like This." Cedric's immersion in a heated game of spades consumes his attention while Eniola sits behind him, browsing Yoruba weddings on Instagram.

"Ennie, you ready?"

"Yea."

Cedric leans forward to rise out of his chair, but one of his cousins Earl makes a strong play. Cedric slams a card on the table, one-upping Earl and he wins the game. Earl's wife Justina—a petite Afro-Indigenous Latina from the Bronx—is hysterical at

Cedric's bragging, inspiring a tirade of bravado commentary.

"How you like me now, nigga?! The title will *always* be mine, every year!" Cedric releases a rare cackle while standing up to spread his arms in victory. Eniola smiles, pretending to find him funny.

After the frenzy dies down, Eniola stands as he gives everyone daps or hugs before their departure. Eniola waves, uncomfortable with any other form of close contact, especially with Justina.

Cedric moves quickly towards Yvonne. She packs a to-go plate covered in foil and hands it to her son.

"Thanks, Ma." Cedric takes the plate, kisses her on the cheek, and escapes without another word. Eniola says her goodbyes and follows suit.

***

Eniola rubs several yards of shiny, decorative fabric while awaiting to get her gele wrapped by a professional in a high-end hotel room in Long Island. Her friend Jumoke nears the completion of her gele wrap service, wincing in her chair when the paper like material is tied tighter and tighter for a perfect fit. After her wrapper is done, Jumoke breathes in relief and gets up to join their third friend Sherifat in applying makeup. Most women hire makeup artists for events, but they attend outings often and gained application skills that rival professionals over the years.

Eniola arises from the bed, next in cue for a gele wrap, only wearing a white slip undergarment gown and a lace top assigned for their festivities that evening. Her lace wrapper is lying on the back of the chair.

Sherifat glances at Eniola's mid-section as she moves from one end of the room to the other. "Ennie, are you pregnant?!"

Eniola doesn't answer as the ladies turn their heads in a hurry for confirmation.

"No, no, no…" Jumoke freaks out and paces in front of the mirror.

"Congratulations, O!" Sherifat squeals. She remains a sucker for love in spite of countless experiences with heartbreakers. Sherifat investigates without hesitation. "When are you due, is it Cedric's and what of marriage?"

"Of course, Cedric is the father. He's the only man I've been with in years." Eniola frowns, ignoring everything else asked.

Sherifat's eyes sway back and forth from Eniola's belly to her face. "Why aren't you excited? Don't you and Cedric love each other? Isn't he like the type of guy you always wanted?"

Eniola fights back her embarrassment with a tightened jaw.

"I knew it." Jumoke claps her hands, rubbing them together like a Yoruba auntie. All of these women existed in the Diaspora for ten years or more and their recent entry into their mid-thirties is shifting the stakes with decisions that seemed minor years prior.

Their Nigerian identities sustained throughout their friendship and their engagement in the Nigerian community that often gathers for weddings, parties and other occasions. They could wrap their own geles, but it would be obvious that they are amateurs and thus would attract resources or men that are on the level of their traditional wear. It's better to show out completely with head wraps that resemble perfectly bloomed flowers, accompanied by glitzy chunks of jewelry. Saint Laurent, Gucci and Fendi purses scatter both beds. Louboutins line up on the wall next to the hotel door.

"Know what? What is it now, Jumoke?" Eniola snaps. She gets defensive when her friends tell her the truth. Her mouth sharpens in the companies of these ladies who are more like frenemies since she upon dating Cedric four years ago.

Jumoke snaps back in equal irritation. "I'm sorry but I don't like this Cedric guy. I never did," she says in a mashup of a Nigerian and American accent, waving her finger to emphasize her point. "He's dragging you along."

"Ah—Moke, chill now." Sherifat says in a delicate tone.

Jumoke ignores her. "This is the same guy who asked you to calculate the square footage of your rented apartment to distribute bills and then had the *nerve* to ask you for an extra $50 dollars over your use of closet space. You suspect that he's being unfaithful, you said he's not that good in bed, he's not proposed, you make just as much if not more money, and now he's impregnated you. *Eni-o-la, what are you doing?*" Jomoke's Nigerian accent is more pronounced with every gripe.

Sherifat's eyes crease in patronizing sympathy. "I just want to know when you are due and why you didn't say anything."

Eniola's grimaces from the pain applied to her temples as the wrapper fixes her gele. "I wasn't sure what I was going to do and no, he hasn't."

Jumoke scoffs. "Let me tell both of you something. I'm the only one in here that is married. And for not my husband, I would not have children. You have to have the right partner. Otherwise, it's *very, very* hard."

Sherifat jumps in to Eniola's defense. "She's already here. What do you want Ennie to do?"

A silence befalls the room at Sherifat's question that none of them can adequately answer.

Jumoke isn't letting up. "Sebi, why can't she do that thing they do here? Child support or whatever it's called." Jumoke is waits for Eniola to engage her and Eniola remains silent, inspiring her to continue. "You already did family law when you first started practicing, so you can protect yourself. Why not drop him and go that route?"

Eniola's gele is finally wrapped. She stands up and straightens out her top, moving her vision to Jumoke. "I'm staying with Cedric and we are going to figure it out. He wants to be more than just another baby daddy."

Jumoke rolls her eyes and finishes her makeup next to Sherifat, annoyed at Eniola's desperation. She's boastful now, but when Cedric acts up for the umpteenth time, Jumoke is the first person Eniola calls in tears. It was shady to reveal the rent issue which was a secret between the two of them, but she needed to justify her negative response to the pregnancy. Eniola's behavior in mixed company shows her lack of gratitude for Jumoke's loyalty, which she struggles to maintain in their lopsided friendship. When Jumoke needs support for her life as a married woman, Eniola does commit and she suspects it's out of jealousy over finding a husband first. Jacob picked Jumoke out from their trio at a 70th birthday party years ago. Eniola assumes everyone wants her the most because she is the prettiest, but Jumoke's self-assuredness is most evident, and that won him over quickly despite some extra weight.

Sherifat squeezes Eniola's hand before sitting down to get her gele wrapped. "Let us know if you need anything and we'll of course plan a baby shower."

"I doubt I'll have one, but thank you." Eniola brags about showers, parties and weddings all the time—her answer is not aligned with what they know about her. She turns her back to them, facing the window while putting on her lace wrapper.

***

A crowd of 20 people await Kofo's arrival while Tunde tricks her into a birthday dinner at Del Frisco's near Rockefeller Center—a restaurant with four dollar signs on its Google profile. He arranged a surprise group dinner their private dining room. For a couple that prides themselves on patronizing Black-owned businesses, they don't celebrate important milestones on their premises.

We just finished at the spa, should be there in 15-20 minutes, Tunde texts Eniola with Cedric peering over her shoulder. Eniola wonders if he needs a real-life manual from her sister's boyfriend on how to fix their relationship.

Janelle sits across Eniola's seat, giggling at a corny joke made by Kofo and Eniola's nerdy cousin Maroof. He's one of the few Black startup founders in New York City, which somewhat improved his swag.

He needs to take his button-downs to the cleaners for proper pressing, similar to the wrinkled shirt he's currently wearing. He can benefit from a nice shave and a teeth whitening procedure. Nothing will convince Eniola that Janelle wasn't after anything other than his recent company acquisition. Her pursuit of a trophy wife's life is ruthless. Eniola plans to call him tomorrow to warn him about Janelle's trick 'em and leave 'em ways. He would never recover from her schemes, considering how much he's ogled over her throughout the years.

Speaking of Janelle, Eniola wonders why Tunde didn't include her in the planning or coordination of the dinner. She and Kofo have a decent rapport, justifying her involvement. Eniola sees herself as a surrogate mother to Kofo because their mother was busy trying to live up to communal norms. Eniola resents her mother as a result, and Kofo resents her sister. If Eniola or Kofo doesn't keep their mother happy, their father will get the wrath that is Morenike. Akeem subdues them with hush money, keeping his daughters a bay to prevent them from pushing the boundaries of Nigerian femininity.

"We have 15 minutes guys!" Cedric belts out to everyone, and they nod at his baritone voice. Eniola wants to be the one who shares updates, irritated that he took another choice away from her. Whenever she prepares to speak to the other guests, her throat has an uncontrollable itch. She smiles at her boyfriend to prevent herself from arguing in front of her sister's friends and colleagues. Her subdued anger prompts a heat flash, causing her weave ponytail to stick to the back of her neck. She starts to fan herself with one of the smaller plates on the beautifully set table while looking down at the prix fixe menu. The plate is ivory white with gold trim. They serve high-end bar food, but the experience trumps it all. She prays Cedric is taking notes.

Her birthday is in mid-September and she is predicting he'll gift her another affordable dinner with paper napkins and acrylic cups. Eniola pretends to enjoy it, but the thought of her being worth so low feels insulting. The fancy table settings remind her that she will tell Cedric that she wants to go to a high-end spa and a Broadway show later that same evening. If she's hungry, they will end the night at The River Cafe with a prime view of the Manhattan skyline, while downing juicy steaks. She wants the fantasy of her ideal relationship to come to life.

Five minutes away! Tunde's text makes her phone ring. Cedric prepares to belt out, but Eniola puts her hand on his thigh and clears her throat to speak.

"Guys, we have five minutes." Her soft voice cracked from a pitiful attempt to raise her volume. Cedric yells out "Five minutes", and it sends everyone scrambling. Eniola looks at the attending waitress who turns off the lights. Various rounds of "Shh" fill up the room as they all wait in anticipation.

Eniola hears her heavy breaths in the midst of the silent group. She feels her baby kick as if it is also excited to surprise her baby sister. She hopes Kofo doesn't steal any adoration her child should possess only for its mother. Eniola fans herself with a small salad plate, rubbing her growing belly that's getting harder to hide under loose clothing.

Maroof is on a mission, ignoring the current task at hand. "I bet you Kofo knows it's a surprise. She gets to the bottom of everything," he says with a smooth, flirty voice to Janelle instead of remaining quiet.

"I think she's totally clueless." Janelle might as well be speaking about herself. Another loud "shh!" comes from a guest at the far end of the table.

Eniola's phone goes off again with a text from Tunde. *Walking in.*

"They're coming!" she whispers, as everyone adjusts in their high-end seats. She likes hearing everyone move to her command.

Moments later, Tunde and Kofo walk in and everyone erupts into a chorus of "Surprise!!!". Kofo breaks out into instant tears of joy, kissing Tunde passionately.

After they all feast on fancy versions of modern American food, Kofo clicks her glass to make a speech. Eniola feels another flash coming on and wipes her forehead, staining the cloth napkin.

"Shit," she mumbles under her breath. Cedric chats up Kofo's biracial coworker Marina who works in the legal department of Palette Cosmetics about recent contracts. He nods, indicating that he wants to continue their discussion later and looks at Eniola, then her napkin. He swaps out their napkins then proceeds to watch Kofo wipe more tears of joy from her face.

"Thank you all so much for coming today." The crowd cheers as Kofo composes herself. "Not too long ago, I was at a low point in my life and in an unfulfilling relationship with someone who didn't value me. I was also lost and not following the vision for the life that is in my destiny. Since then, I decided to let all that baggage and energy go. And that manifested my Tunde."

"Aww," the crowd coos while she stares longingly at Tunde.

"I found someone that really understands me. That pushes me to focus on things that will only feed me. To see myself as the queen that I am. To know that I am favored and blessed."

Marina cheers, letting out a resounding "Yasss!!!" that pierces Eniola's ears.

Kofo goes on. "I hope you all can take my testimony as something to inspire your own journeys. I am really happy now, and tonight is another way for me to focus on my joy." Kofo raises her glass of champagne. "Thank you all, and thank you Tunde. I love you." She kisses Tunde again.

Eniola smiles without teeth, then clears her throat to sip on water while everyone downs their glasses of champagne. Something about Kofo's speech felt insufferable. Kofo's a bursting ball of self-righteous optimism since dating Tunde. Whenever Eniola tries to lament to her sister about her pregnancy, assuming it's a safe space—Kofo cuts her off, then tells her to "change her mindset" and that her "negativity is the cause of the disconnect" with Cedric. Kofo sounds like a social media meme, disregarding any grey space coloring in their experiences. Eniola wishes she could walk her sister through everything she's going through, but anything that doesn't sound like it'll feed her "glass half full" theory is disregarded as unworthy of her time. What Kofo doesn't get is that Eniola experienced a lot of things as a child so that Kofo can benefit. Her parents made all of the mistakes with their first born. Kofo has the opportunity to explore socialization beyond the Nigerian community and can view life outside of the approval of her parents, elders or other Nigerian peers.

Akeem walks in, fashionably late with high-end Ankara garb. *That's odd*, Eniola thinks to herself. Her father doesn't attend events like this and they celebrate birthdays for anyone in her immediate family in Long Island. He also hates American food. He's *never* offered to show up at her family gatherings. Akeem waves at the group as the waitress grabs him a chair.

Eniola freaks out because she's successfully hidden her pregnancy from her mother and is hoping she doesn't emerge into the room behind her father. Whenever Morenike comments on her recent weight gain, Eniola tells her that she got diagnosed with an autoimmune disease that causes inflammation. She can't remember if she told her if it was hypothyroid or endometriosis. She might have thrown fibroids in there too. Her mother goes overboard with prayer requests for her daughters, worrying for Eniola's life and fertility. Hypothyroid sounds more believable due to hot flashes occurring for some with the condition. She stays glued to her seat, refusing to offer her father a proper greeting.

Moments after Akeem settles in, Tunde bends on one knee. The crowd screams, startling the stuffy diners throughout the restaurant.

"Oh my God," Eniola whispers. Tunde *never* mentioned a desire to propose. It's been seven, *maybe* eight months. Her father watches Tunde, completely composed. The only giveaway of her father's surprise is the fidgeting of his napkin resting on his lap.

"Zeenat Kofoworola Adebayo—will you marry me?" Tunde says to Kofo in a tender voice. He must really be otherworldly for them to be discussing marriage so soon. Kofo took damn near a decade to walk away from Fahad.

The crowd holds their breaths, anticipating Kofo's answer.

"Yes! Yes, I'll marry you!"

Everyone squeals and Eniola gives a fake laugh, clapping for what seems to be joy. Cedric whistles and screams "Yea!" like a coach watching a great play. Eniola sips some water to hide her feelings of exclusion while the dinner group rallies around her sister's new life development. Sisters are supposed to talk or at least hint about these kinds of matters.

CHAPTER 5

Tunde lays in bed naked, waking up from making love to the woman of his dreams three times the night prior, still in disbelief that he's engaged. He turns to his right, staring at Kofo's closed almond-shaped eyes, button West African nose, deep brown skin, high cheekbones and full, plumped two-toned lips. Brief moments of solitude in the morning give him an opportunity to gawk at her sleeping face. She wore pounds of makeup when they initially met and frequently braided her hair in extensions, claiming to have a busy schedule. Tunde assured her that her natural beauty is far more striking and flattering. They negotiated and while she still loves to doll up, her true features are more apparent with fewer adornments to her overall look. He noticed a subtle growth in her confidence since.

Tunde rolls out of bed, picking his boxers from the floor and grabs his phone on the nightstand next to his side of the bed. Tunde pulls up WhatsApp to make a video call to his family in London after quietly tip-toeing to the living room. His mom, Adepeju, picks up the phone.

"Hello?!" she yells, as if she expects a poor connection. Her calls to Nigeria comprise of her screaming over static and continuous phone freezing.

"Mommy!" Tunde smiles, crust in his twinkling eye.

"Haven't you bathed?!" She uses every opportunity to remind him of how he can do better in every area of life. Adepeju assumes she sets an example, sporting a stocking cap under her bleached, low-cut hair that protects blotchy, scarred, dark brown skin. Her naked body hides under a casual earth-toned Ankara wrap, revealing plump arms on her thick, shapely body. "I'm making your favorite—egusi stew with goat meat and pounded yam."

Tunde moans in ecstasy, wishing he could ship an entire carton of his mother's cooking to New York City. "Mommy, I need to tell you and Dad something. Where is he?"

"Olumideee!!!" she yells again, wandering around their London townhouse for her husband. Tunde mutes his phone, fearing that he will wake Kofo up. Too late, as she's standing under the archway of the living room. Kofo moves to the couch and snuggles under Tunde, but he stops her.

"One-second babe." He squeezes her hand, smiling, then refocuses his attention back to his phone and meets both parents on the screen. His legs shake, yearning to blurt out his next thought before the moment passes. *Fuck it*, he says to himself. "Mom, dad… I'm engaged."

Olumide frowns as though he was just insulted. "What?!"

"Yea, you know the American girl I told you about that's from Brooklyn?"

Adepeju creases her 60-year-old forehead, wiping her damp face from the steaming pots in her kitchen. "Yes, the Muslim one?"

"Yea, we fell in love. We live together and I proposed last night!" Tunde beams, anticipating enthusiasm from his parents, who grew irritated with his deliberate avoidance of Black women in London. He's had phases of different types—blondes, Irish redheads, South Asians, East Asians, Spaniards, Russians—they figured Tunde's younger brothers and sisters will continue their Nigerian lineage after scores of discussions, campaigning to find his "own kind" more attractive. They were mistaken as his two younger sisters are both dating Caribbeans and his baby brother is with a woman from Turkey.

Olumide is insistent on being a wet blanket. "Isn't it too soon, Tunde?"

Tunde's smile fades as he thinks of what to say to his father. Kofo watches this uncomfortable exchange in her favorite chair across from the couch. He shared many discussions with his fiancé about his father's grumpy discontentment with being an African man in the same country that colonized his forefathers. Yet he raised his children in an English-speaking home, emphasized the superiority of British amenities over Nigeria's, constantly placed emphasis on going to their finest schools despite the lack of diversity and inclusion in these spaces, and complained about Tunde's mom encouraging them to carry foods that will "infest their offices with that foul stockfish smell" in their place of work.

"Dad—sometimes you just know when someone is it for you. That's what I'm saying right now."

Both of Tunde's parents are silent, familiar with this scenario. Tunde is a glutton for attention as the former fat, Black kid. He was teased mercilessly in primary school and a perfect target for unrelenting bullies. Tunde fought back with his fists, but he also fought back with the gym and extreme dieting, slimming down into a handsome playboy a year into secondary school. He eats a salad or a smoothie for lunch daily to avoid creeping up in sizes, knowing that he didn't win the genetic lottery of metabolism, thanks to Mommy dearest. He's spent most of his adult life trying to feign off his addiction to the adoration of the opposite sex upon realizing he is more attractive than most.

While his transfer to New York is an exciting new venture for Tunde, his parents worried he might come back with a baby or another "exotic" American wife. How bittersweet that their prediction came in a Nigerian package.

Olumide opens his mouth to blurt out another critique, but Adepeju puts her hand up to stop him. "Kofo, right?"

"Right."

"Congratulations, dear."

"Thanks Mom." Tunde nods, appreciative that her love for her eldest child won over skepticism.

Olumide purses his lips, holding back. The last time Tunde had an in-person exchange with his father, they fought over the burden that Tunde felt with supporting his younger siblings. Tunde worked two part-time jobs in addition to his full-time entry-level finance job once graduating from university to help his family take care of the college tuition for his younger siblings. He limited his life to London throughout his twenties and wanted to see what else was available beyond the burdens of cultural obligation. Olumide couldn't fathom this perspective and took immediate offense. Why wasn't Tunde content enough with the life that his doting family afforded him? Were they not good enough for his businessman dreams? Tunde tried to explain that their investment in a better life wouldn't pay off for generations if he and his siblings didn't expand. Since meeting Kofo, he gets where his father is coming from. His parents were worried that he might never come back if he seeks comfort outside of his culture. Kofo is literally a dream come true on paper. A total class upgrade with the combination of resources. Their future grandchildren will be global citizens of three nations, all three powerful in their own right. The world will be for the taking.

His mom is an owner of a takeout restaurant in South London, and his dad does taxes for a hefty sector of the West African population in the same neighborhood. They aren't what others would consider "well off", but did their best to at least buy a modest house. Tunde shared a room with his baby brother before moving out on his own, which also prompted Tunde's interest in dating to crash on a bed away from his childhood home. He wanted privacy away from peeping—and snitching—siblings.

"I want us all to meet. Can we come to you in a week or two? Maybe the end of August?"

Kofo becomes wide-eyed and frantic at her fiancé's suggestion, waving her hands at him in dissent. He glances at her, then focuses back on his phone.

Olumide looks down at the bubbling pot of egusi, and Tunde hopes it'll be enough to quell his concerns. "Okay." is all he can muster up to his son.

"Sure, you can come and stay with us. We have a room available and will make it nice for you." Adepeju moves the phone away from Olumide, only capturing her face.

"Thank you, Mommy. Love you, I'll call you with updates."

"Okay dear. Let's arrange a call with Kofo's parents soon, please."

"Absolutely."

"Greet her for me."

"Bye."

Tunde hangs up, sighing in relief. "Woo!" He leans back onto the couch, oblivious to Kofo. After a few moments, he remembers she is standing by for his thoughts on the call. A blush-colored silk nightgown with a hem that grazes her knees drapes her crossed legs. She's a beautiful class act, even when she's worried.

Tunde sits up again, alert. "Babe, what's wrong?"

"I can't take time off so soon. I just started my job at Palette."

Tunde groans, forgetting, and smacks his forehead. "Shit!"

"Why don't you go without me to smooth things over? It might be better, actually."

"They want to get to know you, babe."

Kofo gives him a yea right kind of look.

"Look, they always do this shit. It's like they never believe my decisions. But Kofo, I know they are going to love you. Trust me."

"Go without me. We'll return in a few months."

Tunde gets up, kissing Kofo with his chapped lips.

"Clean that sulfur bomb before you kiss me."

"Not until you come to London with me."

They play fight as Kofo tries to get Tunde's hot breath away from her nostrils. Without confirmation, they both understand that Kofo won't be going to London.

***

Tunde strolls out of his Virgin Atlantic flight that just landed in Heathrow International Airport, pep in his step. He reflects on just finishing his only first-class flight experience with his future father-in-law by his side. Akeem trails a spellbound Tunde with a small bag that can only accommodate a computer and a few books.

"Mr. Adebayo, you didn't pack any clothing?" Tunde asked. Akeem strolled onto the plane as the last passenger before takeoff, late for his flight. He walked into his first-row seat, assuming that the plane would never take off without him aboard.

He smirks at Tunde. "I have a place here. Let's go." Akeem moves with complete domination, using his 6'4" frame to damn near trample all the Londoners that won't move out of his way. Tunde taps him, pointing to the arrow directing them to the subway. Akeem continues to the arrivals section of the airport, shooting Tunde a dirty look. "We have car service." Akeem doesn't skip a beat and Tunde falls right in line.

***

Their all-black, slick SUV pulls up in front of Akeem's semi-detached brick house in Dartford, a solidly middle-class London neighborhood. It's a newly constructed, three-story structure with metal details and updated grid windows held up with a dark-colored finishes. Once the driver unloads Tunde's luggage and pulls away, Akeem whips out his phone.

A woman pulls an ivory-colored curtain back and then opens the door for them to walk in. She's a petite, Black woman who appears to have maid uniform.

"Good afternoon, sir." Tunde spots her Nigerian tribal marks on her almost cat-like cheekbones. He hates watching this woman who is old enough to be his grandmother avoid eye contact with them both.

Tunde's head spins in one hundred directions, staring at the intricate details of the home as he enters the unassuming exterior. The house is something out of a magazine. High ceilings expand its size, glazed brass rods hold up sheer curtains, plush microfiber white couches fill in the parlor and soft tan rugs cover glossy wooden floors. The walls are painted in an eggshell shade, and modern floodlights add a touch of modern interior design—it's the kind of home Tunde dreams about. Tunde walks further into the house, getting a better look at the all-white kitchen with pure marble countertops and brass-colored appliances. A thick wooden dining table surrounded by velvet chairs is adjacent to the rear of the first floor. The entire black wall is made of accordion glass panels, revealing a properly landscaped backyard.

"Tola, collect Tunde's items so he can bathe, and finish cooking so we can prepare for a meal with his family," Akeem grumbles as he hypnotizes himself with his phone. "Make sure our dinner is prepared for seven seats by sundown."

Tunde wants to tell Akeem that his mother will bring food that'll probably taste better than whatever Tola puts together. He instead opts to follow Tola upstairs to his room to freshen up after a long flight. She lugs his enormous suitcase with much struggle as she ascends to the top of the stairs. He attempts to help her by reaching for the top handle of his luggage, but she shakes her head in refusal.

"Thank you, Aunty Tola." He tries to cup the bottom of the suitcase as she groans on the last step.

"Call me Tola when you're downstairs. I'm Auntie up here." She slams down the handle of the suitcase, smiling from the victory of having the heavy luggage on a leveled surface.

Tunde scoffs at the suggestion. "I would never."

They smile at each other, understanding that this is all show for Akeem. Tola stumbles her achy body down the stairs, leaving Tunde to finish the job of getting settled in a well-furnished guest bedroom.

***

Tunde buttons his pressed, long sleeve, fitted shirt underneath a plaid blazer. It's summer in London, but he cannot survive Akeem's blaring air conditioner without a jacket on the ground level for longer than a few minutes.

As Tunde descends the stairs, he spots Akeem laying his feet on a wood trunk coffee table, similar to the way he unwound in his Brooklyn apartment weeks before. A tailored, native outfit in a navy shade is his attire of choice, with the knees slightly wrinkled, but overall, he looks sharp and his cologne consumes the room. Maybe Akeem is the inspiration behind Kofo's favorite color, Tunde says in his head.

"Have your parents updated you?" Akeem asks while watching the BBC.

"Yes, they are parking now." His parents are late by at least ninety minutes wherever they go because his mother is managing a full calendar of domestic duties, and tonight is no exception. Tunde looks at the prepped the dining table and thankfully Tola placed the food in the serving coolers that Nigerians often get as event parting gifts to keep their food warm.

Tunde looks at Tola scrape her uneven nail against a sticker from one cooler that outlines the details of the celebrant.

"Was the party that terrible?" Tunde jokes to Tola, and she giggles quietly.

"I never want those tacky details on my dinnerware. I mean, who goes to parties for parting gifts with the celebrant's name and face plastered all over it? How gratuitous," Akeem complains.

"I don't mind it," Tunde says, indifferent to Akeem's musings.

Akeem peers at Tunde with a quizzical look of judgement.

Tunde twists his hands in discomfort, hanging aimlessly near the kitchen island without a mission.

Minutes later, Tunde hears a car door slam and his mother's voice. She's on the phone, finishing a catering order in Yoruba. He sighs, annoyed that she never reserves her amplified self for more private settings, such as her own front lawn. As Tunde heads to the door, Akeem sits up, outraged.

"What are you doing?!" He barks.

Tunde leaps back as Tola jets to the door. "Oh. Sorry about that."

"Never answer the door," Akeem growls, adding a pit to Tunde's already unsettled stomach.

Tola swings the door open, revealing Adepeju who hangs up, and Olumide trailing behind her.

"Mommy!" Tunde realizes how much he misses her and they embrace for several moments, happy to be reunited after almost eighteen months apart. Her body is warm, as though it was ready to greet him. Adepeju's look is appropriate for a fancy dinner— she wore her highest quality natural colored wig and her makeup has gold undertones against her rich, chocolate skin. She threw on a shiny Ankara skirt and blouse ensemble, and fancy Italian sandals with a matching purse. She even wore the Chloe perfume Tunde purchased for her the year prior.

Olumide pats him on the back. "Hi Tunde." They smile, avoiding close contact. Olumide isn't wearing traditional clothes and sports the same outfit as his son—jeans, a button-down shirt and a blazer. He's also wearing cologne that Tunde shipped to them from New York. The packaging is shaped like a cigar and that sold him immediately when he passed the storefront on 30th and Broadway in Manhattan. His dad loves the film "The Godfather", and Tunde used to wrap paper bags with tea leaves in a mock cigar, pretending to mimic Don Corleone wandering around the house as a preteen. He kept his father in stitches with this act until his mother found out and gave him a severe whooping for idolizing a "criminal lifestyle". Tunde got beatings for damn near everything growing up, but they lost their stride after their first two children. Rather than applying physical force, both of his parents settled for tirades, yelling and abusive insults to keep their remaining children in line.

Tunde studies Akeem's reaction and notices his focus on the tension Tunde displays towards his father.

Both of Tunde's parents prostrate for Akeem and he politely chuckles.

"Oh, no. Please, stand up." Tunde watches him lie straight through his teeth. Had they not prostrated, he would've given them another notch down in his tabulations of social decorum.

Akeem turns off the television and leads them to the dining table. Tunde's siblings rang the bell not much later.

"Ayeee!!!" Tunde's sisters Bisi, Abeni and his youngest brother Seun, all greet him with a group hug when Tola lets them in.

"This house is amazing!" Adebisi says with a South London accent more pronounced than Tunde, flipping her purple weave with long, colorful acrylic nails.

"Yasss, it's too bad." Abeni marvels and brushes her hands against the marble counter, wide-eyed. Seun follows them, nodding in agreement. Tunde sits at the table, watching Akeem stare them up and down in disapproval as they walk in.

"Good evening, Mr. Adebayo," they all say in unison.

"Hi. Have a seat." He cuts a piece of meat and dips his pounded yam into the stew. Tunde realizes that he never saw Akeem eat swallow and wondered why he ate with a fork when the moment finally arrived. Tunde's parents follow suit with Akeem and grab their utensils after stealing a glance of annoyance at their son. His siblings, who were also confused, join in eating their favorite delicacy with a fork, looking at their food with baffled stares. Tunde's seat is opposite Akeem at the other head of the table.

"Tunde, why not let your father sit in your position?" Akeem asks, cocking his head sideways.

Olumide waves off Akeem's suggestion. "Oh, it's fine, sir. Tunde is practically the head of our house."

"Please, call me Akeem. We are age mates." Akeem turns his body towards Olumide, who is sitting next to him. Tunde leans forward, ready to play stand by for his father. Olumide nods, nervous at Akeem's stance. "So how is Tunde the head of your household? What do you do?" Akeem shoots a brief look at Tunde while questioning his father.

"I'm an accountant."

"Are you at a big firm?"

"No, I work with private clients, mostly immigrants."

"I see." Akeem sips on water. He skips the Guinness sitting next to his cup.

"And what about you, Akeem?" Olumide asks.

"I started my career in petroleum rigs in various states outside of Lagos, and now I'm using my

93

money accumulated from that to transition into real estate."

Tunde comes to his father's defense. "Really, Mr. Adebayo? Kofo told me you were working on import, export and then something about solar energy with the Chinese?"

"She's correct, but I have since transitioned out of that and want to establish multi-unit estates throughout Lagos, since it's a big industry."

"Well, my dad has helped several small businesses gross millions because of his bookkeeping abilities. That's how I got my interest in finance, by assisting in his shop and watching him work."

Akeem doesn't acknowledge Tunde's comment. "And what about you, Mrs. Bakare?"

"Oh, I am a Nigerian restaurant owner."

Akeem raises his eyebrows. "That's nice, is it—
"

Adepeju drops her cutlery, fueling the discomfort of the table. Tola is on standby, but rushes upstairs once she spots Adepeju's aggression. "It's a takeout in Tottenham. We have mostly working-class patrons. My husband went to the University of Ibadan and got a PhD in economics and we met while I studied for my business degree there. We immigrated in the early 80s initially in the United States, but didn't like it and brought Tunde here with us here where the rest of our children were born."

Tunde's eyes race across the table and his sister, Bisi, contributes. "I'm an art professor. Abeni is a social media consultant and Seun is deciding between medical school or dentistry."

Olumide nods and smiles while cutting a piece of meat.

Akeem leans back in his chair, sighing for a few moments. Everyone anticipates his next move. "I think we should get down to business and cut all the niceties at this point. Olumide and Mrs. Bakare—I want you to really explain how you feel about the engagement of our children."

Tunde refuses to eat, only consuming a small piece of meat on his plate. Adepeju notices and kicks him under the table, directing her eyes to his plate. Tunde tastes a small dab of stew on his fork. His mother's food is better.

"Well…as Tunde's father, I certainly have questions about Kofo, her background…we are very devout Christians, we want to know her story—"

Akeem snorts in offense. "There's nothing to worry about on that end regarding my daughters or my family in general."

"What my husband was trying to say is that we want to get to know her and your family better. For example, we would've loved it if your wife could have joined. But time will work with us and we can of course travel to the U.S. if needed." Adepeju sips on some water to cool herself down.

"We can arrange that." Akeem gives them all the phoniest of smiles.

Akeem politely kicks them out with an announcement that he is behind on his prayers less than thirty minutes later. Tunde and his siblings file out while Adepeju slowly walks to the foyer with Olumide behind her.

"Akeem, you're welcome to stop by my restaurant for a free plate of traditional cuisine," Adepeju says to Akeem.

Akeem twists his mouth into a smirk. "I like my food home cooked, but thank you for the offer."

"Okay. Goodnight then." Adepeju releases herself from Akeem's judgement and walks outside.

Olumide shakes Akeem's hand with a firm grip. "Thank you, sir."

"Anytime." Akeem pats his shoulder as he passes through the front door.

Tunde nods at Akeem and Akeem stands still, returning a nod before closing the front door.

***

Tunde sits behind his father's driver seat in a champagne-colored Mercedes on the way back to their house. It's a fifteen-year-old five passenger vehicle with a worn leather interior and a loud engine. Tunde offered to replace it with a Volkswagen, but his dad said "Mercedes or nothing else". Tunde leans his head on the window, sullen. He fears that the dinner shattered his dreams of taking his life to the next level with Kofo.

Adepeju stares at her son via the rearview mirror.

"Tunde, are you alright?"

"Yes, Mommy."

When they arrive at their narrow terrace style house in Greenwich—a modest neighborhood of Black immigrants in southeast London—Tunde's body feels a sense of dread as he pulls his suitcase from the trunk. Their house has two windows across its width as opposed to Akeem's, two floors, and faded bricks throughout that need restoration.

What if Kofo calls off the engagement? Tunde thinks to himself. He probably wouldn't be able to stay in New York. It would be too painful.

Tunde drags his belongings to the spare room—his sisters' old room in the three-bedroom home—and closes the door. It is small, narrow, and dimly lit with shades of pink furniture and textiles that are thrown off by their old camel-colored carpet. Tunde hates the carpet and negotiated to get it replaced but Olumide wants to get a few more years out of it to feel like he got his money's worth. Their family can afford to sell this house and buy a nicer place, but Tunde's dad refuses. "I earned every pound for this house," Olumide would boast when Tunde sent him listings of better, bigger spaces in their budget. Being in this room feels like his father is winning in reeling him back into the same mindset.

Tunde plops on the bed, staring at the pink and white wallpaper.

Mommy wanted Kofo to stay here? He wonders. He would've rushed them to the "poshest" hotel, positive she would be unimpressed.

He heads to the one bathroom in the house to shower before bed, and again—not much has changed. The curtain needs to be replaced and there is mold along the caulk that's rimming the bathtub. He rolls his eyes, frustrated at more reminders of why he needed to get the hell out of London. Taking this on would require energy that depletes Tunde.

Once he gets out and enters the corridor, he overhears his mother whispering in Yoruba what Olumide should've said to set Akeem straight. Tunde goes back into his room to sleep for the night.

***

The next morning, Tunde gets dressed when he hears a knock on the door.

"Come in!"

Seun walks in. "Hey bro."

Tunde detangles his trimmed beard with a small toothed comb, leaning down in front of the pink and white vanity mirror to view his progress.

"You alright, man? Last night was rough."

"Yea, yea…I'm straight. Wanna eat breakfast down the block at our spot on me?"

"Mom and Dad want us to come to church. They're already there and mom left us some fried eggs and yam. Here's your robe. I grabbed it from one of the drawers in our room." Seun is already in his all-white robe that drapes over his jeans and t-shirt; a customary ensemble for their Celestial Church.

Tunde groans, irate. He snatches the garment from his brother and puts it on.

"I hope this girl is worth it man. You know mom and dad always say that Nigerian Muslims are fanatics."

Tunde's head pokes out from his robe and he shakes into the sleeves, aligning it with his shoulders. "She's not like that. She's more classy and refined. She's…basically like us. A little bit Nigerian, a little bit American. You get?"

Seun laughs. "She sounds like *you*."

Tunde sucks his teeth. "Let's go. I still want breakfast." He hits Seun chest with the back of his palm, and they leave the house.

***

Seun slips off his shoes as soon as they walk into the Holy Temple of Christ K&S Church, reminding Tunde to do the same. They are late for service, sliding right into the back rows. Adepeju and Olumide are in the front, both in all white. His mother has her usual white cap while they both shout "hallelujah!" in unison with the other congregation members as the pastor moves them with a gripping sermon.

Tunde never connected with the church and often spent his time surfing the internet on his phone or texting girls to meet up later whenever his parents requested his attendance for special occasions as he got older. Tunde prays on his own time when he's dealing with seldom life-related challenges. He didn't want to perform his religiosity to a group of people he barely knows. Tunde's relationship with God is intimate and quiet, and he prefers it stays that way.

The spiritual aspects of their church spooked him out—he suspects that it is more occult than following the ways of Christ. Nigerians from other churches and religions frown upon their church, citing them as a cult with a Jesus cherry on top.

Seun predicted that he would become an atheist if he married interracially or a Muslim if he stumbled upon an African from the other dominant religion on their continent. His brother isn't entirely wrong; Tunde prays every morning with Kofo, who shares similar values regarding her relationship with a higher power. They are learning each other's spiritual routines and Tunde promised to fast with Kofo during the next Ramadan season. They share feelings of an entity speaking to humanity under one universal language, and agree that people complicate the interpretation of God's words. One more reason to make it work between them.

All of the church mommies and daddies participate in the procession from their seats down the aisle, heading to the back of the church. If there is anything that Tunde loves about church, it's the music. It motivates his interest in Black American gospel, thus leading to an obsessive admiration of blues, funk and soul genres. He and Kofo vibe for hours on the subject, comparing notes on whether James Brown's original samples or the hip hop acts that followed his legacy better utilized the genius instrumentation played by his band. Kofo has amazing taste that's she's shy to admit to some of her friends that would much rather bob to the mellow R&B vibes of the 2020s. He reminds her that she will have a captive audience in him when it comes to her taste in art. They were both born in the wrong decade.

"Tunde! Come, come!" Adepeju summons him to the upper right-hand corner of the church, leaving the other mommies behind. Olumide rises out of his seat as well. "Pastor Folarin is ready for you."

"Mommy, no…"

"Tunde. We need answers. Let's go."

Tunde turns to the back where Seun is seated and they make eye contact. His little brother shrugs sympathetically. He feels like the baby of the family in this moment.

"Tunde…it's been a while, great to see you son. What questions do you have for me?" Pastor Folarin annoys Tunde. He's dipped in gold jewelry, crisp suits and an outdated flat top weekly. Where is he getting all this money from? Tunde ponders every time he encounters him. Why can't it be used to make aesthetic tune-ups to the old building? Or a scholarship fund for the poor and working-class families that are a part of the congregation? Adepeju swears he makes an honest living as a "religious consultant" but Tunde feels like he's a fraud. And so are his so-called premonitions. His parents swear by them, but Tunde actually has predictions of his own through his dreams that feel more comforting. He predicted his father getting into a car accident as a toddler and his mother vowed he would lead a life as a pastor or a prophet. She was heartbroken for years when Tunde declined her suggestion to take on that path, preferring to let her rely on Pastor Folarin as an alternative. He doesn't want that level of pressure on his intuition.

"I don't have a question for you." Tunde looks at his parents, rebelling against their attempts to lure him to Pastor Folarin. He doesn't want anyone in his congregation to know about Kofo. The only benefit is that all of the mommies would finally stop trying to hook him up with their daughters or nieces.

Olumide fidgets in impatience, spewing out his queries in Yoruba. "Our son just got engaged and we want to make sure it's a good match. I also want to make sure we get details on their family, specifically the girl's parents. Her name is Kofoworola Adebayo."

Pastor Folarin pulls them farther to the back of the pulpit, away from a group of other churchgoers that are waiting in line to speak to him. Tunde sighs, wishing his parents didn't believe in this. They are waiting on Pastor Folarin to open his large eyes so they can get on with their day. Pastor Folarin starts, also speaking in Yoruba.

"It's a good match." Wow. Tunde is shocked. "She's a good person, very different from other women you dated prior, Tunde. I like her for you a lot."

Tunde doesn't respond but is now invested because he likes what he's hearing.

"And the family?" Olumide questions.

Pastor Folarin tortures them again for several moments by closing his eyes.

Can he even see anything, why do they always close their eyes? Tunde wonders.

"Her family has a lot of problems. But Tunde you cannot tell her. She will leave you if you tell her because she will tell them that you are the source of the information. They will suspect you're into charms. Let her find out about her family on her own, especially her father." Tunde frowns, afraid to find out more. "Keep a cool head around her family, don't talk much and stay out of the way. They don't like you because your addition to the family will expose things. Your fiancé has an older sister, right?" Tunde nods, doubly shocked at that accurate detail.

Disappointed, Adepeju clasps her hands to the sky as if it will magically change what they heard.

"Mommy Tunde—don't worry. Your son will be okay if he takes my advice. You both should be happy that he found a nice Naija girl. This is what Tunde needs."

What I need? What does he know about what I need? Tunde refuses to give him the satisfaction of acting like he wants to know.

"Wait. Who has children out of wedlock?!" Pastor Folarin looks at Tunde in offense.

"Ah!" Adepeju looks like she's about to faint.

"It's not us, Mommy, it's her sister." He touches his mom's shoulder, calming her down.

Adepeju breathes and yelps loudly, concerning some of the folks in line.

"Tunde—it's not her sister. It's someone else. Stay out of it."

Olumide is not satisfied. "What can we do?"

"Nothing. Let your son be happy." They all stare at each other, unsure of what to say next.

"God Bless you. You can put your tithes in the box at the front." Pastor Folarin nods and walks off for his next post-service pulpit reading.

CHAPTER 6

Kofo is in a meeting for work, bored about another pointless discussion that is preventing her from getting home on time to meet her fiancé when he flies back into town. Her performance is satisfactory, but her fulfillment is not. She keeps remembering what Tunde said to her about the way his job makes him feel. Kofo wishes she could access the same level of importance, but all in the name of what? It's another job in a corporate setting, doing meaningless work that feeds a company that sees her as disposable, with boring happy hours, annoying, needy colleagues that want to dump on her with venting sessions about their personal problems, and not to mention the racial politics. Aside from the salary, Kofo is not sure of the point. She was taught to get a job to have a title and make a lot of money, but no one told her it would be this disappointing.

Kofo listens to her boss Katie go on about the entire department needing to use the summer months to strategize their fall and holiday marketing strategy at the head of the conference room. Most of the burnt-out employees are peering at the clock on the flat screen monitor as the time creeps from five forty-five to six, signaling the end of the workday. Katie is unfortunately one of the most long-winded people on their team. Kofo's observation of Katie is making her more invested in what the representation of Katie means—an upper-middle-class white woman that lives in the West Village and doesn't have a balanced life, who pressures her subordinates to join her unhealthy binges of workaholism. She latched on to Kofo within the first week of her starting the job because her husband is also an investment banker and invited her to lunch to the dismay of her jealous, catty coworkers. Kofo went in naïve, assuming their meeting would be an opportunity to discuss diversity on their next campaign, or in the actual office. Katie spent the entire lunch complaining about her recent discovery of her husband's affair with a colleague, warning her to be mindful of dating a "finance man." As if Janelle's scolding wasn't enough.

These lunches continued until Kofo made herself less available, realizing that she couldn't grab that feeling Tunde described. She chases it, looking for it in every crevice of her office and until she settled on being content with simply getting a paycheck every two weeks. The last straw was when Katie cornered her in the bathroom one day, angry about getting six weeks maternity leave and decided that "women can't have it all". She said she was going to put in her two weeks, but that was almost a month ago. Thank God Kofo didn't gossip about it to anyone. She's a recluse in the office and likes it that way. Less drama, even if it's at the cost of her next promotion. Her experience at work is peaceful in the meantime.

Her days are filled with zoning out to emails, calls and meetings while looking forward to her brief reading sessions of historical biographies on her commute and during lunch. She met some local friends at the coffee shop who are kind enough to engage all of her recent thoughts about the findings in these literary works. But that's as far as her interests go. Tunde keeps encouraging her to never give up on finding that feeling. At least it's in her personal life, so she has an idea.

Her phone rang for the third time and she could no longer ignore Eniola's back-to-back calls. She sends her a text.

I'm in a meeting. What's up?

Wanna go shopping with me for some baby gear at our favorite splurge spot?

Kofo doesn't want to go to Target at City Point, but who else will join her lonely sister? Certainly not Cedric. She's been needier than usual, and Kofo noticed her friends aren't coming around as often. Something is up, but something is always up with Eniola.

Okay. I should be done in 20-30 minutes, so give me an hour to commute. I'll text when I arrive. Kofo turns her phone face down on the conference table.

***

Kofo meets Eniola with a cart full of gender-neutral clothing items for a newborn. Eniola grabs a chocolate bar from the checkout line and takes a large bite. Kofo scans the overfilled cart with a look of concern.

"I'm going to pay for it Kofo, relax."

"Okay."

Kofo grabs some baby wipes and dumps them in the cart. Eniola puts it back on the shelf.

"That'll be on my registry. Let someone else pay for it."

Kofo looks down again at the cart, estimating almost thirty items for a six-month-old baby.

"I didn't know you wanted a baby shower. The window is closing to plan it."

"No, it's not. I planned Jumoke's in two weeks." Eniola charges forward to another section of the baby clothes area with a less enthused Kofo following her.

**

Kofo lugs six heavy bags worth of non-essential items for her baby to DeKalb Market food court. Eniola loves to eat, and this pregnancy is the perfect excuse for her to overindulge. She bites into a burger.

"This is so good. I love that I get to eat meat again during my pregnancy."

Kofo smiles, unsure if she should call her sister out on pretending to be vegetarian or vegan when she saw her chomping on a piece of fried goat meat at a wedding a few months ago.

"Ennie… when are you going to tell Mommy? You can't hide this under your long gowns anymore."

Eniola puts her burger down, staring at it for several moments.

"I wanted to talk to you about that." Of course. Eniola's requests for quality time are always driven by a self-serving need. "I think we should tell Mommy about our updates together."

"What?! Why?"

"Because I know she'll be disappointed, and I think it'll be better to gently tell her about both at once."

Kofo knew Eniola had issues, but this is a new low.

"I can't believe you think my engagement is bad news."

"To Mommy it is. She doesn't like Tunde."

"So what? She'll enjoy saying, 'my daughter is getting married,'", Kofo responds with assertion.

"You barely know him. She doesn't know his family, he's Christian... come on, Kofo."

Kofo scoffs, regretting her decision to join her sister.

"You can't even pretend to be happy for me."

"I am not jealous."

"I will not lessen the blow of your decisions, Ennie. You're a grown woman, tell Mommy yourself." Kofo grabs her belongings in preparation to storm off, but reminders herself of the bags surrounding their table. She can't leave Eniola behind—she's not supposed to be carrying heavy items in any capacity. Kofo sits back down, still blown away by Eniola's audacity.

"Kofo. It's alright. Just go, I don't want your help."

"Ennie, you can't—"

"I said go."

Kofo ignores her, waiting for her sister to finish eating in silence.

***

"Babe, there's no way in hell we can agree to Ennie's idea." Tunde unpacks his suitcase in their bedroom closet. Kofo notices his rapid stuffing of clothing in their closet, showing eagerness to re-establish himself in his preferred home.

"We can look at it as a good news versus bad news situation. We'll be on the side of good news." Kofo convinces herself as she tells Tunde.

Tunde plops on the bed, and Kofo joins him, leaning on his shoulder.

"I don't understand why she can't bring Cedric along to tell your mom. What is that dude's purpose?" Kofo can't tell him because she doesn't know.

"Tunde… babe. My sister is really going to need help with this situation and my worry is that my mother's anger about Ennie will overshadow us if we don't share both at the same time."

"Kofo—no. I can't agree with this. Either we tell her on our own or we need to rethink things."

"What do you mean, *rethink*?"

"Kofo, I faced both of my parents like a man and told them straight up."

"Oh, is that why my father had to play backup with you in London? I thought we were a family now. Isn't that what you told him?!"

Tunde smirks, shaking his head. "Your father didn't back up shit. Trust me." Tunde rolls up a blunt he takes out from the nightstand on his side of the bed. Kofo grabs it and throws it all onto the floor. "Kofo, what the fuck?!" Tunde gets up, arms spread in confusion.

"Do you or do you not want to marry me?" Her eyes are flaming hot at her fiancé.

"Am I the type of person to ask someone to marry me if I'm not sure?"

"What happened to you before the play?"

"What are you talking about?"

"Our first date. You said that you couldn't figure out the trains a year after moving here when your 125th street stop is around the corner from your house and it's literally like five stops away, a straight shot. You're great with directions, I know you were lying. Where were you?"

"What does that have to do with anything?"

"What are you hiding from me?!"

"Kofo—nothing. I just don't want to experience every aspect of our lives with your family. This announcement is overkill. I'm not on board. Let's do it on our own time."

Kofo storms out of the room, livid. Tunde grabs another bag from the same nightstand to finish what he started.

***

"I feel him though," Janelle tells her friend while wrapping up a Reiki session with Kofo on a massage table at her office in Thompkins Avenue in Bed Stuyvesant, Brooklyn. It's on the ground floor of a cozy brownstone walkup with creaking wood floors, orange walls, bronze and brown decor, African masks and incense in the air. Janelle manages the spaces, including the rooms she rents out to a rotating cohort of other Black wellness professionals in several disciplines. She's pushed for Kofo to take advantage of the family and friends' discount for ages, but Kofo was reluctant until the epic disagreement with Tunde that occupies her mental space as of late.

Kofo sits up on the table, her short legs dangling about a foot from the floor. "This is our first fight ever. I assumed we would never do this."

Janelle cocks her head to the side. "What do you want to do, Kofo?"

"I want to marry Tunde. But I want him to accept how my family operates. We are tight-knit."

"I think you are letting Ennie manipulate you."

"Here we go."

"No—look. You're about to be married and sometimes that means choosing your partner."

Kofo raises her head, rolling her eyes. "Janelle, enough already!"

Janelle steps back, taken aback by Kofo's anger. "Where is all this energy coming from?"

"Why can't you just be my friend? I don't want you to psychoanalyze me and talk to me like I'm a fucking idiot."

"Kofo—you don't want me to psychoanalyze you."

Kofo looks at Janelle with a look that invites being torn to shreds. Janelle goes right into the task.

"Fine. Your family is a group of enablers. You need to stop taking money from your father—he's not allowing you to figure things out on your own. Ennie resents your relationship with him and is jealous that he loves your more. Your mom... where do I begin? She's literally your obsession. You can't accept that she will never be what you want and you should take her as is." Kofo responds with a manic laugh, finding Janelle incredulous. "And you are in a codependent relationship with Tunde. Y'all are trauma bonding over being westernized misfits when it's all bullshit. Y'all are Nigerians that don't want to accept who you are—a mess like everyone else out here trying to figure things out."

"That's enough Janelle—"

"No, it's not. You wanna talk big shit? Lemme tell you what you need to fucking hear because, despite my feelings about Tunde, I know you want his ass. And you will lose him if you keep letting your envious sister drag you into her nonsense."

Kofo hops off of the bed and grabs her purse.

"This is what you always do, run. Where are you gonna run to Kofo, your daddy? He can't pay your way out of this."

"Fuck you, Janelle."

"I love you too, Kofo. It'll be one hundred and fifty dollars. Discount's over."

Kofo rams her hand into her purse and slams the money on the table.

"You're just salty because no matter how many peer-reviewed essays you write, you still can't keep a man."

"Ok, now you can get the fuck out before I drag you out of here." Janelle steps to Kofo, about to pop her in the mouth. Kofo slams the door, too chicken to fight her now former friend.

***

Kofo fumes with rage, power-walking down Halsey Street to nowhere. The past two days have been supremely uncomfortable, and judging from the status of her two major confidants, she's not sure if arguing with anyone else is a good idea. Eniola called and texted her today to find out if she will agree to the dual announcement.

Why is everyone making this such a big deal? She says to herself. Kofo and her sister meet with their mother frequently to share announcements, and she told Tunde about prior gatherings. He never has a vehement reaction. *Does he want their announcement to be an olive branch to her mother so she can come around on their relationship? Does he want to tell her alone?* She rambles on in her head. Kofo is confused at the chaos arising from Eniola's proposal.

Kofo reaches Halsey and Bedford, realizing that she walked from one end of Bed Stuyvesant to another. She veers right on Fulton Avenue to catch the shuttle at Franklin Avenue Station so she can go home. Kofo decides she will call Eniola once she gets off at her destination. She will be there during the pregnancy announcement, but will opt to share her engagement at another time.

Kofo makes it to the Franklin Avenue Station, watching the sun set behind the roofs of brick walk-ups flooding Bed Stuyvesant on the elevated platform. The shuttle pulls in, and right before Kofo walks onto the train—Eniola texts her in all caps.

CALL ME. MAY DAY.

Before Kofo could even pull up her phone's home screen, Eniola calls her. When Kofo picks up, she hears her sister sobbing uncontrollably on the other end of the line.

"Ennie? What's wrong? What happened?"

Eniola gives her a heavy breath, taking a few moments to speak.

"Maroof. He told his mom, and she told mommy."

Kofo closes her eyes, sighing at what Eniola thought was sympathy but is an incredible sense of relief.

CHAPTER 7

"Miss—we need you to move out of the way to start our work." A Brooklyn carpenter in his 20s steps into the ladies' bathroom of Al-Ahmed before Morenike's Saturday afternoon prayer. Her role as the head of the sisters committee involves volunteering her weekends to monitor renovation projects. Her initial response to this commitment was annoyance, but over time, she grew to enjoy the quiet time.

Morenike rises from the bathroom bench that sisters in the mosque use to perform their wudhu. Despite her refusal to go to counseling when it at the suggestion of her daughters, this building serves as an outlet for reflection without judgement. The last thing Morenike wants to do is spill her innermost thoughts of imposter syndrome with some shrink that only knows of poverty, tragedy, and war from African society.

These weekend sessions at Al-Ahmed are all the outlet she needs. Only her intimate thoughts and Allah; no one has access to this exchange. The role of her mosque community is to provide information to enhance her relationship with him through the sermons and classes. Lots of other congregation members have opposite complaints about their experience. They constantly moan about overhearing gossip, long waits to perform wudhu to prepare for prayer, the time it takes members to file out after the Friday night prayers are done, the distribution of take away foods... but where else will the elders go, especially the Mommies? They are all struggling to parent their children who are consumed with the ways of America and need space to talk about it.

Morenike has a reputation for being private but will drop a nugget here or there to some of the nosier mosque members. One time she laughed with them about her reaction to Kofo moving in with Fahad, assuming it was a precursor to marriage. If she told them about Tunde—another boyfriend Kofo is shacking up with, they would assume that both of her daughters are immoral and loose.

Morenike almost fainted when her junior sister Folade called, congratulating her on having her first grandchild. She checked her calendar to make sure it wasn't April Fools—her sister is a jokester and secretly enjoys watching Morenike's life unravel. Morenike picked her apart when they were teens and young women, assuming that her disinterest in being a 'plain jane' would leave her without a husband. Not only was she wrong, but Folade is happily married to a presumably faithful, dedicated husband for over twenty years. She used to live in Queens but moved to

North Carolina when he secured a Senior Vice President job in the IT department at his company. Folade's son Maroof moved back to New York after college and is now a millionaire.

Morenike concealed her shock, pretending to be excited and hinted at marriage for Eniola and Cedric. She then hung up and called Yvonne to ask if she had any intel on her son proposing, and they both came up with nothing. How could her daughter be so stupid? She regrets listening to Akeem when he told her not to pressure Cedric into popping the question. Morenike warned her daughters that if a man doesn't discuss marriage after eighteen months, dump him because he's unsure about you. Her advice is informed by waiting on Akeem for six years.

During every Friday night service at the mosque, Morenike prays for her creator to put a ring on one of her daughters. She questions why life is unfavorable to her when she is so dutiful. Morenike picks up a Quran, opening it to a random page. She does this whenever she has something on her mind, and the verse is often the answer to her problems. Her grandmother taught her this when she was a young child back in Lagos.

Hours after nodding off to reading the Quran, the carpenter rests his hand on her shoulder, waking her up.

"Miss, is your name Ms. Adebayo?"

Morenike opens her heavy eyes. "Yes."

"Someone named Coffee is here to see you?"

She chuckles. He reminds her of Cedric. "Yes, that's my daughter. I'll let her in." Morenike struggles to get up from the floor.

"Don't worry, I'll tell her to come."

"Thank you." Morenike remains on the floor in surprise as Kofo walks in with pressed beige slacks, a silky gold top and an ivory hijab. She looks beautiful when dressed modestly and wishes Kofo did it more often. Morenike senses an announcement based on the ensemble. On any other day, Kofo would wear tight jeans and a fitted top that shows off the shape of her petite body.

"Hi Mommy." Kofo smiles while her mother looks for clues on what is to come in this quiet moment between them. Kofo kisses her mother on the cheek and sits down, crossed-legged.

"Salam, Kofo."

Kofo surveys her mother for several seconds before speaking.

"Daddy told me you would be here for most of the day." Morenike nods, looking down at the open Quran. "I heard you found out about Ennie."

Morenike doesn't respond and is embarrassed to discuss it in a public setting, despite no one else being in the room.

"I also have to tell you something."

Morenike closes the Quran as if the creator can hear them if she left it open. "What?"

Kofo pauses, giving a reluctant grin. "Tunde and I are getting married." Kofo takes out her ring from the chest pocket of her shirt. "He proposed on my birthday." Morenike gawks at her daughter, unsure if she got a tip from her aunt to play another trick on her. She takes the ring, inspecting it closely. It's absolutely stunning—she estimates an eighteen-carat gold casing on a fat square three carat rock with perfect clarity, surrounding another outline of glistening diamonds. It's a high-quality piece of jewelry. She places the ring back in Kofo's palm.

"Mommy? Are you okay? Do you need some water?"

Instead of addressing Kofo, she closes her eyes, puts her hands in an Islamic prayer position, and cries. Crying tears of joy, of relief that her prayers weren't in vain. Akeem won't be happy about this news, but Morenike dismisses the thought. He is the parent campaigning against his daughters marrying one of their own. "They can't handle Nigerian men", "religion is more constant than culture", is all Akeem says to clarify his perspective and Morenike complies against her better judgement. But her gut instincts push her towards joy at this moment. She doesn't care what Tunde has going on and will stand by her daughter, honoring her genuine desires to remain competent in the Nigerian community and in her religion.

Morenike is certain of her grandmother's presence in their midst. The tears won't stop overwhelming her with the power of faith. Her friends pray with vigor for their daughters to find a good man, a worthy man, a man that wanted to marry their baby girls. All the male children are coupled, mostly with non-African women. But who is choosing all of their educated, beautiful, ready, marriage-minded girls?

The mommies frequently convene on this issue, agonizing as the years for their daughters' lives progress, creeping up closer to 30, 35, 40, 45… and when they are too old to conceive, the mommies accept that most of their grandchildren would be out of their culture in a generation or two. They resign themselves as the sacrificial lambs of the African community—casualties of western achievement, designated to pass resources back to their families and enrich their loved ones sticking it out in Nigeria. Most gave up on their wish for their offspring to find value in claiming their lineage after seeking much comfort on American soil.

Kofo continues watching the tears rolling on her mother's face, unsure of the motivation behind them. Afraid, she touches Morenike's shoulder.

"Mommy? Mommy?"

Morenike rocks back and forth, weeping while reciting "Ya Allah", over and over and over… until she embraces Kofo. Kofo returns the affection, teary-eyed as well.

***

After Kofo announces her engagement on Instagram and Facebook, endless amounts of praise pour in from all over the globe.

During the Friday service following Kofo's engagement, all of Morenike's friends congratulate her and order her favorite parting meal—asaro with croaker fish and fried plantain. Her win is a win for them all. Despite the flattery, Morenike didn't get comfortable. She comes early for Friday service to extend her prayers and on Saturdays to read the Quran before the carpenter arrives, whom she now knows as Kevin. He overheard someone discussing the update and congratulated her family's future. Morenike made a note that he will get a nice tip on his last day of work.

Mommy Bola has the hook up on the fabrics, considering her extensive planning experience three times prior for her three sons. She knew where to get the best deals and the highest quality lace in the fabric district from stores owned by Middle Easterners who lined their storefronts with rolls of the finest materials.

"Many of those guys think Nigerians have money and are thieves," Mommy Bola claims when they walked up and down midtown Manhattan. They browsed the first couple of visits, having a blast with the mounds of fabric. While the shopping thrilled Morenike, nothing she saw was the right fit.

Then the unthinkable happened. Kofo calls her with Tunde on FaceTime one evening.

"Mommy... Tunde and I want to have our wedding in Nigeria."

Morenike couldn't believe her ears. These two—the American and the Londoner—want to go back to their cultural land for the most important day of their lives. Morenike is speechless.

Morenike experiences Kofo trying to get her attention with repeated calls of "Mommy? Mommy?" whenever talking about her engagement, wedding or marriage. Conversations with Kofo prior to the engagement often ended with her seeking patience, and have transitioned to anticipation for the next bout of positive news when they speak again in present day.

"Sure. We can plan something quick for cheaper. Let me know the dates and we'll work together on everything else," Morenike replies.

"Mommy, you sure? What about all your friends and our family stateside?"

"Whoever can make it will fly out. Don't worry." Morenike could care less who was there except for her child, son-in-law, and Allah. Everyone else is an optional attendee as long as the venue fills to its brim.

Akeem is still away on business and when Morenike told him the news, he pretended to be shocked. She knew from his tone that he was already aware. Of course, Kofo already shared the news. Morenike tells him to hurry and get back in town to arrange the smaller, intimate Nikah. The Imams badger her with questions on his return every week and she is running out of excuses.

Eniola's pregnancy is still an impending issue. When Morenike found out, she responded with awful insults that included calling her daughter a whore and prostitute, only able to respond with uncontrollable rage. Morenike dodges questions of Eniola's growing stomach, pretending to be unsure of an alleged wedding date. Kofo's real wedding is the perfect excuse to divert attention from shameful news connected to the Adebayo family.

***

Morenike walks into her owner's suite after a long day of discussing wedding logistics with Kofo and Mommy Bola, plopping onto her favorite chair. This is the chair where she reads, answers calls, pays bills, and watches TV until sleep takes her out—it is a microfiber dream. It's also right next to her house phone that blinks with messages on rare occasions. Morenike presses a button to play one voicemail.

Hello, this is Arlene from American Bank for Akeem Adibaya? I am reaching out to follow up on your request to modify your residential loan. I've tried your cell a few times this week and haven't heard back. Call me back at your earliest convenience. Thank you.

Kofo sends her mail to her apartment and makes fun of her parents for still having a house phone. She mentioned nothing about a house loan or intentions to buy property. Kofo and Tunde make decent money, but they would need help with the crazy prices of New York real estate. Or are they moving out of state? To London? Or Nigeria? Eniola is considering buying property with Cedric, so the loan likely won't involve them, and Akeem would never give either of them a dime, anyway. Morenike's body gave in despite her desire to call Kofo for more details. Moments later, she knocks out, falling asleep with her head leaning on her favorite chair until the next day.

***

Morenike finishes her morning Fajr prayer, sipping on a cup of English Breakfast tea with sugar and condensed milk in the dining area. She drafts a text to Kofo, asking her about the loan because it will disrupt their wedding planning process. They have to have a wedding.

Morenike missed the opportunity to experience her own because her family insisted that she and Akeem come back to Nigeria for a proper celebration, but Akeem resisted, urging her to be content with an intimate City Hall ceremony and dinner at a local restaurant.

She met Akeem at a house party in the ritzy neighborhood of Ikeja during the Christmas season in the 1970s when he was on holiday break from undergrad at Texas Tech. He flew back and forth from Texas to Nigeria every four months, fully obsessed with his long-legged, gorgeous new girlfriend that came from a poor family but was destined for bigger. He loved her arrogant, demanding, fearless personality that could out-haggle most Lagosians. She knew exactly what she wanted and had zero qualms about getting it. Akeem adorned their courting season with fancy dinners, strolls and Picnics on the beach on Victoria Island. Morenike was at his side at almost every outing when he came to visit her in Lagos.

During the process of petitioning for Morenike to immigrate to the United States, Morenike got pregnant with Eniola. They got engaged, and her pregnancy sped up her immigration application for a fiancé visa, but she bombed the interview because of her nerves and listening to envious friends that gave her questionable advice on what to tell the immigration officer.

She applied for a visitor's visa months later. Their plan was to have her travel to the states, and they would marry immediately. They encountered suspicion from the courthouse officials in the small Texas town of Lubbock, and Morenike grew disinterested in fighting racism in the States. She flew back to Nigeria, sending them on an eight-year journey apart, until she finally agreed that raising a daughter amidst the growing instability of post-colonial Nigeria was unsustainable.

When Akeem moved his wife and daughter into his two-bedroom house, things were steady until Morenike's less privileged family constantly asked for money, placing an immense amount of strain on them financially, and Akeem put a stop to the requests. She felt guilty shutting her family out of her new life and got a job cleaning houses to own the burden of sending her family recurring funds. After six months of sacrificing her time away from her daughter, who went to a subpar school and realizing that her family was blowing her money on anything but essential items, she cut them off. Morenike assigned her sister Folade to distribute the money she sent, and it went missing, straining their relationship since.

Morenike's family drama is familiar to many Nigerians, but not Akeem. Akeem seldom spoke to his parents, who divorced and frequented travels from one end of Nigeria for their businesses. He is the only child between them, making him accustomed to a solitary life that involved visiting them in separate locales. Akeem indulged in his accomplishments without interruption, enjoying the advantages of having privileged parents who offered nothing beyond verbal accolades for his growing salary.

"Mommy, our child comes before a wedding," Morenike complained to her mother whenever she pestered them about consecrating their marital union in Nigeria. Her mother caused a ruckus and even got Morenike's beloved grandmother involved. They campaigned to arrange a wedding ceremony in Nigeria and started the initial stages of planning. The timing couldn't have been worse because Akeem was up for a promotion and he couldn't travel out of the United States for "a while." He claimed that the wait would be a year, but it turned into two, then three, then four. Each year, Eniola's expenses grew for school supplies, after-school programs, transportation, and doctor visits. Everything in America comes with a hefty price tag. That's the fine print they don't tell folks who immigrate here.

When Akeem was on the verge of getting rejected for a promotion again, despite his dedication to neglecting his new family, Morenike had enough. She demanded he figure something else out. Akeem applied to more jobs throughout Texas to no avail but found a job with an Urban Planning firm in New York City. They offered him a Director of Development in their "Africa" department.

Akeem moved his family to New York with Eniola creeping up to nine years old. Morenike thought they were "moving on up" like her favorite American television show, "The Jeffersons". Akeem assured her that the fancy life was coming, but they needed to downsize with him generating the sole salary. In the meantime, they rented another two-bedroom in a Flatbush prewar building that was poorly managed with roaches and occasional mice sightings. Morenike tried to get pregnant again with no luck, which made her question her destiny with Akeem. Just when she was on the brink of considering moving on, she got pregnant a few months after their move to Brooklyn with Kofo. Their second baby girl gave them a renewed sense of purpose on their journey.

Morenike loved New York City the minute she stepped off of the plane. It is her American home because it reminds her of Lagos. Texas was too slow and weakened her grit. The swarms of anonymous bodies in the concrete jungle grant Morenike the space to project the grandness of a socialite without questioning.

Akeem liked New York at first but is tired of the hustle at his older age. He left Nigeria to jump out of one boiling pot to enter another. New York City exhausts him. He grew weary of the long commutes with faulty trains, the grumpy people walking down the street, high levels of homelessness and not to mention the safety concerns of raising two young Black girls in the inner cities of Brooklyn during the 1990s. He stressed about his three ladies every day while at work when they initially moved to Brooklyn, unsure of how to secure a future for them that met his standards.

Akeem waited three years for his director position to materialize some meaning beyond empty press releases that discussed intentions with no action for the African continent. He called a meeting with his boss about his future at the company. His boss wasn't pleased and inferred that Akeem should be happy to have a job "at a company like this." Then he proceeded to say that he fought to hire and keep Akeem because several people wanted the position to travel to safaris and Egyptian pyramids.

Akeem quit on the spot, shocking his boss who assumed he would fall in line. That evening was the only time Morenike saw him cry. Akeem said he would never work for anyone ever again. Morenike advised him against this idea, considering her enrollment in law school. Akeem refused to accommodate her, and that was the turning point in their marriage.

Morenike breezed through her courses and made him watch Kofo whenever she was in class or studying. Akeem bonded with his baby girl in one hand and held the other with a phone that grew his Nigerian Rolodex. Finally, one of his old classmates named Kunle suggested he fly to Lagos for a few months to learn more about opportunities in the petroleum industry.

Akeem agreed and flew out to Nigeria during Morenike's summer break. He told her he would be back in four weeks and four weeks turned into four months. When he returned, Akeem promised her he wouldn't disappoint her with another failed pipe dream. Akeem gained his footing and earned enough to convince Morenike to go back to being a stay-at-home mom once she finished law school and took her bar exams. Morenike didn't object and continued practicing law when her husband gained more success as an entrepreneur.

Akeem didn't see a return on his petroleum investment until a decade later. Most of the money Akeem made along the way, he spent it on other women that he met while in Nigeria. Whenever he was in New York, Akeem occupied less of his time at home, claiming to "network" with other Nigerian businessmen over dinner, a fancy bar or a community-based event from their new friends at the mosque such as a wedding or birthday party. Year by year, month by month, day by day... they drifted apart, committed more to the routine and duties of marriage, rather than the feelings that sustain a marriage.

He kept his promise of providing his wife with a high-class lifestyle and moved them all out to Long Island. Morenike loves their big house but despises how conservative and unexposed her neighbors are. In Brooklyn, she had neighbors from Virginia, South Carolina, Haiti, Jamaica, Trinidad, Barbados, Puerto Rico, Panama, and Guyana—they were from all over the world and the diversity inspired an international pot luck during their annual block party.

Her neighbors were busy and didn't always have time for long discussions, but they connected long enough in their building lobby or laundry room to share tips on sending each other's kids to the best schools in the city, the best daycares, where to buy school uniforms or anything else that would make a neighbor's life easier. She loved that they were all in the trenches of trying to make it.

Her new neighbors are past this point of needing to prove something and were comfortable within the walls of their big houses. All Morenike can get from them is a wave across the street. One neighbor asked her for a nanny business card when she was unloading her car. Morenike cursed her out and sent the woman red-faced back to her porch. Both of her girls got called into the principal's office for minor offenses at their local, all white school. Morenike spent a lot of time-fighting the school's administration and local district for their subtle discrimination policies. Her law degree came in handy up to a point and Morenike pulled her daughters out to attend schools in Queens using Folade's old address. Morenike hates Long Island, or at least this part of it. It was nice, but it was incredibly lonely.

Something in her gut told her to call Akeem about the loan application. Morenike pulls up her WhatsApp to call Akeem, assuming he isn't back yet because she hasn't seen him in several days. After a few rings, he picks up.

"Hello?"

"Akeem."

"Yes?" Morenike hears airport announcements in the background, but the accent is British. Either he was in the United Kingdom, or he has a layover in the UK. But Akeem hates connecting flights, he likes to fly direct and first class. Unless something went wrong with his flight.

"Why are you applying for a residential loan?" She transitions their discussion to Yoruba.

Akeem pauses. His reactions are ambiguous these days. She can detect if he's lying almost immediately, but at this moment, Morenike is unsure.

Something else must be on his plate. Probably another woman he's going to see once he lands in New York. Or the one he's leaving behind. Whoever it is must mean a lot to him if he's this wound up.

"Why are you asking me that?"

"American Bank called here."

She overhears Akeem's footsteps move to a quiet area with less flight announcements, possibly a business lounge.

"I'm going to gift the loan to Kofo and Tunde. I will be a guarantor for a condo mortgage. But don't meddle, Nike. She's about to be a married woman and we need to give her space with Tunde."

Morenike rolls her eyes at her husband's ironic accusation. "I know how old Kofo is. I want to make sure that we have enough money for the wedding."

Unlike Akeem, Morenike views her family as upper middle class and would rather budget wisely. She will keep a close eye on this.

CHAPTER 8

Akeem was allegedly in Nigeria for the past couple of weeks, straightening the loose ends of his solar energy deals with Chinese businessmen that are making a killing in Lagos. That deal was in motion but fell through and he is in pursuit of a new partnership in real estate, a promising venture with the growing middle class in Sub-Saharan Africa. He's attempted to work with other Nigerians in the past, including some distant cousins, and got screwed. Akeem lost patience with peering over his shoulder when dealing with his people and moved on from working with Nigerians entirely. Morenike's eyes used to light up with excitement whenever Akeem shared some of his pursuits, even when they were no longer on the best of terms. Now she is hearing one pipe dream after another. Facing her with all of his professional obstacles makes him want to hide away overseas when he's in their big house after too many weeks.

He also told Tunde that he's flying to Nigeria quickly to hash out some business and that if anyone asks, Tunde should tell them the same details. Tunde opted out, suggesting that Akeem to call them with his own updates. Akeem didn't protest, knowing that if he further indulged Tunde, he might know more than needed.

A few days following Tunde's departure, Akeem waits in the "Arrivals" section of the London Heathrow Airport. He hates this airport—they operate like Fort Knox towards perceived migrants. Normally he would order a car service to pick up any guests, but this guest is special. He doesn't want to spend much time standing around in fear of being recognized by any Nigerians that are also spending time with loved ones in Europe. Every Nigerian has a cousin, sibling, or relative in the United Kingdom.

After what seems like forever, his guest arrives—her name is Yinka. She's about 5'9", slender, has smooth dark brown skin with a short, cut afro and trendy glasses. Her features are strong, yet feminine. She appears sophisticated, moving with a sense of ownership of her path. Two young boys are at each of her sides as she struggles to keep them in line while hauling all of their luggage on a trolley.

"Daddy!!!!" one of the boys scream, running into Akeem's arms and he picks him up on cue. It's his son Ayo. Ife follows suit, grabbing him by the leg. They both hold on for dear life. Yinka finally reaches Akeem and pecks him on the lips. All four of them head outside to his car, ready to be a family in London.

Akeem hates driving in London because the steering wheel is on the right side of the car. The orientation distorts his innate cognitive response to driving, and he has to be extra alert on the road to avoid crashing, more so with Yinka and his sons inside.

"Ayo, stop hitting your brother," Yinka hisses at their son in a "posh" Nigerian accent. Yinka comes from a normal, middle-class family with roots in Ijebu, the outskirts of Lagos. She went to the University of Lagos to get a degree in world economics and worked part-time at a cement factory until her boss attempted to sexually assault her at the end of a long workday. Every supervisor thereafter extorted her for sex or used her body as a pawn for other authority figures within the chain of command. She opted out of the madness that was the Nigerian workforce for a quieter life as a fabric shop owner in the Lagos middle-class neighborhood named as Lekki. She dated several men, all of whom presented impressive job titles but no trackable income outside of black-market hustles after dark.

Being with a married man wasn't a lifestyle she ever considered, but when Akeem swept her off of her feet after she serviced him with a fabric purchase for a gala he was attending, she figured wavering on her values to settle with another woman's husband makes sense. Sometimes Yinka longs for a man with his youthful looks still intact, but compared to a lot of other women she knows in Lagos that are drowning in soul-sucking marriages, she is doing well. Things are paying off nicely with Akeem, and she's glad she gave him a chance. There are no real sparks between them, but he provides her with the lifestyle she wants. She fulfilled her dream of becoming a mother, and Akeem gets a break from the stress of his life in New York when they are together.

"But he took my toy!" Ayo wails as the two boys wrestle in the back seats of the black SUV.

Akeem belts out a hearty laugh, happy to relive another version of a pastime with his American family. The newness of this unit brings back fond memories.

***

Akeem sprawls out on the couch of his London house with his two sons. Cartoons play on the television at a low volume. Yinka takes a break from cooking jollof rice and spicy stewed chicken with plantain to take a photo of them napping together. The adorable visual makes her smile before getting back to preparing dinner. A flashing sound from her brand-new iPhone Akeem bought her woke him up. He gently peels off his sons' heavy arms and legs as they continue sleeping, and he rises from the couch. Once standing, Akeem looks down at his sons, proud of his ability to produce another round of good-looking offspring.

"This is what you've been missing out on." Yinka gently hugs him from behind.

Akeem sighs, unsure of how to justify missing out on the growth of his second family. After several moments of silence, Yinka releases her grip and goes back to the kitchen island that has various pots cooking their next meal. She opens the pot of jollof rice and several grains stick to the improperly cleaned residue from previous meals on the inside, instead of swimming in the juices of the sauce that will eventually fill the rice grains with flavor. She scrapes the rice to get it in the sauce, trying to salvage her recipe while sucking her teeth and banging her wooden spoon on the rim to get the remaining grains off of it as well.

"That Tola woman ruined this pot. I use this one for rice, not stew. Don't bring her back here."

"Yinka, relax. I'll buy you another one," Akeem says with a groggy voice while browsing emails on his phone, rubbing his tired, stressed face. He's seated on a stool opposite her at the kitchen island.

"That's not the point, Akeem." Yinka leans forward, placing her hand over his phone screen to get his attention. Akeem rolls his eyes, looking back at her. "I want this to be our lives. I want our children to have a better education and better opportunities than what they have in Nigeria. This feels right."

"I know Yinka, I'm trying to—"

"Tell your wife in New York. Leave her for me." Yinka glances over at their boys, who are still asleep.

"Not right now, Yinka."

"Why not?", she whispers in an aggressive tone. "Your daughters are grown. Just give her the house you all have there."

"Because we have to finish building our place. It's still in progress." Akeem grabs a large roll of paper leaning on a bookshelf behind the couch, then opens it all on the dining table, with Yinka peering behind him. "This is what I want to finish for you before I decide to leave my wife."

Yinka gasps at the floor plan. It's an enormous home with three floors, five bedrooms and four bathrooms on a plot of land with a massive backyard. She continues to lean further into the floor plan, examining details of the layout.

"When can I see it? I want to see it."

"They just finished framing. There's nothing to really see yet, Yinka." Yinka's face drops at what she expects to be a better update. "One of my daughters is pregnant, and the other is getting married. By the time both events pass, the house will be ready. Trust me. Do you trust me? Haven't I taken good care of you and our sons?"

Yinka pauses. "Yes, you have."

"Give me time. It's almost done."

"The boys need you. They ask of you all the time and are misbehaving in school."

"I'll come to Naija next month and stay a little longer than usual. We'll work something out."

"Akeem—I'm not waiting longer than a year. Eighteen months at the most."

"I won't disappoint you." Akeem looks at Yinka with complete certainty. She kisses him on the lips and heads back to the pot of unfinished jollof rice.

***

A week later, Akeem arrives back at his Long Island house and walks into a wedding planning meeting with Morenike, Kofo, and Mommy Bola.

"Hi Daddy." Kofo rises from the living room couch to give her dad a tight hug, challenging his loyalty to Yinka he contemplated during his flight back to New York. Kofo is truly his favorite child. Akeem's overhead people discount Kofo as rude over the years, but he secretly admires his daughter's ability to speak up without fear.

"Kofo! Hi." He hugs her back, nodding at Morenike and Mommy Bola—his wife's nosy, prodding friend as far as he's concerned. She always has something to say, or her facial expressions tell on her.

Kofo looks at his baggage tag to see where he came from. "London?"

"Yea, I had a twenty-four-hour long layover there. They stuck this one onto my luggage after I returned to the airport for my connecting flight."

Kofo's mouth curls into a grin as her father pulls his luggage upstairs. "What kept you busy in London for a day? You hate shopping and anything other than Nigerian food, so I know those are out."

"I just did some general sightseeing, went to a few museums… and there are a lot of Nigerian places to eat in London. Didn't Tunde tell you?"

"Yes, I thought those were further out into the city. No business meetings for you this time?" Kofo follows him up the staircase.

Morenike overhears Akeem lying to his daughter. "Kofo, please come back down. Mommy Bola needs to leave in ten to fifteen minutes."

"Ok, coming Mommy!" Kofo says from the staircase, still deciding to follow her dad. She reaches the top of the staircase as Akeem rushes into his room, closing the door in her face. She speaks through the door.

"Bye, Daddy! Will probably head out of here soon."

Akeem pokes his head out, still flustered. "Bye, Kofo."

"Are you alright?" Kofo stares at him, looking for details.

"Yea… I just have a running stomach from something I ate on the plane."

Morenike is at the foot of the stairs, looking at Kofo.

"Kofo, come on."

"Alright, I'll call you later.", Kofo says before heading back downstairs.

Akeem closes and locks his bedroom door in relief. He calculated numerous tactics to avoid Morenike's questions about the American Bank voicemail. She's a hawk over their accounts and always finds out about Akeem's spending habits. He had to open an account under Yinka's name to track his finances in Nigeria. Any discussions about the house with the Lagos-based contractor are only via phone from an untraceable, unlisted number. Morenike must have spies. That's the only way he can explain her ability to discover all of his hidden spending, including on his personal accounts. He keeps everything on his cell phone with stringent privacy settings that Kofo established, and changes his passcode every quarter.

He considered having Yinka manage the expenses for the house, but changed his mind because he wants to make sure he moves to Nigeria full time first. He can't be that trusting with a woman he doesn't see regularly. She is as much of a hustler as any other Nigerian he's dealt with. Her phone calls pressuring him to move to Nigeria are more urgent after she saw the blueprint of the house in London. Her wait time for his return changed from a year, to right away. They have a joint checking account for small scale spending in the meantime.

Akeem gifted Kofo and Tunde a three hundred-thousand-dollar loan for their engagement, and they used the money towards a beautiful two-bedroom condo in Prospect Heights, Brooklyn. The price of the condo was one and a half million dollars. Tunde and Kofo applied in the amount of their collective savings—overwhelmingly Tunde's—with twenty percent down in the amount of three hundred thousand. They got outbid by other buyers, so Akeem stepped in as a guarantor, and matched the money they offered to put down. His contribution got them approved over other buyers. Akeem covers their mortgage payments while they plan on re-saving the money they used to pay for the condo.

Tunde had more questions than his fiancé when Akeem offered the gift, requesting account logins and paperwork to ensure they could handle the sizeable sum of money. They were happy with the materials Akeem sent and monitored the first couple of payments with no issue.

While Akeem feels a slight tinge of remorse, he powers through to complete his goals. And Morenike's nosiness is exhaustive. It annoys him that she feels entitled to everything he has when they barely even speak. Although he encouraged her to be a stay-at-home mom, Akeem resents his wife for complying in the long run because she essentially wasted her law degree. Her decision to forego working full time made him stay because his daughters needed a provider. The guilt of wanting to leave the mother of his favorite child keeps his wallet open, but it's getting expensive. He's still paying Kofo's undergrad and MBA tuition, he just finished paying for Eniola's law degree, their Long Island housing expenses, mosque tides, his own personal costs and, of course, his other family.

Akeem made a few million from successful petroleum investment profits with Morenike's legal advisement, but the money is running out in New York. She's also burning more money by planning Kofo's wedding. Cedric is flaky with Eniola, so he's adding expenses with his first grandchild as a possibility.

His daughters work full time, but they are terrible at managing money, with Kofo being the worst offender. She lives life on a whim that includes a slew of luxury items. He convinced her not to purchase a Tesla because of her interest in saving the environment and suggested an auction purchase. Kofo screwed her face at the thought of a pre-owned vehicle and he shut down the prospect of another financial liability completely. New York isn't cheap, but if Morenike taught her daughters to live modestly and to stop focusing on their "trendy" friends, they can make living here comfortably a reality. Sometimes Akeem wonders if they would've been better off in Texas.

***

Akeem stayed in his room for five hours, lying on the bed and watching reruns of "Real Time with Bill Maher". He napped to wear off his jet lag, washed up, pressed his clothes, shaved, and cut his fingernails. Morenike filled his extended absence with loud movements throughout the day, from one end of the house to another.

He heard calls about the wedding, the Nikah, sounds of her cooking, and footsteps up the stairs into the owner's suite. His wife kicked him out of that room for three years when he became more brazen with having other women on the side. All of his clothes are in their massive closet and Akeem grabs them when Morenike isn't home. They attempt to stay out of each other's way.

It's later into the evening and Morenike is deep in prayer on the living room couch. Akeem creeps down the stairs and heads through the kitchen side door. He makes brief eye contact with Morenike through the parlor window—her face fixates on his movements as he slips into the driver's seat of his Audi in the driveway.

Akeem notices a few missed calls on WhatsApp from an unsaved number. The number left a voice note.

Eh… Bawoni Mr. Adebayo. It's Ibrahim, your project manager. I'm calling you because your Lagos wife Yinka has been showing up to the construction site, making demands on the house designs. Some contractors implemented them while I was away for holiday with my family. But I wanted to call you to make sure you approve this before we agree, sir. Her ideas are affecting your budget, so please call me at your earliest convenience. Thank you, sir.

Akeem fumbles, urgently pressing the number, but Ibrahim doesn't answer.

"Ibrahim, it's Akeem. Please do not, I repeat, *do not* make any changes that deviate from the plan on the blueprint. I will fly out to Nigeria as soon as possible to straighten things out with Yinka. Call me as soon as you get this. Thank you."

Akeem drops his head onto to the steering wheel before letting out a loud sigh. His two options include calling Yinka to berate her, which would end their relationship that is molding into an informal marriage. The other option would be to downplay her overstepping her bounds to preserve his bank account until he's settled enough in Nigeria to eventually get rid of her when he meets someone else. Akeem decides on the latter and pulls out of the garage.

***

Funmi bends over to grab a pair of jeans from the hotel room floor, showing off her lace black thong. She and Akeem just went another round, and he's satisfied with his performance. He kept the momentum with her and Yinka in the same week. Akeem prepares to turn on the television but notices that Funmi hides her body, hunching over to grab the rest of her clothes in preparation to leave. Their nighttime routine includes sleeping in bed together until the next morning.

"Funmi, what happened to you?" He goes right into Yoruba.

"I'm fine." She shakes her head, scanning the rest of her belongings sprawled throughout the room.

"Where are you going? Why are you acting like I paid for you?" Akeem is alert, sitting up.

She makes eye contact with Akeem. "I didn't know that you had another wife in London."

Akeem feels like everyone wants him to stop being the person they initially met. "That's a lie."

Funmi drops her personal items on the bed. "No, it's not. I thought I was your second wife. What am I, your fourth? sixth?" Several of the men at Chief Lounge are jealous that he snagged Funmi. One of them likely snitched, but how did they find out? Akeem hopes to God that none of them knows Yinka personally.

What Akeem doesn't know is that Funmi knows a few Yahoo boys back in Lagos that can get intel on any and everybody. She kept in touch with one that used to get her lunch during her break as a street cleaner in Lekki. They made a deal that if she ever needed intel on anyone, he would get a cut of the money she gets from the sugar daddy in question. Funmi knows everything about Akeem and he's not as discreet as he thinks. From his number and Facebook profile alone, her Yahoo boy got access to his text messages and photos, which incriminated him entirely. They also connected iPads, laptops and other devices Akeem works on while he thinks Funmi is asleep in the middle of the night.

When Funmi saw Yinka's text, let me know how it goes with your NY wife and what your timeline will be for moving. She knew she needed to get answers.

"I never claimed you were my wife. We're having a good time. Why are you complicating matters now?", Akeem's face transformed into a scowl.

Funmi starts with the waterworks, slamming her bottom onto the bed with sunken shoulders. She intended to gain security with a man thirty years her senior to make her stay in the United States more comfortable. Her investment of time, energy and humility will never produce a return. She fakes every orgasm and lets him touch her in places that no one had access to. Akeem is the only one here who will walk away unscathed. Maybe she should've done this with an older white guy. But that's also risky—her schemes are new, and she knows Nigerian men like the back of her hand.

"I want thirty thousand dollars. You owe me," Funmi says as her nose flares.

"Are you mad? How do I owe you a dollar? I give you money because I have extra, not out of obligation."

Funmi snatches the remote out of Akeem's hand and holds it tight as she paces the room. "Akeem, if I don't get some cash that they can verify, I have to go back to Nigeria. Work hasn't been steady for me."

"What do you need it for?"

"I want to start nursing school. I need money for tuition."

"I can't pay for that."

"Akeem—remember, I have your wife's number. I can tell her everything."

Akeem has had enough. He gets up from the bed and snatches the remote out of her hand, but she's quicker than him and gets it back. They tussle for a bit with neither party making progress until Akeem calmly lies back on the bed and calls the police on his phone. When he speaks to the attendant on the other line, Funmi hurls an infinite number of insults his way, promising to make his life a living hell. When the reality of her deportation calms her down after greeting the police, Akeem assures the officers that their domestic dispute is resolved. He closes the door, breathing heavily while Funmi stands a few feet away in fear.

Akeem's energy hits with a wave of coldness. "I need you to go. And this will be the last time we see each other."

Funmi continues to cry. "Akeem, I really need your help. Please"

"Out. Get out."

Akeem is calmer than he expected. He decides Funmi is too volcanic for his liking. Her temper is a threat to his peace, which won't work. He has enough on his mind. Akeem walks to the bed to turn on the television, this time surfing aimlessly. Funmi stares at him for a long time, hoping his conscience would give in. When she gave up, accepting that he is resolute—she walks out, sniffling. For the last time.

CHAPTER 9

"I don't understand why we need to move to New Jersey," Eniola argues to Cedric as he speeds on the turnpike, almost crashing into another car that is on the same highway lane.

"It's a better location for our jobs and we're closer to my family."

Cedric rushes on the road due to them being late for an open house. He's been obsessing over a four-bedroom, two-and-a-half bath that he found in Montclair for months, and predictably missed his alarm that morning. Eniola cannot shake him awake for missed appointments—her mind fixates on the discomfort of her pregnancy. Cedric complains about her "dragging body", discounting the swollen feet, limbs and her tired back weighing her down.

"What about my family?"

Cedric sneers. "We are renting in Long Island, less than fifteen minutes away from your fam. Name one time they came over. My mom has to trek all the way from uptown to see us."

"Let's just see how the house is." Eniola hates when he reminds her of her family's neglect.

Eniola pouts at the scene of suburban greenery outside of her window for several minutes.

"It's a boy."

Cedric swerved on the road from the news. "Why didn't you tell me?"

"Come to an appointment and you'll know everything you should."

Normally, she would smooth things over, convincing herself that Cedric needs a push in the right direction. Her pregnancy highlights that dealing with her own needs is enough work.

Eniola gave her belly a tender rub when walking out of the doctor's office after the gender reveal, deciding to make the best of her situation. She made amends with her mother, hoping Morenike's apology for her harsh tirade produces changes in her reaction to her first grandchild. Her mother's primary focus was not to tell anyone. "We don't say anything about pregnancies in our culture until the last trimester," Morenike warned. Eniola remembers her mother sending congratulatory wishes to extended family members around her age much earlier in their pregnancies, but they were all married. Since suggesting they take a discreet approach to the new baby boy of the family, Morenike moved her focus to Kofo's wedding. If it isn't about Kofo's wedding, Kofo's fiancé, Kofo's job, Kofo's everything—Morenike cuts their discussions short.

Cedric doesn't respond to the shot Eniola threw in his direction. He refuses to attend doctor's appointments in protest because he claims they were not in a financial position to raise a child. Yet he's been going on about buying a house for at least a year. He sacrificed lunches, boys' night out, canceled his gym membership to jog at a nearby track field, and cut down on shopping.

The maintenance of Cedric's wardrobe is a sacred endeavor and is one of his biggest financial investments. They had to get a two-bedroom apartment to store his sneaker collection in their spare bedroom alone. He frequently brags about his favorite pastime of being online for the latest Jordans in high school. Cedric claims to be too old for that now and would rather scour sneaker enthusiast websites, bidding against other sneakerheads across the world for four-hundred-dollar kicks.

When he approached her at a day party while hanging out with Jumoke and Sherifat years ago, it shocked Eniola that a guy so "fly" wanted her. She later found out through one of his friends who tried to hit on her that he was turning a new leaf away from being shallow. That same friend claimed to be attracted to women with her look and propositioned that Eniola dump Cedric so he could pursue her instead. She told Cedric about it and he's since cut that guy off. Eniola thinks of him and his offer periodically. He's just as cute and accomplished as Cedric, but less fashionable and understated. He was "simple", Cedric complained with smug resentment.

Maybe simple is a better deal, Eniola says to herself while remembering the conversation.

Cedric compliments her cute face and "fat ass", but never her hair or her outfits. She used to solicit his input on her style and hated all of his suggestions. He pushed her to wear red bottoms that gave her corns on all her toes and tight leather pants that barely gave her room to breathe after eating. Her hair came up sparingly and Cedric advised her to relax it, or try to grow her natural hair longer. She watched countless YouTube videos and saw progress, but told him she needs to braid her hair for a few months to get it to his preferred length past her collarbone. He fussed about her suggestion with the opinion that braids are "ghetto" and most girls that wear them are "bald-headed". Eniola settled back onto her weaves since he wanted the appearance of long hair, if nothing else.

***

They arrive at the open house to a crowd of millennial couples. Cars are double-parked all along the block, aggravating Cedric.

Eniola pulls up her phone, avoiding eye contact. "You can check it out. Just double park here and I'll wait inside. Take pictures."

Cedric raises his eyebrows, pausing. "You sure?"

"Yes. Go for it."

Cedric pulls up behind another car, dashing out of the vehicle to charm the real estate agent on the porch in the midst of upper-middle-class New Yorkers that want relief from the Big Apple. He is the only Black person in attendance and goes right into "professional" mode, engaging the real estate agent that responds with a smile and touches his shoulder before they go inside. Eniola looks up from her device, admiring his ability to code-switch. Sometimes he gets rid of his Harlem accent entirely with much effort.

The house is nice at first glance. But that was it—just nice. Being in New Jersey doesn't excite her. It reminds her of Long Island and the dreary suburban days of her adolescence and early adulthood. She vowed to stay away from places like this—the boredom sends her mind to self-destructive places. The malls have the same type of clothing, people live in isolation and it's unlikely that her friends will visit, forcing her to start over with a new crowd. The thought of living in this house with Cedric prompts nausea and she opens the door to vomit, alarming the agent who up close appears to be a Persian woman.

"Oh my God! Miss, are you okay?"

She's beautiful. Eniola thinks to herself once she looks up to respond to her slight accent. She has on a stylish fitted wide-legged gray suit that hugs her slender body, wine red lipstick, olive skin, hazel eyes and a big head of deep brown tresses that perfectly frame her oblong face. Her manicure is an ox blood red shade, and she smells like expensive perfume.

Eniola heaves, leaning back into her car seat with the door open. The woman notices her pregnant belly.

"I'm so sorry. Let me get you a bottle of water." The real estate agent dashes to her Range Rover across the street, and brings back a large bottle of Essentia—the only bottled water brand she and Cedric allow in their house. Eniola takes it, gulping it down, and uses the remnants of the bottle to wash off small drops of her mess from the car door.

"I have two little ones, so I know how you feel. Sometimes I think I'm crazy for wanting more with how uncomfortable it all is," the agent says, revealing a mouth full of straight teeth.

Eniola continues to catch her breath, her head spinning. "Yeah. Thank you," is all she could muster because her intuition would not rest. Other parts of her body tense up and she feels a heat flash coming. Something about this woman bothers her, despite her kindness and beauty. Something is off.

Eniola catches her breath while the agent rounds up a discussion with an Asian couple on the lawn. The wife carries a small baby, exposing a shiny diamond ring set. Probably three to four carats, Eniola guesses. She looks genuinely happy to be there with her husband, but the agent delivers news that drops their smiles at the end of their conversation. The prospective buyers all appear disappointed after getting final words from the agent. Eniola looks straight ahead, hoping that Cedric will get them out of there. She closes her eyes to cool down, waiting for sleep that never came.

***

"What did you think about the house?" Eniola cuts a piece of salmon she made with fried rice on the living room couch. Cedric browses his laptop, shopping for furniture while glancing at a basketball game on their flatscreen television.

"We should get it. The agent wants to work with us." He avoids eye contact with her, his eyes only moving back and forth from the television to his phone.

Eniola has had enough. Her hormones inspire courage, and she turns off the television by grabbing the remote on the coffee table, annoying Cedric.

"Why did you do that?"

"You didn't send me any pictures of the house. You only described it."

"I forgot. I'll send it now."

"How much is the house?"

"$600,000, we have to put 20% down."

"Do you have that kind of money?"

"I thought we were doing this together?"

Eniola shakes her head, wondering how she got here. All she could hear was Jumoke's voice. En-i-ol-a—what are you doing? It's easier to disregard her friend in the company of others to preserve her reputation. But in this quiet moment, she can't dismiss the question that haunts her mind daily. Eniola doesn't know what the hell she is doing and as the days progress, she hates that she can't figure it out.

"How do you know the agent?"

"I found her online. Why?"

Eniola looks at Cedric with an expression that only wants the truth.

"Who is she, Cedric?"

Cedric sighs, looking ahead with his eyes tracing the floor. He then stares at his laptop monitor.

"We used to date when I was in undergrad."

Eniola nods, remembering the Essentia bottle. "And you're still sleeping with her."

"I never said that—"

Eniola cries. Cedric is an asshole, but she's a bigger idiot for staying. Nothing is going to make him commit. Not her outfits, not her mother's approval, not her fucked up weave, not their baby.

Cedric drops his phone, kneeling in front of her. He looks sorry. But it's not enough.

"It was only one time last year. We never did it again."

Eniola breaks into a loud sob, wishing she could kick him across the room. "You want to live in that house with her. Buy it on your own. You don't want me, Cedric."

"I have my issues, but babe—that's not true."

Eniola can't stop crying. This conversation pains her, but it's also a relief. She takes a loud deep breath, releasing everything she's felt for a while. Letting him go isn't as hard as she thought it was going to be.

"Let's co-parent. I'll move back home in a few weeks."

Cedric stands, angry at the suggestion. "Ennie, don't do this. We're about to have a baby. You sound crazy right now."

"So why won't you propose?! Why are we almost five years into this and you barely say that you love me? Why won't you listen when I told you I don't want to live in a fucking sewer called New Jersey?!"

Cedric paces, furious. "Why didn't you ask your doctor about changing your birth control when we talked about it last year?"

Eniola, enraged, leans forward and holds her belly. Her first inclination was to curse him out filthy, but the most important thing she wanted to say is already out in the open. "It's okay Cedric. I can figure this out on my own. You can continue with your phony ass life."

"Oh, word? Were you not right next to me, being full of shit with me or not? You're not mentally well to raise a baby on your own. You cry over everything lately. I don't trust you with our baby alone, which is part of why I'm staying to watch over your unstable ass."

"Unbelievable. Fuck you."

"Yea, whatever."

Cedric snatches his car keys and storms out. Eniola consoles herself for a few moments before making her way to their bedroom.

***

Eniola and Kofo grab the last of her suitcases and bags into her childhood bedroom. Thank goodness Eniola asked her mom to get her a queen bed as a teenager. The room is big enough to fit a crib and a desk for her to do any work after hours.

"At least it's closer to the train versus your apartment." There goes optimistic Kofo again.

Eniola called Kofo for assistance with moving to avoid the "I told you so" vibes of her friends. Tunde works the hardest amongst them all, running up and down the stairs with boxes and random items she managed to pack on her own.

"Thank you, Kofo. I know you're busy with everything and it's a lot for you guys to help me with moving." Her stomach turns to say this to her younger sister, but it makes no sense to dismiss the need for humility at the moment.

"Of course, Ennie." Kofo unpacks a box of beauty products, remembering how Eniola set them up in her room years ago. "Have you finally come around on a shower? You would benefit from one with the gifts."

The thought of having a baby shower as a single mom horrifies Eniola. "Can't I just do a registry?"

"You'll get much more with an actual shower. You need a lot."

"Cedric will contribute, Kofo. He's not a deadbeat." Considering how explosive their argument was after he returned from his drive, he might not. She's unsure of his interest in raising their son.

"Humph," Kofo responds. "Just let me know so I can make sure I'm available to help with planning."

Eniola pins her hair up, afraid of another flash coming that will force her to wash her hair, which she hates doing. "Speaking of planning, how's the wedding going? What's happening with that?"

Kofo gets visibly tense, piquing Eniola's curiosity. "Well… we're gonna have it in Nigeria."

Eniola frowns. "Isn't that far out for your guests?"

"No… it's actually the perfect middle point for both of our families. Plus, we want to sanction our marriage in a sacred place. Nigeria makes sense. We'll have a small Nikah in New York for anyone that doesn't want to fly out for our wedding."

"I see." There's nothing sacred about Nigeria to Eniola. She's more than happy to renew her family lineage in the States. Every visit she makes to Nigeria is filled with family drama, liars, chauvinists, and corruption. For whatever reason, Nigerians exhibit much better behavior overseas towards her. She likes the diasporan version of her people.

Kofo halts her unpacking, visibly annoyed. "I'm going to check on Tunde real quick and see if he needs anything."

"Ok, sure." Eniola smells a rat. Is her marriage to Tunde not what she thought? Are they having problems? A part of her would feel validated if that were the case.

***

"$500 worth of 6-month-old clothes. Why Ennie?" Morenike shakes her head, questioning Eniola.

After the attendant at Target gives Eniola her return receipt, she stuffs it in her purse, hiding more details on her previous splurge when shopping with Kofo previously. "I need a few essential items, Mommy. Do you want to wait in the car?" Eniola grabs a shopping cart.

Morenike dumps her purse in the cart. "I'll join you."

They peruse the aisles in silence, forming no discussion. Eniola realizes she hasn't shopped with her mother in years. The walk through the store reminds her of playing hide-and-seek with Kofo behind television boxes and racks of clothing. Morenike committing to this mundane task speaks volumes—she isn't in a rush to leave or head somewhere else; no one is fighting and neither of them feels a need to fill up the space with aimless discussion. Eniola drops some formula, wipes and eco-friendly baby soaps into the cart.

"Ok, I'm done."

Morenike chuckles. "You need so much more."

"I'm going to prioritize and go slow."

Her mom and sister are the only ones showing up in her life right now. Jumoke remained quiet when she told her about her plans after breaking up with

Cedric, surprised that she didn't want to discuss it any further. Sherifat texted a flat, unengaging, *congrats*!

She suspects Sherifat was jealous of her relationship with Curtis and wanted him to herself because she spotted him first at the day party where they met. He pulled Eniola to the side to seal the deal in getting her number and said, "your girls are cute, but you are bad," before staring at her breasts and her hips. Something told her to wear her fitted sundress instead of a romper, and it worked because everyone wanted a piece of her that day.

"Kofo told me you declined a shower. Why don't you do it at her new condo?"

Eniola stops pushing the cart, pausing from her mother's question. "Isn't her place a rental?"

"Oh. She didn't tell you."

"Tell me what?"

"Your father is helping her and Tunde buy a condo in Prospect Heights."

Eniola feels another heatwave coming over her body. They are both headed towards a new start in different directions. How does Kofo get more when she is in greater need? Her father judges Eniola's financial literacy based on her mistake of blowing Akeem's seed investment for her private practice. She wasn't ready to own a business and needed more professional experience, but her parents kept pressuring her to "think bigger" about her career. Eniola planned on saving the money and to stash it on the side without telling Cedric. But Kofo stupidly told him about the money and he sweet-talked her into using it to support their expenses. Cedric promised he would pay her back and Eniola has yet to see a single dollar.

Her decisions at the beginning of her relationship with Cedric weren't always the best, but she wised up and started saving in secret. Eniola could put a down payment on the Jersey house and have plenty left over, but not one soul knows about her hoarded stash. She touches it sparingly for an occasional splurge item, hence her luxury pieces. One of her colleagues also introduced her to cryptocurrency when she announced her pregnancy. Eniola is dabbling in it with decent results so far.

Kofo is misinformed about her finances and spends beyond her limits. Managing a mortgage at this stage is a bad idea for her little sister. Tunde doesn't seem financially responsible, either. He has a new item from Balenciaga or Saint Laurent every week and splurges on "experiences" as he calls them. The condo should be hers.

"I had no idea. That's nice." Eniola drags her cart to the checkout line, her hopeful mood turned sour.

***

Eniola lays down halfway on her bed, preparing for another early night of sleep. Her swollen feet are in massive pain from standing earlier, and her Morenike gave her a jar of Aboniki ointment to offer some relief. The pungent smell from the menthol reminds her of a hospice. While she stares at her inflamed toes, a deafening silence consumes the room that would've soothed her before hearing about Kofo's condo.

Her mom also gave her a grandma-esque floral nightgown that dusted her calves due to most of her clothing being too tight. In a mirror across from the bed, her double chin pokes out, changing the shape of her face. She removed her weave before bedtime, revealing a dry afro with stringy ends from heat damage. When she picks up her phone, she realizes her screensaver is a silhouette of her and Cedric on vacation in Turks and Caicos.

I'm not gonna cry. I will not cry, she tells herself repeatedly when her eyes well. But there was nothing Eniola could do to occupy her time. Outside of browsing social media, working and going to Nigerian parties—she seldom has anything to do.

As she reaches her arm to turn off the light next to her on the nightstand, Eniola spots a small item that prompts a memory. It is an old coin that she found when her family first moved to Long Island. She wandered farther than their backyard to discover artifacts she displayed in her room and got lost in the suburban forest. When she found a coin using a metal detector that her father bought for her birthday, she sat on the ground and studied it for at least an hour before deciding to keep it. The direction back to the house was unclear, with the fall leaves covering the mud underneath, preventing her from tracing her footprints. A twenty-minute walk from her backyard took three hours, causing her mother to call the police. Morenike made her stoop down for six hours when she got home. Her preteen body was sore for almost a week. She stopped treasure hunting after that.

Eniola turned off the light, letting a tear run down her cheek.

***

Yvonne cuts the damaged ends of Eniola's hair, revealing a short afro at her Harlem apartment kitchen table.

"Now you have a halo." She smiles, gently patting Eniola's hair and giving her a mirror to check it out.

"Thank you so much, Ms. Mathis."

Eniola returns the mirror, rises out of her seat and removes the smock over her clothing.

"Where are you going?!" Yvonne asks in confusion.

"Oh, I was grabbing my wallet. I just wanted a trim. We're done, no?"

Yvonne sighs, sitting down on a chair across from Eniola, shaking her head. Eniola says nothing, unclear about Yvonne's reaction.

"Why won't you let me help you, Ennie?"

"Ms. Mathis, I'm not sure what you mean."

"That's what I'm talking about. *Ms. Mathis*. I told you to call me Yvonne. Or Mommy Cedric like y'all do."

"I'm just trying to be respectful."

Yvonne reflects on her comment, looking down at the center of the table.

"You're a beautiful woman, inside and out. Cedric is my son, but he doesn't deserve you. Let a real man love you, Ennie. Let people care about you. Stop hiding. Let me do your fucking hair and finish it. You're not going anywhere after this except your house. I know you have nothing to do."

Eniola smiles at Yvonne. She assumed Yvonne tolerated her all these years because she wasn't good enough for Cedric. She smiles, timid.

"Okay, Mommy Cedric."

Yvonne deep conditions, steams, moisturizes, and trims Eniola's hair. She finishes with a gentle silk press and shapes it into a chin-length, bouncy bob. Her hair is healthy, thick, and full of body from her efforts of hair growth. Eniola doubts the potential of her mane, but upon looking at the final product in Yvonne's bathroom mirror, a new person emerged. When she steps out into the living room, she finds Cedric in the living room with his mother. He does a double-take, but Eniola is unaffected.

Eniola pulls out two hundred dollars from her purse. "Mommy Cedric… I absolutely love it."

Cedric smirks, but cannot take his eyes off of Eniola's radiant energy. "Since when are you Mommy Cedric?" They both ignore him.

Yvonne smiles and winks, touching Eniola's shoulder. "It's on me." Eniola puts her money away, hugs Yvonne, and applies her shoes.

Cedric leans his head forward in Eniola's direction, expecting acknowledgement. "*Hi*, Ennie."

"Hi Cedric. See you soon." She looks straight ahead to the apartment door and wobbles out of there in a hurry.

CHAPTER 10

It's a Thursday night during the last warm days of September, and the Meatpacking district buzzes as if it's July. Taxis and Ubers drive bumper to bumper, dropping clusters of young metropolitan New Yorkers on graveled roads. Many vie for acceptance into the venues that line up the streets of this trendy neighborhood—yuppie professionals with Schultz stiletto sandals that were on the cheerleading squad in their middle American town and the jocks that dated them, fashionistas dipped in designer labels after waiting in long lines at sample sales in Soho, and crews of queer friends that will settle down from their bustling lifestyles in Hells Kitchen or Chelsea. They all walk different paths, but have one thing in common—desperation for access to the hottest venues in New York City.

    Tunde is determined to own these streets, unbothered by the massive bouncers that turn people away every night, and the promoters with their walkie-talkies that instruct the staff inside on where to place those that get admittance. Wooing his co-workers with jokes and cool stories of growing up in London put him in the position to court foreign colleagues that come into town. The nights include an overindulgence of expensive food and drinks for further networking. One colleague this week is a Swedish guy named Henrik. He flew to the New York headquarters to update Tunde's team on the progress of their office. Tunde liked him right away, impressed by his composure in the office and free spirit off the clock. Another co-worker from the Australian branch named Adrian is representing her office as well. She brought her best friend Suzette along for a first-time New York experience.

"You got a ciggy, Tundie?" Henrik never says his name correctly; he is tired of correcting him at this point.

"Nah mate, only do ganja. Sorry." Tunde stretches his neck out to see what's going on at the front of the line and makes eye contact with the promoter named Julian. He's a muscle-bound Italian American that wears the same button-down shirt in a different color every week.

Tunde told Adrian that they would have to pretend to be a couple in order for Julian to let them in, and Suzette would pair with Henrick. She was initially offended, but agreed after a few drinks because Suzette heard about this area of town and wanted to experience it. Adrian changed into heels after dinner and let her trademark ponytail loose, but the suggestion sullied her mood.

Tunde feels her growing impatience as Julian summons them to skip the line right in time.

"Four? Bottle again?" Tunde nods. "Got it." Julian gives them wristbands, unhooks the rope and they walk right in.

The inside of the club is dark, glossy, with sleek gold details and chaotic lighting. Tunde follows a hostess who maneuvers through the crowd, leading them to a booth while Top Forty music blasts in their ears. A bottle of vodka awaits them, along with juices, ice, and soda. They dig right in, feeding more of their initial buzz from the steakhouse they dined at earlier.

Henrik goes hardcore and downs two shots. As Tunde touches his forearm to ensure he is okay, he saunters off with two twiggy models that likely grace runways during fashion week.

Adrian remains seated at the booth, unimpressed with the scene. Suzette stands next to her, swaying back and forth with a cocktail she prepares in a lowball cup.

Babe… don't wait up for me. The Aussie one is hard to crack. Tunde texts Kofo, then quickly puts his phone in his pocket.

"You alright?" Tunde shouts in Adrian's ear. He needs to make her loosen up. She's killing the vibe.

"This isn't really my thing." Adrian takes a sip of Suzette's drink.

"Do you want us to leave?"

"No—Suzie likes it. What do you have to get me loose?" Adrian stares at Tunde, cocking her head to the side for a satisfactory response.

Henrik appears on cue, as if he heard them across the room. The models are gone and his energy is on ten.

"Guys, we left the office hours ago!" He cackles. "Take a bump with me!"

Adrian's eyes light up, no longer in need of Tunde's ideas. "Yes, give me one!" Henrick gives her a small bag of coke and she heads straight to the bathroom.

"Tundie, you can go after her." Henrick spits in his ear and Tunde can smell his mouth loaded with the scents of cigarettes and liquor.

"I have my supply. You and Adrian are all set!" Tunde rushes to the bathroom and takes care of business.

***

Three hours later, Tunde drags his exhausted body out of the Uber, making his way into his condo. He creeps into his bedroom and sits on an accent chair across his new king-sized bed, in his new two-bedroom condo, watching Kofo sleep.

I own property in one of the most expensive cities in the world. He says to himself.

Windows fill one wall, exposing a view of Prospect Park and Botanical Gardens. The room is half the size of their bedroom less than fifteen minutes away, but everything is brand new. No pre-war faulty elevators, no roaches from dirty next-door neighbors, no loud cranking sounds of radiators. Washing dishes by hand is optional and they don't need to leave the apartment to do the laundry. Everything runs cohesively from pressing a button.

Akeem shocked them with a significant wedding gift. They would never get approved as a couple, grateful that Akeem leveraged his financial

165

history that allowed them to be homeowners in a prime Brooklyn location. Their condo is pricey, but it offers enough cushion to have active social lives as newlyweds in New York City. He's glad he took the leap to move here—life is amazing right now.

***

Tunde jumps out of the bed the next morning, shaving in front of his bathroom mirror while Kofo prepares her morning cup of tea. He's late for work, but his team is understanding when he has outings the night before.

"Babe! Someone is calling you. I think it's from your office." Kofo shouts from the kitchen. She walks to him, handing him his cellphone.

"Thanks Babe." Tunde air kisses her while picking up the phone. "Hello?"

"Tundie—you need to get into the office. Where are you?!" Henrik sounds panicked.

"I'm getting ready. What's wrong?"

"Adrian. She's not feeling well."

"Ok, I'll be there ASAP."

"Please hurry." Henrick hangs up.

Tunde is glad he had his own coke. He knows how to use the right amount, and can time the wear-off of by the minute. If Kofo was awake when he got home, it's unlikely she would recognize anything unusual—colleagues and friends in London taught him how to manage his use of substances. He wants to stop altogether in the future, but it's hard while working in finance because it's done regularly and openly. Weed and liquor are like child's play. The stressful, long hours and crazy deadlines create the perfect environment for a need to wane off the pressures of his job.

***

Tunde slides right into his cube, turning on his work computer. His work friend John—a yuppie from Jersey who looks like he should be in a Ralph Lauren ad—rolls his chair right behind him.

"Dude, what the fuck?" John whispers, darting his eyes all over the office in fear of being associated with Tunde.

"What?"

"You gave Adrian laced coke, man?"

"Fuck no! Is that what you heard?"

"Yes. And she's in the hospital. Henrik won't shut up about it, and he's telling everyone." John gives Tunde a look of worry, but there was something else behind it. Tunde is dreading what's coming and he didn't answer one email yet.

"She was fine when I left them last night."

John shakes his head, rolling away back to his desk. Tunde opens his Outlook and the one email that gets Tunde's attention is from his boss, Cleveland. He's an older version of John with a balding head and a growing pot belly from too much steak and potatoes.

Tunde, I need you to come into my office ASAP.

Tunde walks over to Cleveland's office, preparing for the end of his career that he built with seamless precision until this point.

***

Tunde slumps on his couch, about to roll another blunt that won't soothe his chaotic thoughts. He just got engaged, moved into a condo in one of the most coveted neighborhoods in Brooklyn, and is jobless for something he didn't do. Cleveland didn't want to hear any accounts of what happened last night. The liability of using drugs, spending money at a venue that isn't covered on his company expense policy, and indulgence in anything other than a professional meeting was too much to take on.

Should I tell Kofo that the company is downsizing? He questions. Kofo is the type to demand details he won't have the answers for.

He hears her opening the front door and feels an overwhelming sense of dread. Clearing the table won't work. She's already aware of his frequent smoking.

"Hey babe." Kofo looks down, focusing on taking off her heels.

"Hey."

Kofo looks at Tunde, who is ineffectual at pretending to be okay. She can tell when he's smoking to chill versus smoking to chill out. "What happened?"

Tunde opens his mouth to tell her the truth, but the words won't come. "I had a stressful day at work, that's all, babe." Tunde takes a blow, handing it to Kofo who shook her head, turning it down.

She sat down next to him. "Was it the girl who got food poisoning?"

"Yea... turns out it was a severe allergic reaction she didn't know about to artichokes from the place I took them to for dinner. Cleveland banged on about how I should've asked about dietary restrictions in the future, blah blah. He's so fucking annoying."

Kofo rolls her eyes. "They'll get over it. You're doing too well for them to let you go." Kofo takes his chin, kissing him on the lips before rising to prepare dinner. "I'll make you efo with meat stew and rice. Your second favorite."

Tunde gives a sheepish grin, watching her sacrifice her desired hour of wind-down time when she gets home from work. "Thank you, babe."

***

Tunde acts out his morning routine the next day, not sure where he was going with a brand-new suit. He gave indications of something being off—he didn't make the bed, he left his clothes right outside of the closet, and he forgot to put the toilet seat down. Kofo typically leaves the house first, but he got out of there an hour before her.

When she sorts the mess that he left right in front of their walk-in closet, she spots his Armani blazer in the pile. This is his high-priced, lucky blazer that Tunde wears when he attends big meetings. She remembers that he wore it the same day he went out with Henrik and Adrian. There are stains on the sleeve and it reeks of cigarette smoke, which Tunde loathes. She grabs it along with some other items, intending to make a quick drop off to the cleaners up the block before hopping on the train to Manhattan.

When she lays the pieces on the counter, the owner, Mr. Fung, sifts through the pockets and everything is empty. Except for the inside pocket of his Armani jacket.

"Woah, look at this!" He lifts a small bag of coke, horrifying Kofo. She snatches it immediately and stuffs it in her purse.

Mr. Fung laughs, amused at her discomfort. They aren't the first and won't be the last in this neighborhood. "Your fiancé likes to party, huh?" Kofo doesn't answer.

"How much is it?" she snaps.

Mr. Fung smirks, handing her the receipt. "You can pick it up in a week."

"Thanks." Kofo rushes out of there with her head down before making her way to work.

***

Tunde travels from one end of New York City to another, taking the 2 train all the way to the New York Botanical Garden in The Bronx, and hangs out at The Bronx Zoo until he finishes lunch. He then takes a bus crosstown to the 4 train and got off at Yankee Stadium, walks across the Macombs Dam Bridge to Harlem and takes another bus down to 125th Street and Broadway. The 1 train to back downtown is his next train of choice, but then Tunde changes his mind and walks east to The Apollo theater. He craves soul food and devours waffles, fried chicken and mac n cheese at Amy Ruths on 116th and Lenox before going to the Malcolm Shabazz Harlem Market. He buys a few pieces of ankara outfits with plans of gifting it to his family during his next trip to London.

He had a day like this when he first moved to New York during a lonely weekend. Finally, he walks the waffles off in Central Park until he gets to 72nd Street and makes his way home. There is no way he would run into anyone that Kofo knows uptown, aside from Yvonne. But he avoided her salon near 145th Street in Sugar Hill on the B and C line.

The fears of Tunde's future haunt him as he transitions from one location to the next. He has a career that spans over ten years and it was taken from him in a five-minute conversation. Cleveland nor his colleagues cared what the "London Bloke" had to say when Adrian blamed him for bringing them to the club, as though he handed the drugs to her on a platter. No one questioned her story, and Henrik happily passed the buck his way. Henrick got "suspended" and Adrian received paid sick leave. His parents warned him about the insidious nature of racism in the United States. Europe is no better, but he naively thought the novelty of his foreign status would provide some sort of protection. Microaggressions are one thing, but being unfairly blamed for this was another.

When he gets to Columbus Circle on the B train, it fills up with commuters heading home. Most have on suits and would merge into his old office. He hopes that none of his colleagues pop up, hence why he avoided any east-bound trains—his office is near Grand Central. With every stop, Tunde prays for rush hour delays to slow down the dreaded arrival of his stop, but the ride is smooth this evening.

***

Kofo reheats the previous night's food at their usual seven thirty dining time when he walks in. He washes his hands, setting the table. There is a bottle of wine in the fridge, but he only pours a cup for Kofo. All stimulants and suppressants are off-limits for the foreseeable future.

They sit down to eat, both exhausted for different reasons. Kofo looks down at her plate, tossing her food back and forth. Tunde eats, gorging on it all.

"How was work?" Kofo tosses a pile of spinach stew over some rice while sipping on wine with her other hand.

"Long day. Nothing crazy," Tunde says in between bites.

Kofo rises out of her seat, goes to her purse that sat on their living room couch and pulls out the bag of coke. She tosses it on the table next to him.

"Where'd you get that from?!" Tunde exclaims.

Kofo sits back at the dining table. "Is this what you were doing before our first date? Is that why you lied about getting lost on the train?"

"Kofo, come on—"

"Food poisoning over artichokes? Really, Tunde? Do you think I'm that stupid?"

"But there are people who actually can't eat it Kofo."

"Would you cut it the fuck out?!"

"Chill out, alright?!"

Kofo buries her head in her shaking hands. Moments later, she picks up her plate of food and drops it on top of the pots in the sink. She goes to the bedroom and slams the door. Tunde remains frozen in his seat. He can't hide anymore. She knows too much. Tunde rises and walks enters the bedroom. Kofo stuffs an overnight bag, wiping her teary face.

"Please don't tell me you're going to Long Island."

"Where else would I be going?!"

"Babe. Let's talk for a second."

"Leave me alone."

Tunde grabs her forearm. "Kofo, stop!"

Kofo looks at everything other than Tunde's face. "I let the weed go cause I do it from time to time also. But coke... coke?! I do not fuck with hard drugs. I'm not interested in marrying a 'Wolf of Wall Street' type of guy."

"That's not who I am, Kofo. I only used it once in a while."

Kofo rolls her eyes, turning her attention back to her bag. Tunde snatches the bag.

"Wait, let's really talk."

"Oh, now your busted ass wants to talk."

"I got fired."

Kofo closes her eyes, breathing into the pits of her diaphragm. "What did you just say to me?"

"Henrik met some models at the club we went to and they gave him laced coke. The Adrian girl took some too along with her friend, but Adrian had a severe reaction to it, and ended up in the hospital."

"No, no, no..."

"She's not dead or anything. But Adrian told Cleveland that this was all my fault because I forced them to go to the club. Fucking bitch."

"Well, wasn't it your idea to go?!"

"I mean, yea... but I didn't tell her to take any of those drugs! I have my stash and I never share it with anyone because of shit like this."

"So, they fired your Black ass and let all these white kids stay on the company payroll." Kofo looks at her fiancé with disappointment.

Tunde hates validating Kofo's complaints about racism. He often dismisses her, saying that merit prevails over race.

"Yes. I was the only one that got let go."

Kofo takes another deep breath, sliding her bottom to the floor with Tunde standing over her.

***

Kofo kicked Tunde out of their bed, assigning him to their guest bedroom. He volunteered to go to a local treatment center and is seeking employment. The meetings at the center are torturous, forcing him to confront his need for approval at his own expense—approval from his dad, from his colleagues, from Kofo's snooty but messy family, and so on. He started using drugs to fit in with his British colleagues and they have all since moved on with intact families. Based on what he sees on their social media profiles and through the grapevine, they are sober and loving it.

When he told Kofo about his revelation, she dryly responded, "so where's the part in this that you end things between us to focus on you?" Tunde insisted that won't happen and he would rather sleep in separate beds for now.

He cannot imagine a life without Kofo on his arm. She accepts him fully and is grounded in her expectations of him as a mate. He thought he had to perform for a Nigerian woman of her stature, but Kofo is content with the simplicity of their lives. Her focus during their conversations is his ultimate fulfillment and happiness, and she presses against his complacency if he is slacking on maintaining his desires. She wants him to be happy. He cannot let her go; he needs a woman like Kofo in his life. The only glimmer of hope is that she hasn't stopped planning their wedding.

Kofo walks to the living room one weekend afternoon, transferring items from her work purse into a smaller bag while on the phone with Morenike. "Kofo, get the fabric from me today. Mommy Bola is coming back from Nigeria in two days. She can't purchase it in bulk if we continue to drag our feet, come by and see the sample so you can approve it," Tunde overhears on speakerphone.

"Mommy, I told you I don't want to wear this color. I want blue. And my old boss Katie is having her last brunch with us today, I have to go."

"This is the best fabric we've seen so far."

Tunde is eager to regain her trust, even if it means he has to endure an afternoon with Morenike. "Babe, I can get it."

Kofo nods and explains to her mother the new pickup plan.

***

Tunde's Uber pulls in front of the Adebayo Long Island house. He's nervous about what he's walking into—everything with Tunde's future in-laws is an all-day, all-consuming affair. Morenike can't help her compulsion for unsolicited comments or questions, Eniola needs not one more reason to be envious of her sister, and Akeem will want to know the latest trade secrets he's picked up in work meetings. The next train heading back to the city arrives in an hour, and he's hoping to catch it in time.

He uses Kofo's key to enter the house, walking into Morenike wrapping up a phone call with Mommy Bola in the kitchen. Eniola is buried in her laptop, preparing various items for her registry.

"Hi Ennie. Your hair looks great," Tunde says.

She blushes, smoothing her hand over her silk press. "Thank you," she replies.

Morenike yells into the phone, similar to his mother. This is an unfamiliar version of her. Morenike's excitement and preoccupation with planning their wedding is intense.

Once spotting Tunde, grabs a six-yard bag of fuchsia colored lace material with metallic undertones and sequins. "Tunde, make sure you are gentle with this sample. We already ordered it. We just need Kofo to eventually agree."

"She doesn't really like this color. Her favorite color is blue. She wants to have a royal blue and gold color scheme."

Morenike waves her hand, dismissing him while answering a question from Mommy Bola that should be answered by Kofo. A few phrases in, their connection gets spotty and the call drops. She places the phone on the kitchen island counter.

"Have you eaten?"

"Oh, no Mommy Ennie. I'm okay. I'm actually going to catch the next train heading to the city in about thirty minutes."

"Let me give you a container to go for you and Kofo."

Morenike's phone rings again from an unsaved Nigerian number Tunde spots in the corner of his eye, and she presses the green button to accept it on speaker while putting up her hand for Tunde to wait.

Ugh, he thinks, fearful that he may miss the train because of her. Tunde wants to get out of there as soon as possible. Any hint of unemployment will prompt Morenike to sniff around for detailed explanations of his status.

"Hello?!" Morenike shouts.

"Hi. Is this Mrs. Morenike Adebayo?" a woman's soft voice asks.

"Yes, who is this?"

"Hello, Ma. This is Funmi again."

"Funmi? Funmi from where?"

There was a long pause. The woman sobs, confusing Morenike. Tunde leaves the kitchen and moves to the living area, but he can still hear the woman's voice.

"I was seeing your husband, you called me a few months ago. I thought I would become his second wife. He promised to take care of me and I got deported because I didn't have a steady income that he said he would supplement. But he lied and just used me for sex while preparing himself for another woman in Nigeria. Her name is Yinka."

Morenike takes the phone off speaker mode.

"What's her phone number...Uh huh, okay. I will call you back later. Thank you." Morenike hangs up.

"Tunde, come and get your food," she demands. She doesn't miss a beat and Tunde matches her energy, fearful of any sudden reactions. He glances over at Eniola to gauge her reaction to the phone call and she purses her lips, rolls her eyes and continues on her computer. Tunde cannot fathom his father bringing this mess to his mom. He would kill him with his bare hands.

Fifteen minutes remain to catch the train. When his Uber arrives, Morenike follows him outside the front door.

"Tunde… don't tell Kofo about this."

Tunde looks at her for a few moments. "Can I ask you why?"

"She thinks her father is a good man. It's better for her sake and your own as well. Don't do it. Thank you for stopping by." She touches his shoulder and walks back into the house as he approaches the Uber.

CHAPTER 11

Kofo grimaces when Tunde hands her the fabric—it does not resemble her taste in the slightest. It's gaudy, too shiny and not in a shade she would ever consider wearing. The last time Kofo wore bright fuchsia was in high school—likely a hand-me-down from Eniola.

"Did you tell her I hate this?" Kofo says to Tunde, shuddering her head back and forth.

"Of course. She thinks you're going to come around on it."

Kofo groans, wishing he was effective in making her mother back down. She wants to believe Tunde is worth it—he's doing his best to keep his hold on to her. She vowed to never date a "project" again. How could she end up in a situation with another broken man? What is she doing that makes room for this? She picked up on one of Tunde's major insecurities earlier in their relationship. He changes his accent around non-Black people to a "posher" word arrangement, and wears subdued, blander clothing with less logos. Kofo assumed he was in work mode, playing a role like most Black people out of necessity.

"I tried to tell her you wouldn't be into it."

Kofo continues staring at the fabric, wishing she could toss it in their incinerator. "I'll figure something out with her. Thank you for picking it up."

Tunde places the fabric on their coffee table and sits next to her. "Kofo... are you alright?"

No, of course not, she responds in her head.

Tunde takes her hand. "I'm committed to being better. You won't have a shred of doubt on the other side of this. I want to be better for me and for you."

Kofo looks at their hands together. They fit perfectly. She loves how his masculine veins pop out, showing strength against his clean-cut nails.

"Why do you want me?" She's been burning to ask.

"I tell you every day, Kofo. I think you're amazing."

"Yea, but like why? Why didn't you propose to all the girls in London instead?"

"Because I want you. You are kind, supportive and understanding... you're gorgeous, sexy and intelligent. You carry a quiet fire inside of you that turns me the fuck on. I feel like we work. You remind me of who I am striving to become every day. You're the first Nigerian woman I dated that inspires me to be myself. I can just be. No woman has ever made me feel that ordinary Tunde is enough."

A few weeks ago, this would melt her heart. Now it's just making it heavy.

"I'm torn, Tunde. You lied to me. You're an addict."

"I know, and it was wrong. I'm trash for doing that. But believe me, Kofo—I am going to win you back. I don't even want to touch that shit anymore."

"What if you get addicted to weed or liquor?"

"I am working on curing my addictive personality overall. That's what my treatment program and my therapy sessions are teaching me."

"Does anyone else in either of our families know about this?"

"Not a soul."

Kofo nods and rises to change out of her clothes from brunch, leaving Tunde with the fabric.

***

Kofo smooths out the sleeves of her dress for her local Nikah, an Islamic prayer ceremony, in her bedroom mirror. The fabric richly combines beige, ivory and gold details. The gown is long-sleeved, with a boat neck and a mermaid style bottom, spilling a tiny train. Her bulky gold jewelry highlights the metallic shades in her dress and is appropriate for the occasion. She used Eniola's gele lady to wrap her gold aso-oke headdress, and she crunched the paper-like fabric onto Kofo's head with perfection.

Kofo is in love with her Nikah ceremony ensemble. Her sentiments towards her Nigerian ceremony are another matter. Her troubled engagement consumes her, and she forgot to decline the fuchsia fabric before Mommy Bola returned from Nigeria. It was too late by the time she told her mom that it's not her style. Kofo ignored her mother's imposition of the fuchsia fabric that is collecting dust in her closet, and starts a search online for blue fabrics.

She lands on a rich, cobalt, reflective lace adorned with curved sequins in the same blue tone. When she sends the gorgeous fabric to her Senegalese tailor Mamadou in Crown Heights, he immediately got to work on her outfit. If she couldn't get her mother to change the wedding party's attire, she will protest on her own.

Tunde emerges from their walk-in closet wearing the Nikah fabric with slim cut pants and a fitted dashiki style top. His gold cufflinks match her jewelry.

"You look beautiful," he says while drooling at her outfit and perfect makeup job.

"Thank you." Kofo grabs a bracelet to add to her accessories, doing her best to not lock eyes with Tunde. Her need for distance as of late feels like she's punishing Tunde, but she can't help it. There are obvious improvements in his daily habits—he cut out smoking and only drinks sparkling cider. His energy levels and mood elevated despite their tension. His diet improved, and he cooks delicious, healthy meals for them at dinner. And he hasn't given up on her. He hasn't given up on them. She didn't object to the quick timeline of their relationship because he was the first guy she's been with that felt like her own decision.

The hard part about the situation is that no one in her circle will listen or understand why she is torn about Tunde. Janelle would pack an overnight bag to help her escape the minute he runs out for his next errand.

They had sex for the first time in weeks the other night, and it was awkward. It felt good physically, but the connection lacked between them and failed to inspire much passion. Before the coke incident, Tunde put a trance on Kofo's body, intuitively knowing how and where to touch everything. He is a skilled, confident, and competent lover. Making love to him gave her a bigger appetite for sex and expanded the way she expressed herself. Taking a break from Tunde revealed the hold he had on her previously. She is experiencing her own form of withdrawal.

"We have to leave in 20 minutes, Tunde."

"I'm on it, babe. I'll be ready in a sec."

Kofo leaves the bedroom and sits on the living room couch. She loves melting into the microfiber upholstery. It feels like a big hug that she needs at the moment.

Tunde walks into the parlor with the air of a real "oga", or boss man, in his agbada outfit. The spark she's suppressing slightly bubbled up to the surface with a quiet smile. Maybe they can try sex again tonight. She gets up near the door while he puts on his shoes.

"You look nice too."

Tunde smiles, kissing her. "We look nice." He's persistent in winning her back.

***

Kofo and Tunde walk into her family home and it's filled to the brim with almost one hundred friends and family members, most of them her mother's friends. Tunde's parents could not attend this local ceremony, but plan on joining them for the official celebration in Nigeria.

Servants pass around hors d'oeuvres such as suya or grilled spiced meat on skewers, fried bean cakes known as akara, fried donuts named puff puffs, meat pies and samosas. A tent in the backyard covers several rows of white, plastic chairs facing a small, elevated platform where the Imam is slated to officiate their Islamic ceremony.

An unrecognizable Uncle pulls Tunde away from Kofo. He recites the common script of an elder. It starts off with, "You don't remember me? Ah! I knew you since you were a baby! I grew up with your parents back in Lagos!" whenever they reunite every five years. Kofo wishes she was better with faces and names to make these encounters more gratifying.

"Hey Ennie! Where's Mommy?" Kofo approaches her sister as she drags her pregnant body back and forth throughout to manage the event. Eniola has on the fuchsia fabric sewn into a simple, long sleeve, V-neck gown that grazes the floor.

"She's still getting ready upstairs. She's running behind."

"Daddy?"

"He ended up having to go on a last-minute business trip."

Kofo can barely stand up. "You're telling me he's on a plane right now? The night of my Nikah?"

"He's at the airport." Eniola's eyes avoid Kofo, hawking the productivity of the event staff.

Kofo snatches her phone from her Fendi purse and slams her touch screen to call her father. The phone goes straight to voicemail all three times. She sends him a text.

Daddy, where are you? It's the night of my New York Nikah.

She sees a text bubble forming a response, then it stops. Then it starts again. *I had a last-minute business trip to Nigeria*, Akeem responds.

Kofo couldn't believe what she was reading as she furiously types back to him. *Daddy, this is my Nikah. What could be more important than that?*

I'm sorry. I wanted to make it but I can't. I'll go to the one in Nigeria.

Kofo's eyes water.

Who else is going to disappoint me? She says to herself. Kofo reflects on the argument she had with her mother about attendance, never getting a hint of her father's unavailability. She tried to get her mother to pause the Nikah until Tunde's parents could attend because they needed time to come up with the funds for their flights. Morenike discounted them entirely, claiming their Christian backgrounds lessens the necessity of their presence and their participation in the Nigerian Nikah should be sufficient. Kofo contemplates that perhaps her mother jinxed this night.

Eniola grabs a napkin from a server and hands Kofo a napkin. "Kofo… I think you should go to the bathroom and get yourself together."

"Did you know about this?"

"I just found out not too long ago."

Kofo heads to the powder room to wash up. She attempts to call him six more times, three of them via WhatsApp, with no luck.

When Kofo emerges from the bathroom more composed, she finds Mommy Bola standing in front of the door.

"Hi Aunty Abidemi!" Kofo has her game face on.

"What did I tell you about calling me that? It's Mommy Bola."

"I've been calling you that my whole life."

"Never mind that. It's Mommy Bola." Kofo attempts to peel herself away from the discussion, furious at the woman who enables her mother's disregard towards the genuine desires she has for her wedding. "You look beautiful. Turn around, let me see." Mommy Bola turns Kofo around on her own, ignoring Kofo's obvious discomfort. Kofo peeps Eniola watching their exchange on the other side of the room and gives her a look that begs for help. Eniola walks in their direction.

"Ya Bola, we're heading into the prayer area now," Eniola pleads to her in Yoruba while grazing her arm in the direction of the backyard tent.

"I'm waiting for your mother. Focus on the other guests," she snaps to them both in offense.

Kofo and Eniola walk away from Mommy Bola, and Kofo ends their path at the foot of the staircase. Eniola grips Kofo's arm, stopping her.

"Leave Mommy. She's about to come right down," she whispers.

"I want to find out what's going on," Kofo responds in a hushed tone.

"Later, not right now. Focus." Eniola won't loosen her grip until Kofo gives in. Kofo continues her quiet dissent by standing at the bottom of the stairs.

Moments later, Morenike emerges, wowing the handful of guests that are lingering around for the last round of appetizers. She wears a pastel pink outfit with high-end gold jewelry, leather Italian pumps, fresh neutral toned makeup and bright pink nails. Despite Kofo's aversion to pink, she admits to herself that her mother looks stunning.

Morenike greets everyone with a plastered smile as she reaches the last step, carrying on like a pageant queen. Kofo charges her mother, keeping a low tone.

"Mommy, where is Daddy?"

"He's not coming. He'll be at the wedding in Nigeria."

"What happened?"

"Last minute business. Let's talk about it later." Morenike heads to a corner with Mommy Bola, who pulls out more fabric from a bag. Kofo spots another batch of six-yard fabric in a shade of orange—it's likely what they are going to impose on her next. Kofo becomes more inflamed as their secret discussion progresses. She wants to react, make a scene, and ruin this sham of an event.

Once the Mommies are done, they all file into the tent with the mosque Alhaji awaiting their arrival except for the bride. Kofo sits on a chair in the parlor right outside of the tent. Kofo reflects on a memory of winning a chess game against her father in the same room for the first time.

When they cue her to stroll down the aisle, Kofo opens the door to make her way outside. She recoils at the sight of countless daddies and uncles who were at their children's Nikahs she attended throughout the years.

Kofo gets to the altar before the Imam next to her fiancé. Tunde holds her hand.

"Tunde, what is your Muslim name?" The Alhaji is ill-equipped for the night.

"Um… I don't—"

"It's Balil." Kofo makes up whatever came to mind. This moment serves as a reminder that she lacks control over her wedding. This should've been discussed during the planning stage of the event.

The Alhaji proceeds with his prayer, followed by a sermon.

An hour later, crowds of family and friends congest around Kofo and Tunde to take photos of the smiling couple. They move like politicians, giving the impression that they were ready to deliver another successful Yoruba marriage to their community. Maroof approaches Kofo, gently touching her shoulder.

"Congrats, cuz."

"Thank you." She gives him her contrived smile everyone is receiving for the night.

"Where's Janelle? I texted her to ask if she was coming, but I never heard back," he says at a volume that makes Tunde glance over at them during a conversation with one of Kofo's family members.

Maroof's question puts a pit in her stomach. She blocked Janelle out of her memory and he rattles the stability she maintains for this event.

"I guess she couldn't make it," Kofo says in an impartial tone.

"She stopped returning my calls and texts, too. I really liked her," Kofo wishes he would shut up. His mother, Aunty Folade, asked about her father a few minutes prior, badgering Kofo about Akeem's whereabouts.

"Let's talk about it later," she says through gritted teeth. His lack of self-awareness makes Kofo question how he became a millionaire. She moves to the next guest, focusing on her memorized answers.

The crowd thins out with only a few friends and family members remaining. Sherifat and Jumoke appear, heading in her direction.

"Hello my Naija bride!" Sherifat spreads her arms in excitement with Eniola watching, smiling uncomfortably. Kofo notices an awkward exchange of glances between Eniola and Jumoke.

"Hi, Sherifat."

"Make sure you get your fabrics to us. I love the pink!"

Kofo swallows, pissed. "You won't be sorry! It's on the way."

Jumoke steps forward in her direction. "Hey Kofo… congrats. Sorry, I won't be able to make it to your Naija ceremony."

"Really?! Why, you always said you can't wait till me or Ennie gets married back home."

Jumoke gives a trembled chuckle. "Yea… I guess hubby and the kids are making it more challenging to travel these days."

Kofo looks at Jumoke up and down with suspicion.

"Okay. You'll be missed."

"Next time. Goodnight my dear." Jumoke gives all ladies quick, impersonal hugs.

Mommy Bola joins the pack as Jumoke gives Eniola a quick smile on her way out. Kofo spots Eniola look away from her friend. The encounter reminds her of her own loss of friendship with Janelle.

Mommy Bola rummages through her purse. "Look at these pictures from a wedding we got inspiration from." She shows the group photos from a lavish pink and orange wedding on her phone.

The viewing of the photos drains Kofo, but Sherifat eats it up. "We must show out to Naija in complete style." She and Mommy Bola share a giggle.

"Ya Ennie, come!" Mommy Bola waves Morenike to their circle and she rushes over, right on command. "Look at this Islamic ceremony with orange detailing. Have the Imam wear a fuchsia kufi to match us."

Kofo is stoic and icy. "Did you find an orange sash for Pastor Folarin?" she asks the Mommies with biting confrontation.

Morenike waves her hand. "Oh, we canceled that part. It was going to take up too much time."

"Thank you all for coming tonight. I'll see you soon." Kofo offers hugs, but they were all thrown off by her abrupt tone as she escapes.

***

The tension in Kofo's body lessens when the party exits, leaving her with her mom, sister, Tunde, and the event staff.

Morenike climbs up the stairs. "Ennie, make sure the staff finishes cleaning by midnight so we don't get overcharged." Kofo barges over to her at the foot of the staircase, fuming.

"Mommy, what the hell is going on?!"

Morenike turns around halfway up and glares at Kofo with a bewildered expression.

"Who are you talking to?"

"Where is Daddy?"

"I told you... he's away on business."

"No, he isn't!" Tunde grabs her, pulling her away. She jerks away with aggression, maintaining her stance. "What did you do? I know you did something. You always do."

Morenike narrows her eyes. "Don't say another word to me. Don't make me come down there."

"And when did my wedding become Aunty Abidemi's?!"

Morenike ignores her, moving more quickly to the top of the stairs. Tunde tries to grab her arm again. By the time he loosens her grip and Kofo runs upstairs, her mother is in her bedroom and locks the door. Kofo bangs, but there is no response. Kofo groans, muffling an eventual scream.

Kofo turns around to head back down, but not before she makes eye contact with Eniola. Their eyes connect, both with defeat. Kofo sits at the bottom of the stairs and hangs her head.

"What the fuck is happening?" She asks, looking up at them both. Neither answer with words, responding instead with looks of sympathy.

Tunde takes her hand. "Kofo... let's go home."

Kofo and Tunde drag their tired bodies in an Uber back to Brooklyn. As soon as the car door closes, Kofo calls her father again on WhatsApp and the call rings out.

"I'm sorry, Kofo," Tunde says.

Her shoulders slump. Tunde puts his arm around her, initiating the closing gap of their decreased intimacy. Kofo leans onto his chest and he kisses her forehead while rubbing her temple. She attempts to call Eniola and Tunde takes her phone.

"If she was going to tell you, she would've at the house," Tunde says.

Kofo sighs and falls asleep halfway through the ride.

***

Kofo wakes close to 5:00am the next morning, unable to sleep. She sneaks to their guest bathroom and calls her father again, assuming he's already landed in Nigeria. He doesn't pick up through regular phone calls or WhatsApp.

Daddy, please call me. I want to talk to you, Kofo texts.

The two checks next to her WhatsApp text change from white to blue, showing he read the message—he doesn't know how to change his privacy settings on his phone and she sets up all of his preferences whenever he buys a new device. Still no response from her father. Kofo switches gears and calls Eniola, who picks up with a groggy voice.

"Kofo?"

"Sorry Ennie, I know it's early. I want you to really tell me what's going on with Daddy."

"Why do you think there's more to the story than what was told? Go to sleep Kofo, it's Sunday. I need my rest."

"I want to have a meeting with Mommy about the wedding. I hate all the ideas."

"Kofo… I need to sleep. Call me in a few hours and we'll figure something out."

Kofo rolls her eyes after Eniola hangs up. Her sister's indifference sends a cold reminder that her father is her only ally in this family.

***

Eniola watches Atlanta Housewives on repeat in Kofo's living room, munching on leftover chin-chin from the Nikah on her couch. Meanwhile, Kofo and Tunde scramble to get ready in their bathroom mirror. Kofo decides on wearing attire in neutral shades, similar to the outfit she wore when confessing her engagement to her mother.

Kofo's afro isn't shaping up the way she normally likes, frustrating her attempts to manipulate her hair using a pick and setting spray.

"Do you need help?" Tunde asks as he clasps his Rolex.

"No, I got it."

Her phone rings with a 1-800 number on her bathroom sink. Kofo does her best to handle their bills, but the absence of Tunde's higher salary is a major hit to their household. Kofo suggested they downsize and rent one of their bedrooms, but Tunde refuses. He's confident that a tenant won't be necessary and he will find work despite countless interviews leading to nowhere. Word spread about his incident and his reputation is preceding him.

He presses the red decline button on Kofo's screen. "We'll deal with that later," he whispers.

Kofo remains silent, leaning her head down to pick her afro from the back to avoid making eye contact with Tunde. Tunde grabs her by her waist as reassurance on the pressures weighing her down. Kofo is receptive to these intimate moments, but she's not completely sold that her fiancé is a changed man. Her guard is up and she needs more time, along with more proof that he is indeed someone she can count on.

Mommy is parking on Eastern Parkway, Eniola texts.

"I'll clean up some more," Tunde announces before leaving Kofo alone, and she lifts her head to review her image in the mirror. Her hands are unstable as she tries to form a twisted plat near her temple. She sucks her teeth, combs it all out, puts a small amount of water on her hair and adds finishing touches to her tinted lip gloss.

She walks into a living room scene of Eniola smoothing out her second silk press. Eniola appears more self-assured lately. The combination of new her hair and the breakup with Cedric did something for her.

Tunde scrambles to hide their sex toys that he used on Kofo the night before because she wasn't getting as wet as usual. Her mind is everywhere between the wedding and her father's abrupt disappearance—sex is far from a priority. Eniola smirks at Tunde and the toys as he struggles to find a home for the instruments.

Morenike makes her way inside their apartment, using a key that is likely Akeem's. More clues that something isn't right. Kofo would never give her prodding mother keys to any of her homes. She'd make frequent surprise appearances, walking in on versions of Kofo she could never stomach.

Kofo's mother is smug and overdressed, strolling into the condo with a disapproving scowl. They haven't spoken at length since the incident at the Nikah a week prior and wedding planning has reached a standstill. Her mother's entry intimidates her, but she refuses to give into her unsettled mind.

"No tea? No stew?" Morenike frowns at the plates of salad and salmon filet on the dining table where everyone else is seated.

"We got in late last night, so we didn't have time to cook anything else." They were working on rekindling their sex life the night prior—a very demanding affair.

Morenike sits at the table, staring at them all. Namely, Kofo and her uneven afro.

"When are you going to do something with your hair? Why not straighten it like your sister?"

"That's not what today's meeting is about, Mommy."

"That doesn't make what I'm suggesting any less true. Your hair doesn't look good, and it's about time someone said something to you." Her mother resorts to these passive-aggressive critiques when she is upset, going for consistent low blows. Kofo's determination to meet her objectives in this meeting overshadows her urge to throw an emotional tantrum of foul language and interrogation.

"Thanks for your input, I'll consider it," Kofo says while opening her wedding planning notebook. She takes a sip of water and then bites into a dinner roll to occupy her hands.

"You need to." Morenike won't stop.

Tunde breaks the icy vibe. "Mommy Ennie, let me make you some tea."

"I want it boiled hot. I don't want anything from that nonsense electric kettle."

Tunde works on a perfectly filtered, stove-boiled cup of English Breakfast tea while his back is facing the table. Kofo notices his jaw clenching from the corner of her eye.

"Mommy... I want to talk to you about two things." Kofo takes a deep breath. "Firstly, I would like to know what's going on with Daddy. Is he really away on business?"

Morenike rolls her eyes in irritation. "How many times are you going to ask me the same question? What else are you looking for? I said he's on a business trip—"

"He works for himself and practically has staff running everything. Even when he has emergencies, Daddy usually comes up with a plan for his team."

Morenike huffs. "Why don't you call him yourself? I know as much as what I'm telling you."

"I already tried. I must've called him fifty times this week alone."

"So then leave it alone. He'll eventually be back. What's your other question?"

"When is he coming back?"

"I'm done answering questions about your father. What else do you want?" Morenike's energy accelerates, but Kofo is unwavering. Eniola stares at the thick, wooden table, entranced by the lines that trace its rectangular shape from one end to another. Tunde maintains his focus on the stove, equally silent.

Kofo takes a long pause, contemplating if she should push more questions about her father. She addresses her next need first before circling back.

"This is actually more of a request than a question. I don't like the wedding colors for my Nigerian clothing."

"It's too late to change it—"

"I will pay for the colors I want. I already have the wedding party buying blue dresses. We can give the fabrics you chose as parting gifts."

"Are you mad? Do you know how much fabric costs?"

Tunde brings Morenike's cup of tea to the table and sits down in an available chair.

"Mommy, there's a reason why I trekked all the way to Long Island every weekend to explain my desires to you and Mommy Bola. I trusted you both to make selections that aligned with what I wanted. If you were going to make these changes, why am I just finding out?"

Morenike leans into the table in Kofo's direction. "Because you're not paying for it."

Kofo's face shakes. Her arduous attempts to make peace with her mother always come back to bite her. "Why are you being so cruel?"

Morenike bursts into a laugh that poorly hides her rage, dismissing her daughter's plea. "I'm showing you the consequence of being irresponsible. The fabrics you wanted are too expensive and are made of materials that won't last as long as the ones we picked out. They also look better. Blue is too masculine."

"What does that even mean? What are you trying to say about me?"

"Well... you always have something to say. Is that something a feminine woman would do?"

Kofo can't hold in her feelings towards her mother's hypocrisy.

"You wanna talk about masculine? You're controlling, overbearing, rude—"

Ennie puts her hand in between them before things get out of hand. "Okay, that's enough Kofo. Easy. Let's focus on the topic at hand."

Kofo looks at her sister, enraged. "I want my wedding. I want my vision."

Morenike chimes in. "Kofo—do you understand what it means to get married in our community? As a wife, you show deference to those above you. Including your mother, your elder sister, your father and your husband. All you do is poke, put your nose in everything, ask questions… we got these colors because it's best for your wedding."

"It's not what I want!!! Don't you get it?! How can I show deference to you when all you do is undermine me?!" Kofo is heaving, her head spinning out of control.

Tunde grabs her arm away from the table. "Excuse us, please." He pulls her in the direction of the bedroom.

***

The minute they are out of sight, Eniola stares at her mother across the table. Her expressive eyes are a combination of worry and pity.

"What are you looking at?" Morenike barks.

"Mommy—you have to tell her." Eniola says in Yoruba, one of the few leg ups she has over her sister.

"No." Morenike sips more tea from her cup.

"Are you going to wait for this Funmi lady to tell everyone and spread this everywhere? I can't keep lying to my sister."

"How would that woman ever have access to our people?"

Morenike's mouth often annoys Eniola, but not at this moment. She's like a difficult client that's about to go through arbitration. Something about Morenike's abuse doesn't sting the same way. She knows too much about her mother's baggage.

"Mommy—tell her. You're going to have to do it eventually, so just do it now."

"You people—first I'm a tyrant and now I'm a liar. What's next?" Morenike clicks her tongue, rambling complaints in Yoruba about her disrespectful children under her breath. Eniola picks up her phone and browses Instagram.

***

In the owner's bedroom, Kofo leans against the window, looking outside, filled with aggression meant for contact sports. Tunde stands at the bedroom door, on standby for whatever she might need a in few seconds, minutes or hours.

Kofo turns around, directing her focus on Tunde. "You never defend me."

He leans his head against the door, sighing. "Kofo—you know how these mommies are. There's nothing I would say that she would listen to, anyway."

"So, should she be wearing this?" Kofo raises her left hand, revealing her engagement ring.

"I thought you said you could handle her." Tunde locks the door, then folds his arms while walking in her direction. "If I confront your mother, you won't have a wedding—the most important day of our lives. You wanted to have this in Nigeria and experience our culture, right? To have both of our families there, celebrating. That's your dream. If you want your dad there and you want him to walk you down the aisle like you always envisioned—play along. Focus on the agenda you have, which is the blue wedding of your dreams, and finding out what happened to your daddy. What can you tell her that will make her do that?"

Kofo rubs her forehead, finally getting it. Her relationship with her mother is a game, and she just got coached. She has to get back into the ring and finish what she started.

"Maybe we should just call this whole thing off."

Tunde jerks his head back as though someone punched him in the nose. "Are you sure? I thought you always wanted your wedding to be traditional."

"I can't deal with my mother. This is too stressful."

"Yes, you can. Some things require sacrifice, Kofo."

Kofo looks at Tunde and scoffs. "Why don't you tell me about sacrifices, Mr. Investment Banker?" she hisses at him. "If we had your salary, we wouldn't even be having this discussion with her."

Tunde squints and gets closer to Kofo with only an inch in between their faces.

"Did I not take care of you before that? You had nothing to say when I was buying a bunch of shit for you back then. I supported you exactly the way you wanted, and because I slipped up one time, you want to penalize me for it? Really? And by the way—by definition, I'm not an addict. I dabbled socially, but I'm not an addict."

Kofo looks at Tunde, still unsure of his suggestion.

"Let's focus on the end goal that will make you happy."

After a few seconds, Kofo bursts out of the room, and Tunde sucks his teeth before following out after her.

***

Kofo storms into the living room, abruptly standing at the head of the table.

"Mommy, I'm calling off the Nigerian wedding."

Tunde sits down and takes a loud, deep breath after Kofo's declaration, shaking his head.

Morenike adjusts in her seat as her eyes flutter.

"This wedding has to happen in Nigeria."

"No, it doesn't. This isn't working for me."

Morenike looks to Eniola and Tunde for help, but they fail to contribute.

"I have to tell you something. Sit down."

"Mommy no. I'm clear on my decision."

"Kofo—sit down!" Morenike yells, almost frantic.

Morenike hasn't yelled at Kofo like that in a while. Her mother's voice transports her to a childhood scolding, accompanied by punishments for the slightest infraction. The subtle hints in her mother's inflections make her agree to sit down.

"Your father has a second wife." Morenike tells her in a somber voice.

"What?!" Kofo glances at Tunde, who appears equally shocked at Morenike's admission. Eniola is calm and unaffected.

"The real reason he flew out to Nigeria is to live with the woman in a new house he built with some local girl he's been hiding."

Kofo shakes her head in disbelief.

Is she this desperate to turn me against him? She asks herself.

She knew her parents didn't have a great marriage, but Kofo assumed they settled into tolerating each other until their last days like many older couples.

"I asked Daddy myself and he told me he's not into having multiple wives."

"When was the last time your father showed up in public with me?" Kofo is tracing her memory for a recent appearance.

"Exactly. But I'm not finished with your father."

"Why not?!"

"I am entitled to everything that man has. He wouldn't be where he is without me. We also cannot have a wedding with almost one thousand people without your father there. Not this family. There's no wedding in Naija without your father's contribution. We have spent half of the budget, invitations, food—"

Kofo holds her hand up, overwhelmed. "Mommy, wait—"

Morenike's energy peaks, and she leans into the table as though she is closing a business deal. "I need you to talk some sense into this man. He needs to come back to his family, and only you can get your father to do it."

Kofo leans back into the back of her chair, away from her mother's overwhelming energy. "I'm not comfortable doing that. I don't want to be in the middle of this, and I don't even know if what you're saying is true."

"What reason would I have to lie to you people?!"

Kofo purses her lips, opting to keep quiet. Her list to address her mother's confusion is too long to fit into the limited time of this disastrous meeting.

"He is already spending a lot on our place on Long Island and for your condo. When I confronted him about the house in Nigeria, he made it seem like it was for our family retirement home. But your father was actually building a house for his other family."

Kofo is speechless. She thought she was her father's favorite and is heartbroken at the idea of him letting them all go just to be with another woman at her expense.

"He took my name off of all of our accounts. Everything I contributed is gone. *Everything.*" Morenike waves her hand in the air with a swift, firm motion.

"Mommy… what do you want me to do with this information?"

"Do you want to keep your condo? Are you not getting me? He could ruin your financial history and credit if he stops paying your mortgage. People are already stopping by in Long Island because they found out the house is on the market."

Kofo stares up at the ceiling for what feels like forever before Morenike jumps back in.

"Are you both working?" Morenike questions, her voice rising. Both Kofo and Tunde don't answer and Eniola shifts in her seat. "Hello?!"

Kofo looks at her mother's neckline instead of her face. "Tunde is in between jobs at the moment."

"Did your father pay the most recent mortgage payment?"

Both Kofo and Tunde shake their heads no.

"Kofo—let's go to Nigeria and get him."

Kofo shakes her leg, quivering.

Eniola leans sideways to reach in her purse and pulls out a spreadsheet.

"Although Mommy doesn't have access to the most recent data, I created a spreadsheet that estimates what he owes you both, in addition to potential assets should he decide to permanently separate from our family." Eniola slides the paper in Kofo's direction and Tunde peers at the document over her shoulder.

Kofo looks at her sister, suspicious. "What about you?"

Eniola shakes her head. "I don't want his money. He'll probably leave you guys on your own to handle the mortgage before you're ready to pay it off on your own."

Hater, Kofo says in her head. Eniola refuses to believe that her father wasn't happy to give her the loan, regardless of the motivation.

"Let us know if you are in on going to Nigeria. I think you both have a right to ensure your assets and expenses are protected," Eniola continues on. She shares some additional details about their entitlement to Akeem's resources, but Kofo focuses on the numbers she sees on the sheet. Her parents were always comfortable and upper-middle class, but her father is a wealthy man. Last she heard, a couple hundred thousand dollars he got from petroleum dried up, hence why he travels frequently in hopes of transitioning into other industries. She also spotted the six million dollar estimate of his net worth.

"How does daddy have all this money?"

"He thought that his petroleum enterprises were no longer lucrative, but I went over several of his contracts from the oil rigging corporations he worked with and realized he is entitled to more than he negotiated. Your father has investments in real estate, dabbling into some other areas. That's why his traveling to Nigeria picked up aggressively over the past couple of years. Also, he invested some profits he accumulated into the stock market, which again was my suggestion," Morenike rants while her nose flares up, embittered.

"We're in." Tunde declares.

"I did not say that," Kofo looks at him, frowning, then back again at the sheet.

Morenike places her forearms onto the table, clasping her hands together. "Kofo—you need to get your name off of the mortgage, or he needs to give you cash for your loan so you can pay it off. Your financial history is in his hands, which is dangerous."

Kofo rises and pulls out her phone while pacing back and forth. "I'm calling him to confirm all of this."

She spots Morenike rolling her eyes, side-eyeing Eniola with an "I told you so" expression.

"He's not going to pick up, he's not answering our calls!" Morenike shouts.

Kofo ignores her mother, letting the phone ring endlessly and hoping to prove her wrong. He didn't answer but sends a text. *I told you that I am away for business in Nigeria. I'll reach you when I return, Kofo.*" Kofo's face drops, hoping her phone pinged with better news.

"Did I not say?" Morenike shakes her head at her daughter.

Kofo plops back into her seat, silent for what seems like forever. "Now what?" she asks her mother.

Morenike leans in like a saleswoman. "Your wedding is happening in a few weeks. I will identify his address and then we will confront him in Nigeria. Once he has no choice but to speak to us, we will demand the money and the family house in Long Island. Ennie is going to draft some legal documents that will threaten him on our behalf."

Kofo appears skeptical, yet intrigued at the same time.

"Kofo—you are the one that gave this family a chance. We are still a unit because of you. Don't allow your father to ruin this. We loved that man unconditionally, supported his frequent travels, spoke highly of him publicly, went to all of his events... we have been there every step of his way. The least he can do is give us what we are due."

A deafening silence fills the room as everyone awaits Kofo's decision.

"I need time to think about this."

"Kofo—"

"Mommy—it's not a no. I just need a minute."

Eniola nods at her mother and they quickly glance at each other.

"Ok, fine," Morenike grumbles.

***

Kofo's meeting with her mom, Tunde and her sister occupy her thoughts incessantly. Everything reminds Kofo of her dad—hearing elders speak with African accents on the train, spotting a bottle of Guinness at a bar, watching Audis drive by in the street, older gentlemen with Italian leather shoes—he haunts her without trying. His absence feels like she's mourning his passing. They didn't speak daily before he left, but they caught up a few times a week. The idea of her father sleeping around with a bunch of women puzzles her. She never heard other women in the background during calls. He never flirted with other women in front of her and he doesn't comment on the beauty of ladies they might encounter in passing. Akeem actually spoke down on polygamists, relegating them to "slaves of old school traditions." She sees her father as a "dad". An asexual patriarch, functioning as a businessman.

Maybe in the 1970s, Kofo tells herself while walking down the street. He wore a lot of loose shirts with the buttons undone to his mid-torso, exposing his chest taco meat layered with yellow gold flashy chains that had big pendants. He had a shaped, full beard, similar to Teddy Pendergrass on his iconic "Duets - Love and Soul" album cover. Kofo can see her father pulling ladies when he looked like that.

Morenike's undercurrent of emotional hostility now makes complete sense. She dismissed her mother as a woman with an envious spirit. There is a lot more to her mother she is discovering.

"Hi. I'm here to recover my diploma," Kofo politely says to the woman behind the counter at her school's registrar's office. "I got my MBA this past spring, and I changed addresses, so it may have gotten lost in the mail during the summer."

The registrar woman didn't respond but furiously types on her computer. Kofo stares at the renovated counters with brand new computers and LED screens. The lighting is bright, almost fluorescent, but still kept the employees unenthused. They are always grumpy, no matter what is requested. It's like they agreed with Kofo's belief that higher education is a Ponzi scheme.

While Kofo gives the woman her address, one of her former instructors—Professor Schultz—walked past the registrar's glass doors. They make eye contact.

"Ko-fu!" he exclaims and walks into the office with a briefcase in one hand, and he adjusts his wired glasses in another. His bald head left little for the frames to hold on to, and he constantly had to adjust them from sliding down the bridge of his nose. "Are you enrolling for your doctorate?!"

Kofo clears her throat. "Oh no, Professor Schultz. I think we both know I'm done with school." He gives out a hearty laugh in response. He forced Kofo to ask or answer questions during lectures, despite her immaculate test and assignment records.

"Well, how is everything? Are you working? What are you up to?"

"Yea, I'm at Palette Cosmetics in their marketing department. I'm applying the theoretical practices of economics that you taught all so well," she says to him in a playful tone while he nods.

"Congratulations, that's wonderful." Kofo smiles at his praise, despite all that she has on her mind. "How's your dad doing?"

"He's doing well, he's doing alright." Kofo's smile gets tighter as she slides her purse closer to her torso on her shoulder. Professor Schultz looks at her for more, but Kofo doesn't give much.

"Well, tell him that my sister and I say hello."

"Your sister? How does my dad know her? I thought you both went to the same university?"

"Oh no, he dated her about seven years ago and he frequently showed up to hang out with us. We are very close. Didn't work out, but they remained good friends."

"Oh wow," Kofo bulges her eyes and looks at the floor. Before her mood gets any lower, she raises her head again. "It's a small world, I guess."

"Indeed Kofou. Look, congratulations on your degree and your new gig. I gotta head to class, but reach out to me if you have questions or need any additional tactics at work."

Kofo nods, her smile more timid. "Absolutely, thank you. It's great seeing you, Professor."

An awkward silence cuts through the conversation.

"It's Kofo, by the way. Pronounced Ko-Foe."

Professor Schultz slaps his forehead. "So sorry, I always screw it up. Your father would kill me if he heard the way I pronounced your name."

"No worries, I'll always remind you."

He chuckles, flushed. "Please do. Bye now." He rushes out.

***

Later that evening, Kofo lays in her bed, staring at her WhatsApp conversation with her father, the only light illuminating their dark bedroom. She tied up her hair in a scarf as Tunde sleeps, his chest heaving up and down each time he snores.

Kofo tries to call her father again, and he declines her call. Kofo sends him a text that reads, *are you divorcing Mommy?*

Of course not, he writes back.

Kofo rolls her eyes, creasing her eyebrows together at what she just read. She then calls her mother, who picks up after two rings.

"Salaam, Kofo."

"Salaam, hi Mommy. I think we should follow the plan you suggested about Nigeria."

"Of course, we should."

"Ok—I will gather all my mortgage documents and the spreadsheet again."

"That's a good idea."

Morenike's voice quivers in a way that feels unrecognizable.

"Mommy, do you want Tunde and I to come to Long Island tonight and join you? We can grab an Uber."

Morenike sighs quietly. "No, no... that's okay. I'm reading my Quran before bed."

"Okay." Kofo feels a well of emotions wash over her suddenly. "Have a good night."

"Good night."

Kofo got only two hours of sleep that night.

CHAPTER 12

Morenike can count on one hand the number of times she's been to Nigeria in the past ten years. Akeem and Mommy Bola pressure her to check on her siblings, but figures of her sobering childhood revive the emotions she shed over the years while reinventing herself in The States.

She walks off of the plane at Murtala Muhammed International Airport with Kofo, Eniola and Tunde all walking a few steps behind her. The air is hot, muggy, humid, and smells like gasoline. Half of the overhead lights are off, bleeding shadows into the airport from power outages. Staff members linger near the ramp right outside the aircraft to observe passengers in need of assistance with wheelchairs or bags. Morenike drags her carry-on luggage on a moving walkway that wasn't working, likely because of unattended maintenance. They encounter a working escalator leading to a brighter room, with three employees standing at wooden podiums to stamp their passports.

After asking the all of the typical questions inquiring about their visit, an attendant says to Morenike, "Mommy—do you have anything for me? What of your daughter's wedding present since I'm letting you through?"

She retrieves her passport, smiling. "Not this time, maybe for the next trip." She signals to her three children and they all escape from his attempts of extortion.

They encounter another checkpoint, where airport customs professionals examine their documents again. Military officials shift and divide travelers into lines between Nigerian and American passport holders for processing. They observe Morenike for a long time, reminding her that wearing a canvas bag and pleather shoes was a smart move. She would never wear these materials back in New York, and stowed away her "good" personal items in her carry-on in the event that they rummaged through her larger suitcases. Kofo and Eniola caught on, but Tunde struggled to pack clothing without labels.

She sighs in exhaustion. This is the last thing she wants to deal with after a ten-hour flight. Morenike can't remember when things ran smoothly at this airport—the sharp turn of amenities in Nigeria causes amnesia of when things were better. Everything in Nigeria is a ten-step process when it should be two steps. The airport is a reminder of why she doesn't mind living her last days in America—it's best for her peace of mind.

Two hours later, they approach the luggage retrieval area, and everyone's suitcase is identified. Her luggage got lost twice before and she heard things got better on that front.

"Mommy, don't you want a trolly?" one airport attendant asks.

"Are those your daughters? Are they looking for husbands?" another questions, almost grabbing the handle on her suitcase.

"Get out of here!" a male voice growls, intruding on their attempts to get money, all of them scattering to various ends of the airport for their next conquest. It's Morenike's older brother, Uncle Bolaji. He's an average sized, brown-skinned man with a clean-shaven beard and black-rimmed glasses.

She called him a few days before they flew out to Nigeria, requesting that he use his connections to greet them at the airport. Akeem would have them go through another check-in process with more ease, but Morenike refuses to beg him for any help.

"Ah, Brother Bolaji! Bawoni?" Morenike prostrates for her older brother while he pats her on the back with one hand. Kofo, Eniola and Tunde also formally greet him and he acknowledges them with head nods. Uncle Bolaji instructs two nearby airport workers in Yoruba to carry the luggage on trolleys and they all head out to his car in the parking lot, swatting off indistinguishable employees, local taxi drivers, and area boys that want to assist with pushing the trolley for a tip in dollars.

***

When they get into Uncle's large black minivan, everyone rides in silence. Uncle Bolaji is in the passenger seat next to his driver, Tobias. In the next row is Kofo behind the driver, Tunde in the middle and Morenike behind her brother. Eniola is in the last row next to the luggage.

Morenike looks to her right outside of the window. She estimates passing a million people after being in the car for ten minutes. Scores of Nigerians move with fervor to their destinations on foot, by car, danfo vans and okada motorcycles that bob and weave through the automobiles blocking their path. The minivan breezes past it all, including pedestrians running across the expressway that neglect the available overpasses.

Uncle Bolaji breaks the ice. "Kofo, how is medical school?"

Kofo looks away from her window in her uncle's direction. "Actually, I just graduated from business school."

"Oh, I thought you wanted to be a doctor?", he questions.

Morenike looks down at the space in between the driver and passenger seats. She told him that Kofo changed her career prior to her start in business school. It's apparent that he doesn't listen during their brief calls.

"No—I work in the digital marketing department for a cosmetics brand."

"I hope they are paying you good money?" Uncle Bolaji isn't reading the room.

Morenike expected more protection from her older brother growing up, but he was consumed with being their battered mother's surrogate husband. As a result, he got most of the resources out of all of their siblings. When Morenike spoke out as the second child in line, Uncle Bolaji convinced their mother to only take care of him and Morenike, leaving the rest with little social standing in Lagos. He justifies it by telling them that their mother doesn't have much, so it's better that the two oldest get inheritances. Uncle Bolaji worked on blowing his mother's legacy as a moderately successful goat farm owner by spending it on women, and Morenike escaped to America. She feels guilty for leaving her other siblings behind, but not enough to make her come back to Nigeria.

"I support her as an investment banker." Morenike feels relief from Tunde's input.

Uncle Bolaji nods in approval. "Wow, that's amazing."

Morenike notices Kofo's expression drop before she continues looking back at the scene outside.

***

The van pulls up to Uncle Bolaji's house in the upper-middle class neighborhood of Lekki—a two-story, mid-sized gated home with a curved, cobbled driveway. It's recently built with a fresh gray paint job, new windows and white, modern finishings. Morenike steps out of the car with the help of her brother's house staff, all of whom appear happy to greet guests, prostrating for the Adebayos and Tunde.

"Thank you," she says to the staff, strolling to the front door of the house while they work on removing her luggage from the car.

Uncle Bolaji walks ahead of her with Tunde in the foyer and she overhears him say, "do you want some Guinness? I want to talk more about how I can open up an account at your bank for some investments

I want to make in America." Tunde follows him to a room she couldn't identify down a corridor.

When Morenike exits the foyer into the parlor, two women await her.

"Ah!" Morenike yelps. The two women rush her to form a group hug—Busayo and Temitayo. They were her primary and secondary school crew—everyone knew them as the "it" girls, running to weekend parties with their best clothes. Busayo and Temitayo snagged husbands from affluent families and Morenike lagged behind them with Akeem. Men were suckers for their long legs, smooth curves, trendy dresses, understated makeup, stylish hairstyles and sassy attitudes for the 1960s-70s. Most girls were too modest and uptight to keep up with them.

Busayo hugs the hardest. "Morenike... my friend—it's so good to see you," she smiles and says to her in Yoruba.

"My judge! How are you?!" Temitayo asks while Kofo looks at her mother, confused. Morenike forces her pressed mouth into a smile with wide eyes, helping Kofo to catch on with assisting her mother in lying.

"All is well, thank you, thank you." Morenike switches into Yoruba with deliberate gestures, mocking a politician's wife.

"Who is this pretty one?! Is this Eniola?" Busayo makes a few steps toward Eniola, looking down at her belly and pulling her into a hug. "Congratulations dear, I can't wait to meet your fiancé."

"Thank you, ese ma," Eniola prostrates, offering no correction on the assumption.

"And Kofo, the lucky bride." Busayo pulls Kofo's hand, invading her personal space in the way that most Yoruba elders do when they put a face to a name. Morenike watches her daughters respond to Busayo's forward nature, hoping they can still maintain decorum.

"Hi, Good Afternoon," Kofo responds but doesn't prostrate.

Busayo and Temitayo jump right into a gisting session with Morenike. Kofo wanders off once their discussion picks up.

"E Kabo, Ma. What of Akeem?" Kafayat asks Morenike, strolling in with slippers and a tailored ankara dress in shades of green. Kafayat is one of Uncle Bolaji's wives and spends to the most time at his house whenever she isn't tending to their three children. She corrects her relaxed nature once she spots Busayo and Temitayo, prostrating for them all before sitting in a chair opposite the couch of the other mommies.

Morenike responds, "He's around, he's staying with family to take care of some things. He should be at the wedding."

"Don't you all have a family home? Why not stay there now?" Kafayat remains persistent.

"Yes, it's still being built, so he's staying in Ikeja, I believe."

"Ah, okay. God willing, you'll be able to rest your head in your Nigerian home for holidays."

Busayo and Temitayo nod in agreement.

"Amin," Morenike says before sitting down. Eniola sits next to her, browsing the internet on her phone.

Temitayo is the most bourgeois of them all, winning over the affection of a billionaire senator and a West African hotel chain owner. Morenike questions his motives in his endeavors, but their friendship sustains her suspicions. They have an unspoken agreement to avoid political corruption as a point of discussion, and instead lament the incompetence of the federal government. Its neutral territory and all class levels face varying levels of frustration with Nigeria's compromised infrastructure and government agencies.

"Haven't you people seen our guest? Bring her food, now!" Temitayo barks at the house girls. They scurry into the kitchen and return with platters of meat pies and tea, placing them on the coffee table. Morenike swallows to hide her discomfort. She doesn't care for Temitayo's methods, but it gets things done.

Busayo pulls out six yards of fabric wrapped in plastic, slamming it onto the couch while the other mommies look on. "Ore mi—I love this blue. Why did you change it now? I was going to head to my tailor today."

"You didn't get my WhatsApp message that we changed it to pink and orange?"

"Pink, ke? Everyone wears those colors. I prefer the blue. I love the deepness of the shade."

"Yes, o," Temitayo agrees while watching one of the house girls prepare a cup of tea for her.

"Oh, really?" Morenike looks around at them all for confirmation of what she's hearing.

"Yes!" Busayo places strain on her response, almost whining and yelling at Morenike at the same time. "If you don't change it back, I'm sewing this fabric o, it's beautiful."

"I might get some for my next gathering. We can hire my lady together. She does in-house service, especially for rush orders." Temitayo says, taking small, careful bites into her meat pie while the other mommies look on, watching her every move to note how they should address hunger during their next social encounter.

Morenike chuckles, failing to address the uncomfortable silence in the room until Busayo and Temitayo start a gossip session about other local Lagosians from yesteryear.

***

Morenike is alone when Kafayat walks Busayo and Temitayo out—they became chatty while discussing the dissolving marriage of one of her neighbors. The story triggered worries about her own marriage. Morenike listened intently to the story, interested in a real-life account of divorce in Nigeria from their social circle.

Kafayat reenters the foyer, walking into Morenike gathering her belongings and sighing from fatigue. She buries her head in a tote bag, searching for ibuprofen.

"Kafayat, we need to talk to Brother Bolaji about borrowing his car for some errands while I'm here. How does he normally work with you?" Morenike looks up at Kafayat's worried face. "Ki lo de, what's wrong?"

Kafayat looks down the corridor and up the stairway to ensure they are alone. Eniola went upstairs after excusing herself an hour ago.

"Morenike—what's really going on? Where is Akeem?" Morenike is shocked at her candor. None of her junior family members speaks to her in this manner. Kafayat is really leveraging her proximity to Uncle Bolaji. In any other scenario, Kafayat would be rude and out of line.

"What do you mean?"

"He doesn't have family in Lagos and you are not building any houses last time I asked."

"Kafayat, I'm fine—"

"Bolaji and I have heard things."

Morenike backs down in surprise that her brother's aspirations of joining the movers and shakers of Lagos have materialized. She dismissed his initial declaration of the goal, citing his chauvinism and "village bush mentality" as the barrier to gaining acceptance from the likes of Temitayo. A lot has changed since her last visit when her mother passed away.

"If you need help with the new women joining your family, let me know. It's better to face it so everyone can come to an agreement."

"What women? Kafayat—my husband will not be juggling me with anyone else."

"Most wives deal with this at some point, Morenike. It's only a matter of time."

"Not for me. But thank you." Morenike picks up her last bag and walks upstairs.

***

Uncle Bolaji assured Morenike that his amenities would properly accommodate Morenike and her children. The next morning of their stay, they ran out of water. Then they ran out of fuel for the generator that is allegedly automated once The Power Holding Company of Nigeria—formally called NEPA—turns off the electricity. Uncle Bolaji claims that having a large amount of guests over-exhausts these resources. His house is appealing at first glance, but beyond the surface, it isn't what she hoped for during her first trip after being away from Nigeria for so long. Her brother said that his house is an experience of nostalgia once you get past the recent construction. Morenike was not amused.

She walks to her daughter Eniola's bedroom in the four-bedroom house. Eniola lays in a pool of sweat, worrying Morenike.

"Come down and eat with us."

Eniola lets out a weary sigh. Morenike remembers the days leading up to their preparation to move out of Nigeria. Eniola was more excited than both of her parents and skipped throughout the airport when they immigrated to the States.

"I think I'm going to stay here until the power comes back on, Mommy."

"You haven't eaten all day. That's dangerous in this climate. At least come down for some water. Please."

Eniola peels herself from the wet bedsheets. Morenike reaches out her hand to help her and Eniola waves it away.

"I got it."

"Everything is going to be working soon," Morenike says to her daughter, almost pleading. Eniola nods, dragging her slippers that loudly scrape across the concrete floor. Eniola is about to pop any day now and insisted she stay behind in New York, but Morenike manipulated her with words about taking for granted her free accommodations. The conversation hurt her daughter, but Morenike is determined to fulfill her agenda on this trip. Morenike's realization that she is putting her first grandchild in danger dawned on her.

Morenike walks out of Eniola's room, then knocks on Kofo's door with no answer. She puts her ear to the door, hoping Kofo and Tunde aren't having sex at this time of the day. *What if the house help walks in on them?* She wonders. After a few knocks, she walks down to the dining room where she meets Eniola, Uncle Bolaji, and Tunde. Eniola picks at her eba and okra soup, eating everything in tiny bites while her brother and Tunde gorge on their meals.

"Where's Kofo?" Morenike asks.

"She was napping," Tunde says before inhaling his stew and eba.

Morenike goes back to the staircase to check on Kofo again. She would send Eniola to summon her sister, but the pregnancy is in the way.

"Kofo! Kofo, where are you?!" she shouts on her way up.

Morenike hears heavy steps that slab on the floor as Kofo descends the stairs.

"I'm right here."

"Oh. I couldn't find you for hours."

"I was cooling off."

"Tunde is eating dinner."

Kofo stops with a few steps left, her face filled with exhaustion.

"I already ate."

"Won't you join him? Just go sit. Everyone has been looking for you."

"When are we going to see daddy?"

"Soon. We'll talk about it tomorrow."

Kofo rolls her eyes, then heads to the dining room. In any other setting, the rudeness of her daughters wouldn't be tolerated. But she's unsure of how to address this experience that is disorienting her. She bathed with a bucket of lukewarm water and got a second bucket from one of the house girls named Fisayo to flush the toilet until they fix the generator issue. She forms slight bubbles of gas from what she thought was spices, but it might be the efo she ate after the meat pies the day before. Or it could be the meat pies. They were on the cooler side and could've spoiled.

Morenike feels like a fraudulent Nigerian. A watered-down, tamer version with her grit totally gone. In her prior visits to Nigeria, she adapted to any lodging scenario with a stomach as strong as garbage disposal. Kafayat is less friendly since their conversation and gives her judgmental looks, assuming that Morenike thinks she's of another class of women above the many polygamous families in their community. Morenike saw the havoc that polygamy caused in her mother's life—she was the second wife because her father's first couldn't bear more than one child, making the first wife insanely jealous. Her mom would ask the first wife to watch Morenike and her siblings while she was at work if Uncle Bolaji wasn't home. She was as hot tempered, abusive, controlling and unstable as her father. Morenike still has a scar on her ear from one day when her father's first wife scratched and punched her, almost possessed by anger over Morenike wearing nude-colored lipstick at sixteen. She said that only "asewos", or prostitutes, wore lipstick at her age. Morenike never stayed at her house after that, preferring to deal with her mother's occasional slaps over coming home late after school. Morenike's mom worried for her future and begged her father to work his magic with a connection at the American Embassy.

Everyone thought Morenike would be the least successful, yet Uncle Bolaji spends much of his energy trying to catch up to his sister. Her guilt in being the one that got "out", and reaping benefits as a wild child is preventing her from convincing Uncle Bolaji to take her money to improve the amenities during the stay at his house. Ironically, Uncle Bolaji asked her if she needed money from him when he found out about her status with Akeem.

"This is an induction period. The dust will eventually settle. All the wives react the way you do," he told Morenike when she sipped her English Breakfast tea and biscuits while they had an early breakfast alone together. She told him she was not interested in being Akeem's property. "Am I some sort of savage to you?" he challenged.

"No—I don't want to share my husband. I don't want to do that." She hates how her peers use customs to covet blatant abuses in their culture. She decided that sharing her heist plans for Akeem's money is a bad idea. Her brother would presume that she's only after Akeem's bank accounts, labeling her a gold digger. The same accounts Akeem wouldn't have grown were it not for her.

Back at the dining table, Tunde sits before an empty plate of food, fully satiated.

"Does she cook like this at home for you?" Uncle Bolaji asks him.

"Somewhat, not this traditional. This is a treat."

Morenike peers at her brother's loud snort. He digs his hand into the last few bites of his meal.

Tunde clears his throat once he takes a sip of his beer. "Babe, can you get me some water and my slippers near the door? I realized I forgot to bring them to the table." Tunde is melding into Uncle Bolaji's world too much for Morenike's liking. She says nothing, continuing to make more observations.

Kofo stares at Tunde with intensity. "You can get it after. The beer will wash your food down."

"This one is just like her mother. I wish you well with these Adebayo women," Uncle Bolaji responds in between bites.

Kofo's mouth turns downward in offense. "What about you? I thought you were married?"

Uncle Bolaji leans in, resting his soiled hand on the table. "Both of my wives live locally with our children. You met your Aunty Kafayat, and my other one has a place not too far from here. I also have friends that drop by from time to time."

Morenike surveys the table, relieved that Kafayat went home to tend to her children's need for help with homework and dinner preparations. Morenike fears her reaction to Uncle Bolaji's lifestyle would make it obvious that she looks down on her.

Eniola disengages the discussion and browses her phone. *What is she always looking at?* Morenike says to herself. It can't be more interesting than everything happening around her at the moment.

"Won't you take my plate?!" Uncle Bolaji yells at Fisayo as she stands in the room's corner. Everyone jumps at his command except for her. She remains cool, familiar with his outbursts. Fisayo removes his dirty dishes from the table, avoiding eye contact.

Another house girl comes with a bowl of water and he washes his stew-soaked hands off. "Tunde, let me know when you're ready."

Tunde nods, peaking at Kofo through the corner of his eye while Uncle Bolaji grabs his Guinness bottle, leaving them all at the table.

"Where are you going?" Kofo asks her fiancé. Morenike is ready to go back to America at this point.

Tunde is oblivious to Uncle Bolaji's attempts to induct him into his fraternizing ways. "His son Jide is taking me to a local club."

"I'm coming." Kofo demands without asking.

"Oh. I didn't think you would want to, but we can go. I'll tell my siblings to meet us there."

"You should."

Tunde reaches out to them on his phone, but his moves are hesitant.

Morenike puts her teacup down and clears her throat.

"Kofo and Tunde, be mindful that we are guests in someone's house. Keep your fighting to a minimum."

"As long as he doesn't get too comfortable with all this, we're good," Kofo says under her breath.

Morenike called Akeem three times, and he declined them all. She also texted him, making him aware that they are in Nigeria and want him to visit at Uncle Bolaji's house. He read every message, refusing to answer. She assumed he would take them more seriously when she touched down on the fort where he enjoys the other half of his double life. Confrontation from Morenike gets Akeem in line—she's barged into Chief Lounge, she's followed him to Queens to meet a woman, and she's sent him pictures of other women she found on his phone. This new woman must mean a lot to him if Akeem is protecting her.

"Be careful what you share at the club. Just have a few drinks. Don't turn this into anything else," Morenike advises the couple. She gets up from the table and spent the rest of the evening nursing her gassy stomach.

CHAPTER 13

Tobias drives with complete confidence on the Lekki expressway at eighty miles per hour, swerving other speeding cars and pedestrians that put their lives on the line on the often congested throughway road. Kofo notices the power outage from the non-functioning street lights. They are relying solely on car lights or buildings that can afford non-stop electricity through large-scale generators to navigate the road. The incessant busyness of Lagos provides a safety net of light in most pockets of the city.

"Can you slow down?" Kofo asks Tobias when he zigzags pedestrians in close range.

Tunde laughs at Kofo. "We'll be fine. He does this every day."

Kofo puts on her seatbelt.

Tobias smiles, unfazed by Kofo. "Welcome to Lagos," he says in a thick Eastern Region accent. He follows her instructions for the next two intersections and then speeds up again.

Tobias turns onto Admiralty Way Road, landing on the bustling nighttime scene of Lekki Phase 1. The streets illuminate from one building to the next and crowds gather before venues like King Fisher, Farm City, The Observatory, Blackbell Lounge, Foodies, and many others.

"Nigerians party every day like this?" Kofo asks Tobias.

"Oh yes. Some of us go out daily, but you should see Naija on a Thursday through Sunday. You also came during the end of the year, the perfect time to see many people on holiday."

"Babe—we need to come back after our wedding."

"Sure, of course," Tunde responds, affirming Kofo's excitement.

Kofo smiles, entranced by the resemblance of Lagos' energy to New York. This version of Nigeria feels like home.

***

Tobias makes a left onto a quiet, dark street lined with waterside venues and flats with modern architectural designs. Young Nigerian men stand in the middle of the road, directing people towards parking spots for extra cash. Tobias shoos one away who is aggressive than the others.

"We've arrived," he says in a flat tone after pulling over.

"Thanks man. I'll text you when we're done," Tunde gives him a small tip in Naira before they hop out.

A group of Hausa-Fulani men dressed in kaftans swarm the couple, asking if they want gum, candies or other breath fresheners. Tunde charges past them towards the bouncers at the venue gate, pulling Kofo along with him.

"Jide said this place is called Bolivar," Tunde whispers to Kofo after they pass the checkpoint.

"I feel like I'm in a beer garden in Williamsburg," Kofo says. The venue is a large courtyard, sectioned off by brightly painted containers. A container with the kitchen is to their immediate left, and another with the bar is to the right. A massive container is stacked above the bar with a DJ booth and more seating. Benches and tables fill up the open space in between the containers, and sectioned off small bungalows are sectioned off with "reserved" signs for VIP guests. The back of the venue is lined with tables and chairs that are positioned next to a body of water.

Clusters of Nigerian professionals, artistic types and expats mingle in their after-work clothing while munching on local treats and cocktails.

A meaty, medium brown-skinned man approaches them. He has on black-rimmed glasses that resemble Uncle Bolaji's trademark look.

"You must be Kofo and Tunde!", he says with his arms outstretched in a loud, deep voice.

"Yes. Hi, Jide!" Kofo says, taken aback by his forward nature—a deep contrast from his father.

"Hey man, I'm Tunde," Tunde says, giving Jide a firm handshake.

Jide leads them to a large bench table reserved for their group. The servers immediately wipe the table down and the other loungers check them out, curious about their status.

"I hope this place is good enough for you. Order whatever you want, it's on me," Jide says in an accent that is Nigerian, but subdued enough for anyone to assume an advanced educational background.

"Thank you. This place is more than fine, but we already ate. Your father really pushes for home cooked food daily," Kofo says.

"Get a drink then!", he belts, startling Kofo. "Are your brothers and sisters still coming, Tunde?"

Tunde looks up at Jide from his phone. "Yea, they're in an Uber and I'm sharing my location because the map reception on their phones is spotty. They're scared to tell the Uber that they're lost." Tunde rolls his eyes.

"Well, is it safe to be driving Ubers out here and at nighttime?" Kofo asks.

A server brings a cold bottle of beer for Jide. He wipes his forehead with a handkerchief, pops it open, and takes a big gulp. "Now Kofo… Nigeria isn't all you see on the news."

"I mean, I know but like—"

"If they have issues, I'll take care of it."

"How so?"

"I work with some local government officials. I own a cyber security company."

"That's cool."

"You're into fashion or something, right?"

"I work in the eCommerce marketing department of a cosmetics brand and Tunde works as an investment banker."

"Nice."

Kofo wants to ask more questions, but any affiliation to Uncle Bolaji makes her unsettled.

"You're Aunty Kafayat's son, right?"

Jide let out a delirious laugh. "No way. My mom is your Aunty Jamilah. She's my dad's first wife and I'm his eldest son."

"Oh wow, what's that like?"

A server brings Jide a platter of spicy penne pasta with large prawns. Jide digs in immediately, blowing off the heat steaming from the pile of food on his fork.

"I'm shocked that you're surprised."

"What do you mean?" Kofo asks in a challenging tone. She looks over at Tunde, who appears nervous. Jide digs into his meal.

"Never mind," Jide replies.

Tunde's siblings approach the table and Kofo watches them all give Tunde hugs of joy and excitement.

"Bruuuv," Seun says to Tunde and they embrace for a long time, patting each other's backs in hard, masculine motions.

"You must be Kofo!" Abeni says in an excitable voice, with Bisi trailing her.

"Yes, I am! Cool hair and I love your accents."

Abeni flips her auburn lace front wig with slick baby hairs affixed on her temples. Her French manicure pokes out like white Chiclets from her nail bed.

"Of course, the *American* likes our accents," Bisi says, playfully rolling her eyes. Her style is more understated, and she has one auburn streak running down the side of her well bumped, swooped, naturally colored wig. Her nails are a plain natural and she's wearing nude, glossy lipstick. Their deep sibling connection is evident, making Kofo an instant fan out of admiration and longing for a similar bond. "Where's your drink, Kofoworola?!"

Seun playfully pushes them out of the way. "Please ignore them. Hi Kofo, it's a pleasure. I've heard tons about you, all good things." He is a muscular version of his older brother and while Tunde is overall more handsome, his younger brother is a perfect runner up.

Abeni pokes her head in between them. "Yes, Tunde can't stop talking about the *Brooklyn* girl."

"Yes, abi o!" Seun breaks into a thick Nigerian accent, and they all laugh.

"Who's treating tonight?" Bisi asks, wasting no time.

"I am," Jide responds.

Bisi's eyes transform into vessels of seductive mystery. Kofo knows that look—it's one of potent attraction. "And you are? I hope we're not related."

"No. I'm Kofo's first cousin on her mom's side. Jide." He extends his hand, blushing at Bisi's flirting.

"An enormous pleasure. Bisi is my name." Bisi takes his hand, grinning. Her siblings and Kofo laugh, shaking their heads in amusement.

***

"How did you two meet?" Abeni asks, pointing at Kofo and Tunde.

"Tunde never told you?!" Kofo grins, reminiscing on the earlier days of their romance.

"Nope. Talking to Tunde is like conversing with an 8-Ball," Bisi says across the table next to Jide, munching on fries.

233

"We met at a chain restaurant called Five Guys."

"Whaaa? Is it like some sort of unique pub location?" Abeni responds.

Tunde shakes his head at his sister.

Kofo's temperament is more relaxed compared to their initial arrival. Moments before their current discussion, Bisi dragged Jide to the bar, and he bought the three ladies two shots each. Kofo joined them during their second round.

"Nooo… it's just a really yummy spot to grab some burgers and fries after hanging out at happy hour if you're still hungry. It's really good. People also like Shake Shack."

"We have both. I just thought y'all would've met at some sexy New York City rooftop. But a burger joint will do!" Abeni says.

"Does your father know you eat at places like that?" Seun asks. "He might want to a gourmet chef to make ground beef patties from scratch with caviar or tuna tartare as a starter in his fancy parlor." He's also tipsy and took four for the team when Tunde refused the shots Bisi ordered for her brothers. Tunde gives him a hard nudge.

Kofo scoffs at the question. "Why would my dad need to know if I ate a ten-dollar burger?"

Tunde shakes head at Seun, rolling his eyes at his brother. "Ignore him, babe."

"No… I wanna know." Kofo's tone grows in aggression. "Is there something I need to know about my dad that y'all aren't saying?"

Tunde, his siblings, and Jide all get quiet. Abeni gently touches Kofo's shoulder.

"Sorry, Kofo. I just think my brother made a bad joke because your family's house in London is really nice. He meant nothing by it."

Kofo scans all of their faces and it's clear that something isn't being said. But they are having such a great time and the last thing she wants to do is ruin the great energy amongst them all.

"It's cool. I've never been to the house," Kofo says softly.

"Oh." Seun says, exchanging a guilty glance with Tunde.

Kofo spots Jide holding up his finger to Bisi, signaling that he'll be right back. Bisi nods, enjoying all the food and the cocktails he left for her to indulge in while he slips away.

Jide breaks the group's huddle and stretches his hand out to his cousin. "Kofo, let's talk. Walk with me to the back near the water."

Kofo hesitates, and Jide shakes his hand, smiling.

"Come on. Tunde will still be able to spot us."

Kofo allows him to pull her up and they walk off.

***

Jide takes her to the back deck of the venue, right next to a calm body of water called Five Cowries Creek. A yacht passes by with music blasting over the already loud music at Bolivar, likely with a wealthy celebrity, a crew of Yahoo boys, or expats.

Jide pulls out a joint and lights it up. He offers a blow to Kofo, but she shakes her head.

"I'm cutting down, but thanks. I appreciate you looking out for us tonight. We just met and you've been so hospitable."

Jide shrugs her off.

"We're family. This is what I'm supposed to do."

Kofo smiles. She feels at ease around him already.

"Kofo… everyone knows about your dad's indiscretions. It's been family gossip out here for a while." Jide says while taking a puff.

"Gossip like what?" Kofo's tone gets defensive.

"Hey look—I'm just trying to talk this out with you, but we can end here if you want."

"No, I'm sorry Jide. It's just a lot to process."

"I know. I went through the same thing when my father started marrying and being with other women. He was my father exclusively for fifteen years. I did everything with him. I went to work with him, I went to parties, I went to every family gathering he attended until things changed. He was my one and only mentor. It's not easy sharing him."

"Are y'all still close?"

"No. I only heard from him today because you are in town. I haven't spoken to him in a few months. We greet each other and it's pleasant, but I don't really know my father anymore. Neither does my mother, aside from what he wants to tell her. Money is tight with all of his resources spread so thin, so I work more than I want to in order to make sure my mom is okay. It's been hard to find a woman that wants to deal with my situation."

"What about your siblings?"

Jide shrugs. "Eh… they're fine. But how much bonding would I want to do with the source of my father's absence?"

Kofo pokes out her lips towards the joint and Jide holds it up for her to take a blow.

"Here's my advice to you. You will always love your father, but they come from a different time, and for you—a different society. From your view, it's fucked up and to be honest, I agree. But it's what they know. You'll be angry for a while. Don't harbor resentment forever. The anger you feel will damage you more than anyone else if you prolong it. He will continue doing whatever he wants."

Kofo casts her eyes downward. "I actually think my father left. I don't even think he wants to juggle his families."

Jide shakes his head.

"When the new wife misbehaves, he'll come back. Trust me."

Kofo's head circles in multiple directions. She thrust into an intimate conversation with someone who is a stranger.

"Thank you. Seriously," Kofo says while watching Jide smoke.

"Anytime. I wish I had someone to talk to. I'm sure your sister does too. Those American counselors can't handle what goes on out here."

Kofo chuckles, afraid to learn the full reasoning behind his statement.

CHAPTER 14

Uncle Bolaji worked with his house staff and local repairmen to fix the generator issue. They succeeded in cooling down the house compared to the night prior.

Morenike, her children and Uncle Bolaji all gather at the dining room table again on their third day, this time for breakfast. Morenike calls Akeem countless times with no luck before she leaves her room, making her the last person to join the group.

"We're going to the tailor with Aunty Kafayat today," she says, forcing a cheerful tone while putting ogi and akara from the center of the table into her bowl.

Kofo eats her food in slow motions, unmoved. "Are the fabrics still the same colors? And when are we going to see daddy's house?"

"Kofo—I told you to wait." Morenike is losing patience with her daughter.

"I don't see the point in going if we aren't going to get the mon—"

Morenike couldn't take it anymore. "Stop it! Just shut up already."

Kofo looks down, fuming.

Morenike exchanges a glance with her brother before he clears his throat. "What are you getting from Akeem, Nike?"

"Nothing. We need to have a meeting as a family before the wedding."

"You better not be asking me for money while chasing your husband, who is with every other woman in Lagos." She bites her tongue, almost causing it to bleed while restraining her embarrassment.

"Kofo and my family have done a lot to have this wedding, Brother Bolaji."

"Well, why not America? Why Naija?"

"Because their father lives here."

Uncle Bolaji opens his mouth, but she interjects.

"That's good enough reason. Please drop this," she pleads.

"Humph," he grabs a piece of akara and puts it on his plate.

***

Morenike washed up after her Fajr prayer earlier in the morning, but her children needed to bathe after breakfast. She tours her brother's house and finds Uncle Bolaji in his den. He's reading the newspaper while soccer—or football, as they call it outside of America—plays on the television.

"Brother Bolaji," Morenike calls out to him.

"Yes?" He buries his face into a newspaper. His tone is detached and laced with judgement.

"Please, show your face," she begs in Yoruba. He lowers his newspaper.

"Your bride is a brat," he says matter-of-factly.

"I'm sorry. We really appreciate all that you've done in allowing us to stay here." Morenike can't recognize herself. She begs no one for favors.

Uncle Bolaji shifts in his seat, leaning into Morenike, who sits down across from him. "Look, Nike—as you know, I am not against Akeem's lifestyle for obvious reasons."

"I know, but—"

He puts his hand up, cutting her off. "What I do not agree with is the way you are walking your children through this. They are not babies. Stop this nonsense."

"They don't know or understand it, Brother."

"See, that's the issue. Yes, they do. They just look down on it."

"Why can't they have an opinion on it? Look at what happened to mommy."

"They may feel whatever they want. But don't intrude on the lives of people who are living this life. It's not proper. You need to speak to Akeem privately, work out an arrangement between the two of you, and introduce your children to your father's lifestyle objectively. That's what our mother did, and that's why we all got along. Stop coddling these kids, especially that Kofo. She'll never see her father clearly."

Morenike pauses for a long time, staring around the room. Her memories of her mother's experience with polygamy don't at all resemble what

Uncle Bolaji said. "What if I don't want my children to know much about it?"

Uncle Bolaji responds with a patronizing smile. "Tunde already knows a lot. He knows more about Akeem than his own wife."

Morenike rises. "I am grateful that you let us stay here. But don't corrupt my son-in-law to your life. I don't want my daughter to sign up for this."

"The young people are doing something different these days. Isn't it called 'baby momma' and 'baby fada'?" He laughs at his realization.

"Please, brother. This is not a laughing matter."

"Okay, okay... just be honest with your children, especially Kofo."

Morenike is quiet for what feels like an eternity. "Look at what it's done to Eniola. I am afraid Kofo will end up the same way."

"Eniola found out in the same way that her younger sister is discovering things. You should consider that if you want a new outcome."

Morenike nods, then walks to the living room to wait for her children to finish preparing for their day.

***

Morenike, Kofo and Eniola all hop out of Uncle Bolaji's car to walk down a forked road on Lagos Island. The streets of Balogun Market fill to the brim with locals shopping for items that could be found in any American superstore. She holds Kofo's hand and Kofo holds Eniola's hand, attracting the stares of Nigerians who watch everyone in their surroundings with vigor beyond people watching—it's more like people hawking. Random men accost her daughters, recognizing that they either are diasporans or come from plush conditions, offering to sell them anything ranging from flat-screen televisions, to water buckets, to pens.

The unpaved roads in Balogun market have shallow puddles and Morenike walks around them all with brisk steps to avoid getting trampled. Two to three-story structures built during Nigeria's colonial era house stores, or stock rooms for the shops at the ground level. Balogun market is an endless maze leading to winding roads and alleys where salespersons poke out, emerging unexpectedly to sell their unattended products. Fifty years ago, a fourth of the crowd would shop along these streets with room to breathe and take in the variety of purchase options. But the current day version of Lagos requires comfort in cramped quarters for facilities suffering from long-term neglect, forcing Nigerian locals to build sustaining shops that accommodate the hefty number of consumers. Morenike spots a path clearing for a handful of East and South Asian men with Nigerian staff trailing them. She wishes she could ask if any of them are doing business with Akeem.

Morenike enters a fabric stop with mounds of Nigerian party lace shelved on the surrounding walls illuminated by florescent lights. She finds Kafayat there, gisting with other ladies who are sitting at the store's entrance in anticipation of customers, cooling from the overhead fan.

Kafayat rises, prostrating for Morenike and offering hugs to her nieces.

"This guy Kayode is overcharging you."

"Why?"

Morenike and Kafayat charge ahead in Kayode's direction, challenging his unapologetic pursuit of more money upon finding out the customers he's servicing are paying him with a higher currency. Morenike relishes in the challenge of haggling. Kayode smirks at their rage, all too familiar with Nigerians that pretend to have tight wallets, expecting him to lose profits from his labor.

Morenike glances over her shoulder at her daughters sitting in a corner of the shop, watching their mother in rare form. Morenike used to live for this autonomy and misses it. Kofo dozes off while Eniola continues browsing God knows what in her phone. Morenike dumps her purse on their laps, expecting them to guard its contents.

When Kofo awakes thirty minutes later, Morenike finds her daughter connecting with one of Kayode's assistants at their sewing machine. She smiles to herself, glad that at least one of them is interested in this tradition.

Morenike's phone goes off in her purse on Kofo's lap. She watches Kofo look at her screen, wide-eyed.

"Mommy, daddy just texted you! He can talk!"

Morenike stretches her arm to retrieve her pocketbook, looking at Akeem's text that reads, *I am available to talk tomorrow.*

Morenike reads the message repeatedly.

We are at Bolaji's, she writes back.

Akeem still pushes for a position of authority via text. *Sorry, I am only agreeing to meet at my place. I'm not comfortable having any discussions at your family's houses so we can do it on another day.*

Morenike wants to grunt and shake him through the phone. *I need to prepare Kofo for this. I will let you know tonight or tomorrow when we are coming.*

He ends his contribution to their conversation with, *Fab. Chaio.*

Morenike creases her eyebrows, confused at Akeem's language. *What is this man saying? Is the other woman some sort of fashion mogul?* she ponders.

When Morenike looks up, Kofo is before her, staring with bated breath.

"What did he say?"

"Let's discuss it later, not here."

Kofo looks around, finally agreeing with her mother for once. She occupies herself with the seamstress until they leave. Eniola picks at her new nails after exhausting her social media browsing—they are almond-shaped claws of fire engine red tips. Morenike hates them, but one step at a time. At least Eniola's hair looks much better than before.

***

Morenike pulls up her phone and texts her WhatsApp group of mosque sisters while winding down after a long day.

As Salaam Alaykum Sisters, I hope all is well. The preparations for my daughter's wedding are occupying my time and will do so in the near future. I would like to assign Sister Aleemat to oversee the bathroom construction in the meantime with weekly progress photos. Please confirm you have received this message and agree to the new arrangement.

The Al-Ahmed sisters send her frequent photos and texts of happenings in the mosque since she left town that would never go on in her presence.

The bathroom project is on hold, their weekly cleaning staff is missing in action and their weekly cook sends incorrect orders. Worst of all, the local police officers that patrol the block during their Friday services ticket them every week for the smallest infractions.

Aleemat agrees to Morenike's proposal after much protest and expressions of disappointment amongst the text group. Aleemat texted Morenike in the morning to report that the brothers attempted to call Akeem for help with the bathroom project and recent ticketing issue. Of course, he was of no use because he would have to redirect them to the real mastermind behind his contrived empire. Morenike is certain that Aleemat reached out to him directly—she competes with Morenike only inspired by delusion, constantly sending signals of her potential to replace Morenike's position of popularity if the opportunity presented itself. It's a better idea to form an alliance with the likes of Aleemat to diffuse any messy outcomes with her husband—she plans to end their affair by killing her with benevolence.

Morenike struggles to tell Kofo the truth, afraid that introducing her father's new identity may inspire her to cancel her wedding to a Nigerian man, even if he is a diasporan. On the ride home, Kofo asks about their text exchange and Morenike texts to her to say that she would rather not discuss this in front of Kafayat. Kofo presses her for details as soon as Morenike went into her room to wash up after a long day, not giving her a chance to catch up on her prayers.

***

Kofo's mood declines during dinner, creating another snide reaction to Tunde hanging out with Uncle Bolaji for the day. Morenike requested Tunde stay behind so that he can get advice on dealing with Akeem and the realities of their family overall. Eniola and Tunde have maturity about how elders operate that Kofo refuses to accept. She and Uncle Bolaji decided they will take Kofo out to lunch the next day to smooth over the news before heading over to Akeem's place. Eniola and Tunde will also be there, but it's unlikely their input will offer value. Morenike is sure that disclosing more details about Akeem's mess in public will subdue aggression in Kofo's response.

Before Morenike heads to sleep, she hears a knock on her room door.

"Come in."

Kofo creeps inside, realizing that she's walking in on her mother during her last moments of a long day. She sits on the bed with her outside clothes, staring at Morenike.

"Mommy—when is he coming?"

Morenike looks down at the bedsheets, wishing she could count each flower on the bedspread instead of engaging Kofo's persistence.

"Kofo, I don't know yet. He needs to send me his availability."

"Why can't we send him ours?"

Morenike does her best to keep a cool head. "I already tried that. We have to work with his schedule. He's going to get back to me. Be patient, you're going to see him. Go to bed."

Kofo looks outside the window at the night sky from one window. Morenike wonders if she is wishing—wishing that whatever she encounters with

---

her father doesn't break her heart. But both she and Kofo know it's too late. Her father is more than just "daddy", he is a man, a messy man. A man that hurts people. A man that knows how to flex his power when needed. A man that changes his behavior when he needs something. A man that can entrap you if you don't study him.

"Ok. Good night, Mommy." Kofo slowly rises and heads out, gently shutting the door behind her.

Morenike grabs her phone and pulls up her WhatsApp to message Akeem.

Please send me your address. Expect us tomorrow evening and do not contact Kofo beforehand.

Akeem responds immediately with, *noted. See you all then.*

Morenike takes a deep breath while looking at their digital exchange. She lies down and goes to sleep.

CHAPTER 15

A sharp abdominal jab wakes Eniola up in her abdomen at three in the morning. She didn't need to look down at her pelvic area to know that it was time for her baby boy to arrive. The pain was so acute that she had an immediate flashback to her discussion with Jumoke, who encouraged her to take baby delivery classes at New York Presbyterian, where she works as an anesthesiologist. Her embarrassment of Cedric's absence in the classes because of their breakup made her refuse the offer.

Eniola wails, surprising herself with her voice's potential. She blows out heavy, loud breaths in the way that many women do during the deliveries she's watched on television.

Kofo runs into her room and turns on the ceiling light. Her younger sister panics and she gathers Morenike, who gets Uncle Bolaji and Aunty Kafayat to bring a local obstetrician. He performs a successful home delivery in four hours.

When the doctor plops her baby boy in her arms, Eniola sobs upon locking eyes with his beady pupils. Despite all she fears, his innocence and comfort in her warm, sweaty, body assure her that this will be the most profound bond she would share with anyone in her life. He ignites a mission in Eniola to produce a man who will never let her down. Gbenga Adebayo will be the saving grace of her new future.

Fisayo and the house girls show up for Eniola with full support, washing both Eniola and the baby during her recovery. They offer her breastfeeding tips and healing herbs, basing their feedback on their own experiences. She's heard mostly horror stories of delivery and birth from her peers in The States, and her experience is quite the opposite so far. Aside from tiredness and soreness in between her legs, Eniola is fine.

"Are you sure you are ready to eat stew?" Morenike asks.

"Mommy… they are not adding any spice. I'll eat it," Eniola groans. Her mother is driving her crazy, running after the house girls like a drill sergeant. Uncle Bolaji demanded that she relax and bring her hounding to a standstill. Eniola's edge wore off when Morenike and Kafayat went to the hospital to register Gbenga's birth in Ikoyi on her behalf.

Kofo takes over monitoring Eniola while Tunde and Uncle Bolaji watch a football match in Uncle Bolaji's den on the first floor.

Kofo looks up from her phone, appearing reluctant to open her mouth.

"Cedric keeps calling me. What's going on, Ennie?"

Eniola rocks Gbenga, soothing his gentle cries. She fears breaking his tiny limbs. "Don't answer the phone, Kofo."

Kofo frowns at her sister. "But he's the father."

She sent a photo of Gbenga to Cedric after the delivery and reblocked his number. Yvonne called her a few days before leaving for Nigeria, pressing her to stay in New York as instructed by her doctor. But Eniola didn't want Cedric in the delivery room, pacing around her privates with his real estate girlfriend while she had a crusty, swollen face and matted hairdo like she does now. The imagery alone infuriated Eniola. He barely checks in on her and fell off on all visits until she ceased communication. Cedric insists he is hesitant as a parental figure because he wants to discuss his involvement with "her baby". She will bother with him upon her return.

Eniola ignores her sister and takes Gbenga's smooth hand. He instinctively wraps his fingers around her pinky.

"Did you at least let Daddy know?" Kofo asks, breaking Eniola's intimate moment with her child.

"Kofo—I just delivered my son. Do you think I am worried about telling people who don't want to be here about it?"

"Don't say that. Daddy would be here if we told him."

Eniola snorts, shaking her head at her sister. "Just like how he showed up for your Nikah, right?"

The rhetorical question silences Kofo, and Eniola pops her heavy right breast out of her bra to feed her baby.

***

Eniola and Kofo wake up from a nap when Gbenga cries for his next meal. Eniola feeds her baby from her left breast this time and the process is painful, but he thankfully latches on. Other than law, motherhood appears to be another area of skill for Eniola.

Kofo's phone pings and she cracks open the door while whispering to Tunde in the corridor. Moments later, Tunde walks in with a couple whom Eniola is sure are his parents. Tunde looks like a perfect blend of them both. He has his mother's perfect teeth and broad, flat nose. His expressive eyes and angular jawline and head are indeed from his father. Eniola gives Tunde a look of surprise as his parents approach her, and he smiles nervously in return.

"Hi Ennie. This is my mom and dad. They heard about your newborn and insisted on visiting."

Eniola's eyes trace them both with discomfort and she covers her exposed body with a bedsheet. "Good afternoon, Mr. and Mrs. Bakare."

"Good afternoon, Eniola. Congratulations on your baby." Olumide says in a thick Nigerian accent with slight British undertones. His speech is impersonal and unenthused.

Eniola smiles and nods. "Thank you, sir."

"We were visiting family not too far away and decided to stop by. Is your mother around?" Adepeju asks.

Fisayo drops chairs into the room and Tunde's parents sit down five feet away from Eniola.

Eniola's eyes dart back and forth at them both in confusion, and Kofo interjects to step in between the two parties, breaking their view.

"Actually, our mom should be home soon and my dad is staying nearby with other family members. Do you want Fisayo or any of the house girls to get you refreshments?" Kofo inquires.

Adepeju shakes her head while her husband sits beside her in silence. "That's okay. We are here to meet you all and become acquainted."

Eniola looks down as Gbenga finishes eating. She gently covers her breast and exposes him to her in laws, unsure of how to respond to this bizarre ambush.

"Well… it's certainly a pleasure to meet you. I wish Tunde would've told me you were coming so I could've prepared for your arrival." Eniola stares at Tunde with fiery eyes.

Adepeju rises and stands next to a flinching, uncomfortable Eniola.

"Eniola—don't be upset with your brother Tunde. We forced him to let us in. We thought someone could offer us some details about your family."

"About what?"

"We want to know what's going on with your parents. We want to know the complete story of what's going on."

"Excuse me?"

Kofo rises and gently touches Adepeju's arm, but she doesn't flinch.

"Peju, sit down!" Olumide yells at his wife.

Tunde's mom goes back to her seat.

Eniola sighs at the sobering reality of her family. *Even the ones that are marrying in are insane*, she complains in her head.

"Mr. and Mrs. Bakare—"

Before she could finish, Morenike bursts in with Kafayat.

"Ah—"

Eniola watches Kofo patch this mess up together by explaining to Morenike whatever story Tunde's parents concocted to justify coming over. Morenike appears thrown off initially, but she salvages it with typical Yoruba greetings and offerings of refreshments and dinner. They eagerly oblige.

***

Kofo attempts to engage in conversation with her in-laws, using her "work" accent and speaking in perfect English with explanations of her Master's degree and fancy job title. Eniola feels embarrassed by her oblivion—her sister doesn't pick up on their indifference. Tunde's parents are more self-assured than their parents. Eniola's ex-boyfriend, Tope, has a similar family. His parents went to an Afar—an Islamic spiritual advisor—who instructed them to break up their relationship because marrying into the Adebayo family will doom male children. Apparently, Akeem's past inspires the worst of any men, including those that join the family.

Eniola watches the concerned faces of Tunde's parents, who appear to know more than they're letting on with their lingering stares. Tunde knows about Yinka by way of being in the house the day Funmi called… but a sidepiece isn't a new issue or a shocking revelation for a typical Nigerian family. His parents must know about the loan, or about another big secret.

Adepeju shifts in her seat, breaking the ice. "Eniola—what of your fiancé? Is he around in Nigeria also?"

Eniola hesitates. "Not at all. I dumped him."

"Oh. I'm very sorry to hear that. What happened?"

She shrugs. "Well… I think we were both settling for each other in a lot of ways."

Morenike jumps in. "Eniola, be mindful of your words."

Eniola ignores her mother and proceeds with her thoughts. "I spent several years trying to make it work, but I'm not his type or what he wants. He actually was never my fiancé, he was just a boyfriend. And now the father of my baby."

"Eniola, keep quiet!" Morenike screams, her face growing with rage at Eniola blowing up their contrived story.

Eniola complies, but she boils with resentment. Resentment for years of being held silent when her mother swore it would pay off and make her more likeable. But no one respects Eniola. Her thwarted voice brings unnecessary complications. Her discretion subdues conflict at the expense of her own fulfillment.

Feeling, touching, and connecting with the body of her son raises the stakes for all the things Eniola secretly desires. One thing Eniola longs for is to speak as freely as her sister—to be unafraid of unbridled honesty. She experiments with a more straightforward approach of communication, leveraging Adepeju's desire for candor.

"Mommy, let's face it. It's the truth. He was never going to marry me. He's a lot like Daddy in many ways, actually."

"Shut up your mouth, Eniola! You are speaking like a fool, shut up I said!" Morenike barks before grabbing Eniola's hair and shaking her head several times.

After Morenike releases her grip, Eniola feels a pain in her chest, and she winces before crying. Morenike's rage was dormant for years, but Eniola often feels it bubbling beneath the surface as of late. She looks at her son sleeping peacefully in the carriage next to her. Eniola is determined to free him from the damage of abuse and neglect that she and Cedric inherited but expressed in different ways.

***

Morenike pretends to play it cool on the phone with Mommy Bola while Tunde's parents sit in silence at the scene they witnessed. Eniola wishes they would leave so she can go to sleep. Kofo can try to woo them another time.

Morenike hangs up, and the room falls silent. Eniola looks at her feet, hypnotized by sadness.

Adepeju clears her throat. "Excuse me, Mommy Ennie."

Morenike rolls her eyes and looks up. "Yes?"

"I apologize if I am overstepping my bounds here," she starts in Yoruba. "But don't you want to know why Eniola feels the way she does about her father?"

Morenike smirks, proud as ever. "My daughters love and admire their father. He is a loving figurehead of our family. Eniola is just crying for attention."

"Eniola... do you want to share?" Adepeju asks.

Morenike puts her hand up in protest. "I don't think it's your place to ask my daughter that."

Eniola lets out a heavy sigh and hesitates.

"It's a long story, but I'll share some of it. He's been in and out of my life since I was a young girl. He is physically present, but that is the extent of his parenting towards me. His inability to be an involved father created feelings of invisibility and loneliness that plummeted my self-esteem. I suffer from severe depression and anxiety. I have been suicidal since I was a teenager and attempted to end my life twice while away in college because of my upbringing with frequent beatings, verbal and emotional abuse, and pressures of living up to the expectations of what my parents want the world to see about the Adebayo family. Please excuse my mother, Mrs. Bakare—she is also finding out some of these things for the first time."

Tunde's mom nods at her in concern. Eniola glances at her enraged mother but carries on.

"I've been on medication since my second incident and have been fine... well, sort of. But I don't think I can handle the toll a man like my father would take on me mentally and emotionally. My ex-boyfriend isn't the nicest guy, and I don't want my son to be anything like him. I want to keep my child safe. I still have a lot of work to do on myself also. So, yea... that's why."

Eniola picks Gbenga up from the carriage to avoid stares of pity.

Kofo touches her thigh. "What if Tunde and I help you raise him?"

"You guys need to focus on yourselves. I'll be okay."

Tunde stands straighter, opening his mouth after hours of silence. "I'm sorry you had to go through that, Eniola. We are here for whatever support you need from us."

Eniola exchanges looks with everyone except her mother, a sincere smile on her face in a long time. "I appreciate that. Thank you for creating space for me to speak freely. It was comforting."

Olumide speaks up since first entering the room. "And don't forget to lean on the Almighty for answers. He won't lead you astray as a mother. You can do it."

Eniola's face transforms into a pensive stare at her baby. "God hasn't favored my life, but we'll see."

They all hold off on responding to her innermost thoughts.

***

Morenike left the room shortly after her revelation and Tunde's parents stayed until eleven in the evening. Eniola exchanged contact information with them and promised she would bring Gbenga with her to London whenever she visited in the future. Eniola enjoyed their company and wishes they were her actual in-laws. Kofo remained awkward throughout the visit, unsure of how to connect with her fiancé's parents. Eniola will school her when they get back to New York.

Uncle Bolaji slides his way into her room right after she changes into her nightgown.

These people won't let me rest, she grumbles to herself.

"Eniola—what did you do to your mother?"

"Uncle... please. Today has been enough for me."

"She said you insulted her? Why?"

"That's not true. I just told Tunde's parents some truths about our family. It was obvious they wanted information and already knew something."

"Ah! Why now?!"

Eniola closes her eyes, tempering herself. She sits down on the bed and rocks Gbenga to sleep. She shares in detail with her uncle many accounts of her childhood that correspond with what she shared with Tunde's parents. In typical elder fashion, he tells Eniola that her that her mother just wants "the best" for her and then she told him about her mental health challenges dating from her college days. He couldn't wrap his brain around it all, encouraging her to pray to Allah, and offered to raise Gbenga with Kafayat's assistance. When Eniola clarifies that there is no way in hell she will allow that, he agrees to tell Morenike to accept how she wants to parent her baby.

She follows her uncle to her mother's room, and they find Morenike in hysterics.

Morenike rises and stands in front of Eniola with energy that feels unrecognizable.

"I'm so sorry," she says in between heavy sobs.

They embrace for a long time and Uncle Bolaji leaves them alone to sort out the rest of the night.

CHAPTER 16

Sleep escapes Kofo the night prior—she is still digesting all that occurred. Tunde apologized for his parents' pop up and she apologized for what they witnessed between her mother and sister. This is not what she envisioned for her first meeting with her in laws. They are nice people and she hopes none of what they observed is used against her.

And Ennie—*poor* Ennie Kofo thinks briefly when the memory crosses her mind. Kofo vaguely remembers her mother being harder on Eniola while Kofo was a small child, ordering her around to assist with essentially raising Kofo. A lot of memories that Kofo towed away overflow to the surface when Kofo lays up at night, thinking about her sister.

Kofo remembers when Morenike would beat or slap Eniola over adding too much or too little spice to their meals. Their mother crumbled and threw her exam papers at Ennie whenever her grade was lower than an A. Calling her an idiot, telling her to shut up whenever she spoke up or asked questions while being reprimanded. The worst incident was when one of Eniola's male friends from school called the house. Morenike told him to forget their number and to never call the house again. When she hung up, she beat and scratched Eniola's neck with destructive force, leaving her sister with a small scar at the nape of her neck till this day. Akeem told her to stop, but Morenike's anger engulfed her as she continued beating Eniola. When he realized Morenike was determined to put the fear of God in their daughter, he sucked his teeth and stayed in the parlor to watch the evening news. Eniola locked herself up in her room for days, refusing to interact with anyone.

Kofo was terrified of her mother and begged Akeem to tell her to stop after that incident. Things calmed down when Kofo was a teenager because Akeem often intervened. While Morenike wasn't as physically abusive, she was still hostile, critical and overbearing. The less intimacy Kofo pursued with her mother, the better their relationship. Eniola's behavior towards Kofo makes sense now that their childhood memories are less hazy.

Kofo and Tunde rummage through their luggage after taking a shower, dressing up for another daily itinerary dictated by Morenike.

"Uncle Bolaji is taking us to Terra Kulture today for lunch," Tunde tells Kofo while she checks out her baby blue sundress in the mirror attached to the dresser.

"That's cool," Kofo says with forced enthusiasm.

Kofo opens her carry-on suitcase, the one where she stores her valuables. She wants to wear her chunky chained brass bracelet that she often sports for weekend brunches. She opens her side zipper where she stores the necklace, only to find it empty.

"Wait—" Kofo blurts aloud, as she unloads her luggage.

"What's wrong?" Tunde stands over her, gently placing his hand on her upper back.

"What the fuck!" Kofo shouts.

"Babe, what's wrong?"

"Where is my bracelet? My wedding jewelry? And my Gucci shoes?!"

"Are you sure you put it in this suitcase?"

"I'm positive, of course. I always put it in my hand luggage."

Kofo's eyes race to every crevice of the room, and her hands follow suit, both moving in frenzied motions. Tunde is behind her with measured steps, repeating searches at each checkpoint in the room in case her emotions cause her to overlook minor clues. They are unsuccessful in finding Kofo's items after wiping the entire room clean.

Kofo storms out, heading to the ground floor where she meets her mother and Uncle Bolaji. The house staff prepared a mid-morning snack of English Breakfast tea with condensed milk and biscuits. Kofo pays no mind to the stillness of the scene, barging in with full force.

"We've been waiting for you all. Are you ready?" Uncle Bolaji munches on a biscuit. Kofo doesn't answer him.

"Mommy, did you take my jewelry and shoes from my carry-on suitcase?"

Morenike sips her tea with careful precision, refusing to dial up her energy to Kofo's level. "No, I don't even know what you're talking about."

Eniola walks in on their discussion, freshened up with Gbenga in her arms. "Are you sure you packed it?"

"Yes, I'm absolutely positive. I always pack my jewelry and shoes in there when traveling. The shoes are in a velvet dust bag. Did you see them, Ennie?"

Eniola shakes her head no, leaving everyone to stare at Kofo without offering much intel. Kofo doesn't back down, determined to make it clear that she's not crazy.

"Someone took it."

Morenike puts her cup down and repositions herself to sit upright. "Kofo—no one took your things."

"Yes, someone did. I know I packed it and we searched my entire room."

Uncle Bolaji purses his lips in restraint. Fisayo walks in, pouring more hot water into the thermal kettle on the coffee table tray. Kofo approaches her. She gave her a generous tip the day they arrived.

"I want to see your belongings," Kofo demands. Fisayo doesn't answer, but tightens her shoulders, appearing confused at Kofo's demand.

Morenike gets up, glancing at her wide-eyed daughter. "Kofo! Stop it!"

"No! I know what I'm talking about, I'm not crazy. I'm so sick of this. You have us running all over this godforsaken city! Where is my father?! I want to talk to him!"

Morenike makes careful steps in Kofo's direction. "Kofo, if you don't stop—"

"You need to listen to me. I know what I am—"

And before Kofo could finish her thought, Morenike slaps her with energy that hasn't emerged since Kofo was a teen. Kofo stumbles back, almost losing her balance out of shock. Beatings hurt, but there is something humiliating about a slap. The complete assertion of domination, control and submission.

"How dare you accuse my brother's workers of being thieves!"

Kofo's chest moves up and down in aggressive motions as she hunches over, cupping her face. She stares at her mother through the corner of her eye with contempt.

"You're a monster. You've always been," Kofo snarls, still panting while her mother looks on, frowning. After a few moments, Kofo turns around and heads back upstairs. Uncle Bolaji remains seated, leaning his head into his palm.

"Where do you think you're going? Get back here!" Morenike yells. Kofo ignores her, going where she desires.

***

Once she re-enters the ransacked room, Kofo slams her belongings in her suitcases. Eniola gently walks in, watching her sister scour the room that reflects Kofo's current mental state. She whips out a fan, calmly waving it on her face to keep cool.

"Kofo, you can't leave here, we have a plan to—"

"Just shut up about this stupid plan already! How can we get this done if we don't even know what the fucking plan is?!"

Eniola stops fanning herself, strolling towards her sister.

"Who the fuck do you think you're talking to? You can't just cause a scene like this and then walk out of here."

Morenike's yelling and scolding of Kofo is audible from their room, serving as background noise.

"You have no backbone," Kofo says as she finishes packing her last suitcase.

Eniola grabs her by the arm firmly, startling Kofo.

"Don't you dare go there. I'm in Nigeria because of you. And all you've been doing is pouting like an ungrateful brat like you always do."

Kofo wiggles free from Eniola's unrecognizable grip. Everyone's energy is out of character today, it seems. She takes a few steps back, attempting to regain balance from a reaction she wasn't expecting from Eniola. Kofo studies her sister, not sure how to respond to this new version of Eniola.

"I never asked for your help!" is all Kofo could come up with in response.

Eniola sits on the bed, wiping her sweaty face with a rag while rocking her baby.

Kofo avoids any further invitations for discussion. She walks out of the room with her belongings, locking herself in a bathroom down the hall. Her hands shake as she pulls up her WhatsApp account to send a text that reads, *Daddy, I am in a serious emergency. I need you to pick up the phone when I call you.* Kofo sits on the toilet for several moments while staring at the phone screen. She types again, but her instincts push her to call instead. He picks up on the second ring.

"Daddy?!"

"Hi Kofo. What's wrong?" Akeem's tone is calm and unresponsive to Kofo's high-strung energy. She can hear her father lowering the volume of a BBC News announcement in the background.

"I know you know I am in Nigeria."

"Yes, I do."

There's an icy silence on the line between them. Akeem's cool tone towards her is unfamiliar. Or was Kofo's interpretation of her immediate family skewed all along? *Who is this clinical man on the line that often was cheery when his baby girl came into the room? What did being in Nigeria do to her family?* Kofo reflects while closing her eyes, wishing all of this away.

"I need to stay with you for the duration of my trip. Tunde is coming with me."

"Is your mother okay with this?"

"No, she isn't, but I'm coming anyway. Please have someone pick us up as soon as possible from Uncle Bolaji's house."

"I will have one of my drivers come. But you are on your own regarding your mother."

"Okay, thank you."

Kofo hangs up the phone, unsure of how her next encounter with her father will feel. She sends a text to Tunde. *Babe, I'm packing a bag for you. We're going to my dad's place.*

He writes back with, *doubt this will end well. But okay.*

When Kofo gets down to the living room hours later, Morenike rises from her seat on the couch.

"Where do you two think you are going?!"

"I'm going to Daddy's. You know the address, so no need to send. I'll see you at the wedding."

Morenike continues to rant epithets in Yoruba and Kofo is unfazed, walking outside to the driveway with Tunde. Eniola trails them and her mother taps her arm before she walks through the front door.

"Talk to your sister, please."

Eniola nods and exits. She finds Kofo and Tunde in the backseat of a tinted luxury car as the driver places their suitcases in the trunk. Eniola knocks on the window and Kofo rolls it down halfway open. Tunde sits next to the opposite door, looking away from them both.

"Mommy was really trying to get him to meet on neutral ground, Kofo."

"Trust me, this will work. Worry about your baby.", Kofo says in an overconfident voice.

Eniola rolls her eyes. "You need to apologize for cursing at Mommy. And also, to me."

"Not right now Ennie."

Eniola shakes her head in disapproval.

"You better fix this, and soon."

Kofo counters Eniola's demand by rolling up the car window.

****

When the car pulls up to Akeem's Ikoyi driveway, Kofo is unsure of what to make of her father's house. It's a big, gated, Victorian mansion with a large, freshly cut lawn, tall palm trees and a water fountain in the center of a mowed lawn. It is two times the size of their Long Island home. House sprawl throughout the exterior of the house, working on various assignments.

Kofo continues to make detailed observations of her surroundings as the driver unloads their items.

Kofo and Tunde walk into the foyer, marveling at the understated, grand, architectural design of the house in tones of grays, blues and whites. The tiles on the floor, high ceilings and intricate carvings of the marble stair railings indicate elevated decorative taste, which her father does not have.

An older gentleman from the house staff descends the stairs. Kofo pulls out a twenty-dollar bill, but Tunde stops her.

"Tip before you leave." She agrees, putting her money away.

Kofo walks further into the house, gingerly stepping into the den where the television plays. The news broadcast is an immediate reminder of her father. Plaques hang onto the walls and stand on console tables, most of them recognizing her father's "innovations in the world of petroleum technology."

"This used to be in our house," Kofo says, reflecting on one of the older plaques. Tunde raises his eyebrows.

Not much time passes before Akeem makes his way over to the couple.

"Hi, Kofo." He gives her a comforting, big hug. Kofo fits right into his embrace, slumping her tight shoulders.

"Hi Daddy."

Akeem looks at Tunde, smiling. Tunde's mind flashes back to London, eliciting a slew of negative emotions when Akeem pushes an open palm in his direction.

"Tunde—it's good to see you." Tunde shakes his extended hand, and they firmly grip each other. He doesn't smile back at Akeem and maintains a neutral expression.

"Likewise. Thank you, sir."

"The food is ready. Come with me."

Kofo and Tunde follow him to the dining room set for a group of eight with freshly cooked Nigerian dishes. The aromas of tomato stew, ginger, spicy peppers and other ingredients are prominent.

"Tunde, I hope my house help cooks as well as your mother."

Tunde smirks. "That's a tall order, but I will keep you posted."

Kofo stares back and forth between them, wishing she could chime in with commentary on the trip she didn't attend.

Akeem stares at his plate with focus, ready to eat. His house attendant stands by, awaiting Akeem's long list of needs.

"Bring Yinka and the Boys!" he yells at no one in particular.

Kofo almost chokes on her cup of water.

"The boys?" she asks.

"Yes, your brothers."

"Blood brothers?"

Akeem takes a beat. "Yes."

Kofo looks down at the table, frozen.

***

Uncle Bolaji's dining room is eerily quiet except for the sounds of silverware hitting the plates while Morenike, Eniola and Uncle Bolaji eat dinner the same night. The house girls tiptoe around them, praying they go unnoticed while pouring glasses of water before staying put in their stations throughout the corners of the room.

Eniola eats the ogbono stew, amala swallow and ewedu vegetables with ease. Gbenga coos is in his carriage behind her.

"I hope these ingredients are okay with your food sensitivities, Ennie?"

Eniola takes a piece of fried fish from the stew before mixing it with other dishes on her plate. "Yes, thanks so much, Uncle."

Morenike picks at her plate, unable to eat with much intention.

"Nike… let it go. She'll be back," her brother assures her.

Morenike looks up at her brother with eyes of worry. "Brother, I'm so sorry that my daughter made those comments—"

Eniola jumps in. "I think she is right, mommy." Eniola can't believe what she hears coming out of her mouth. Agreeing with Kofo on anything is a rarity, and more so when expressed to their mother. She hopes Morenike and Uncle Bolaji don't resort to being offended by her honesty.

"I'll confirm that she isn't," Uncle Bolaji says. He charges to the kitchen, approaching his house staff. "Fisayo! Bring your bags!"

Morenike and Eniola exchange a glance before rising fast in the kitchen's direction. They walk into Uncle Bolaji storming towards his barefoot, tired house girls. Their ankara outfits and worn t-shirts are soiled from sweating through a long day of tasks. Fisayo packs leftovers from dinner in a plastic container. Morenike takes a step into the kitchen towards her brother.

"Brother Bolaji, it's fine. Stop it."

He disregards her, focused on cabinets, drawers, and corners of the entire kitchen. All the house girls cram near the door leading to the back of the house right next to the refrigerator.

"Bo-la-ji!" Morenike calls, and he increases his commitment to making his point, searching with more speed. He pokes his head into the cabinet shelf below the sink and finds a black plastic bag filled with items. When he opens it, there is a velvet bag with gold Gucci sandals and several pieces of gold jewelry. He allows his surprise to set in, he looking up at his sister and while placing it on the kitchen counter.

"Ah—"

Fisayo steps up from the cluster of ladies. "Mr. Modupe, I didn't take it…"

One of the other house helpers, named Tolani, grabs the bag from the counter and gives it to Morenike, then tries to run out. Uncle Bolaji grabs her by the arm.

"Are you crazy?!" he screams, causing her to flinch.

Eniola steps into the kitchen from the doorway. "Uncle, it's okay."

Uncle Bolaji releases Tolani, turning back to the other ladies and scolding them in his most aggressive Yoruba insults.

Morenike leaves the entire scene, heading back to the dining room. She clutches the bag of Kofo's items, letting out a weary breath. The background noise of her brother berating the girls is another trigger, reminding her of the many days when yelling was commonplace between her mother and father.

Eniola stands over her with an empathetic gaze. She leans in and wraps her arm around Morenike.

"Over shoes Ennie. This is too much."

Morenike picks up her phone to call Kofo, but Eniola takes it out of her mother's hands, putting it down on the table next to her half-eaten plate.

"Let her see who he really is, mommy."

Morenike's body gives in and she returns to Eniola's embrace.

***

Kofo picks at her fried rice and fried stew chicken, unable to enjoy her meal. Her father always orders her rice and chicken to eat when Nigerian food is on the menu, believing his daughter can't handle the spices of his native cuisine. Kofo is riced out and would rather dine on traditional meals that set her tongue on fire. Before this moment, her father's attempts to protect her abdominal lining charmed her. She never viewed it as a concealment of his culture. Akeem doesn't want her growing curiosity about her identity to blossom into something that would force Kofo to come with her father on one of his many supposed business trips. Kofo becoming a devoted Nigerian will place his own comforts at stake.

Yinka walks in and Kofo notices her trendy hairdo, high-quality makeup and freshly manicured pearl-colored nails. She looks like a younger, slimmer version of Morenike. Akeem has a type—Nigerian women with bourgeois aspirations. Two young boys walk in behind her.

"Kofo, this is your Aunty Yinka and your brother Ife, who is six, and your other brother Jide, who is eleven."

Kofo's brothers sit down in their seats and their mother sits at the other head of the table. They all seem comfortable. So settled in.

"Hi," is all that Kofo has to give, mainly to her brothers.

Jide eats a scoop of rice, chewing quickly. "Hi. Are you the sister that is getting married?" *His Nigerian accent is adorable*, she admits to herself.

"Yes. It's really nice to meet you," Kofo says with a slight smile.

Akeem ruins the window of opportunity for them to genuinely bond. "Kofo, you can't say hi to Yinka?! Get up and say hi."

Kofo looks at Yinka expectant stare for her proper greeting. Akeem's tone catches her off guard. It's unfamiliar, as though her dad is wearing a new costume—one of a textbook traditional, authoritarian dad. Despite his threatening tone, Kofo refuses to be formal with her.

"Hello."

"Hi Kofo. How is the wedding planning coming along?" Yinka asks in a posh Lagosian accent.

"Fine."

Yinka looks at Akeem for help, but he shrugs. Kofo sees their exchange, disappointed by another display of apathy from Akeem. Digesting all of this would be easier if he was the same person from New York.

Kofo looks at Yinka's smooth hands, concluding that she couldn't be over forty, which means that her father scooped her up during her mid-twenties. She repulses at the idea of her father having sex with a woman too young to be her mother.

"So how old are you?" Kofo's curiosity got the best of her. "And how long have you two been together?"

Yinka hesitates in shock. "Um, well…"

"Kofo, you don't ask elders these kinds of questions," Akeem jumps in.

"Daddy, may I speak with you privately?" Kofo wants answers and this light fare conversation oozing with denial is not satisfactory.

"After our meal."

Kofo's eyes bulge out while she watches her father scoop up a pile of rice, shoveling mounds of starch into his mouth. Tunde gulps down a glass of water, Yinka eats with her head down and the boys remain occupied with their own playful imaginations.

"Who am I talking to right now, daddy?"

Akeem puts his fork down, leaning back in his chair to withhold his impulse to answer Kofo's question with more aggression than she can handle.

"Follow me downstairs."

Kofo rises, glancing at everyone's lowered heads at the table. It's clear that this version of Akeem is familiar to them all, including Tunde. Kofo moves with purpose behind her father, furious at the realization that one of his biggest supporters knows him the least. Before Kofo disappears from Tunde's view, he says to Kofo,

"Do you want me to come?"

She turns around to face him. "No. I got it."

Akeem leads her to a set of marble stairs with a translucent glass railing. The tiles get colder with each step down, reminding her it fits perfectly with her real-time experience. He stops in front of a wooden, oak-colored, carved door. Akeem opens it with a lock, leading her into a large study.

Wooden shelves line all the walls in the room, piled with books, files, plaques, Yoruba indigenous wooden carvings, and office supplies that appear in bulk sizes—likely from Costco in the United States. Floodlights popcorn the ceiling, giving the room a fluorescent tone. Kofo hates this type of lighting. It's her father's favorite to get work done. He told her she should give it a try, that "it'll make you just as productive as me", he joked years ago.

Kofo still stands at the doorway, unable to move into the room until she takes in every detail. His executive-sized desk stands opposite the door, and Akeem pulls out a brown leather office chair behind it to sit down. When Akeem faces her, they lock eyes, both unsure of what to say next. Kofo spots an air conditioner that lets out a soft electric buzz. Goosebumps rise on her forearms, signaling her to shiver.

"You don't need an invitation to sit down," Akeem points to an empty chair facing him on the opposite side of the desk. Kofo steps into the room, carefully placing one foot in front of the other before following his instructions.

Akeem's desk has a titled plaque and pictures of Yinka with the boys. None of her or her sister. Or her mother. Papers pile metal office racks and he has a large, papered calendar on the flat surface of the desktop. This office is regularly occupied.

"Why didn't you decorate your office back home like this?" Kofo looks down at the calendar with meetings scribbled on it.

Akeem gets up to close the door for privacy.

"I know this is shocking, but you cannot talk to your new mother like that."

Kofo looks at Akeem with bewilderment, the fire rising in her. Suddenly, the room isn't as cold.

"So, this is what you've been doing on your Nigerian trips? Bearing children with other women and pretending to be some kind of chief?"

"I wanted another wife. What is the issue?"

Kofo scoffs, shaking her head. She looks at the walls, hoping there was something she could pull out with information on handling his family affairs. In the past, Kofo recommended bell hooks, knowing his interest in her was a long shot, but she thought it was because she was Black American, and allegedly couldn't relate to her experiences. Not because she was a feminist. He didn't read Chimamanda Adichie either. He only reads books about business, and how to manifest a better ranking within the scales of societal wealth.

"You told me you would never take on this lifestyle."

"Circumstances have changed, Kofo. And I think it's time for you to know what's really going on between your mother and I."

"How can you ask us to be one big, happy family? This is crazy."

Akeem's expression drops, sighing.

"Your mother and I have been unhappy for a long time. We only stayed together when she got pregnant with you after trying for so long. And I'm tired, I need a break. I'm not someone who performs for the community. That is what your mother is about."

"I highly doubt Mommy hid her ways before you married her. You benefitted from Mommy's choices too, Daddy. So many people helped you start and grow your businesses, especially from the mosque."

"You're right. But it was to make her look good. There is a lot your mother and I did for the sake of culture. It's none of your business."

"Does Mommy know about my brothers?"

"Yinka told her when your mother got her number somehow. Yinka wants your brothers to have a relationship with me and would prefer if I lived here for the majority of the time to handle expenses, especially since you and your sister are adults. The boys are having some behavioral issues in school and it hasn't been easy for her to raise them alone."

Kofo closes her eyes, taking in everything she is hearing.

"Your mother suggested I wait to tell you and your sister, so my hands were tied."

Kofo looks down at the floor when she finally opens her eyes.

"I didn't realize you lied this much." Akeem doesn't answer her. "I ran into Professor Schultz when I picked up my diploma."

"Oh, how is he?!"

"He's fine, he's doing well. And so is his sister."

"Why would he tell you that?!"

Kofo shakes her head, aghast at her father.

"Maybe because he assumed you weren't married and already told me, Daddy."

"We're just friends."

"Not seven years ago."

Akeem rolls his eyes. "Kofo—why can't you mind your business? How does this affect you?"

Kofo makes piercing eye contact with her father as her eyes well up.

"Why are you crying, Kofo? Stop it. You and your sister are grown women. I stayed with your mom until I felt it was appropriate for you two to move on. It's time."

"So, Mommy is our job now?"

"Well, with Ennie's baby and I'm sure you'll conceive soon—that should keep her occupied enough."

"Just so I confirm—are you telling me you are no longer a member of our family? Because you told me you're not divorcing Mommy."

"I'm not. I'll come back when I'm ready to. In the meantime, defer to your uncles in the mosque."

"They're not our blood relatives. Do you even know any of them that well?"

"Kofo—just do it and stop this already."

Kofo stares at the desk calendar for several moments.

"You told me to always prepare my arguments when I didn't agree with someone. Do you have a Quran down here?"

Akeem rolls his office chair to a nearby shelf to grab a Quran and then hands her the book. She opens it, familiar with where to reference the book for their discussion.

"In Sura-four or An-Nisaa, it says, 'if you fear that you shall not be able to deal justly with the orphans, marry women of your choice, two, or three, or four, but if you fear that you shall not be able to deal justly (with them), then only one, or that which your right hands possess. That will be more suitable, to prevent you from doing injustice.'"

Kofo takes a long, careful look at her father, hoping for him to tell her this is all a joke. But Akeem doesn't flinch. More moments pass while Kofo notices his dyed beard hairs. Akeem remains cool and unmoved by what she just read. Kofo accepts that this might be the last time they will have a moment alone together.

"Is it just to make the condo a liability for me? To take away a lifetime of earnings from mommy because you want another wife?"

"You see? I'm just a bank to you people."

"You promised to take care of us! Daddy, you were the one that begged me to take your money when I told you that Tunde and I would sort it out and continue renting."

"And yet here you are."

"I wouldn't even be here if you didn't ask me to rely on you."

"I knew he would do this to you. I knew he would disappoint you."

"In the same way you are, currently, I'm assuming?"

Akeem rubs his mouth in restraint. Kofo wishes he would just spit it out.

"Look Daddy—if you don't want to be an active father, fine. But you can't just leave us high and dry when you agreed to provide for your family—"

"Not as adults!"

His anger shakes Kofo, but she remains dedicated to her mission.

"Your mother was abusing my money for material items."

"So, what exactly is this house? Or the car that picked us up earlier?"

Akeem smirks. "Kofo—I can afford to buy these things for myself or whomever I want. I worked for my lifestyle. Your mother is a housewife that leisurely practiced law when it suited her. She could've been a working mother if she really wanted and she chose not to."

Kofo frowns at her father's arrogance.

"I wish I never saw this side of you."

Akeem's pompous grin disappears as he is impacted by Kofo's comment. He rises and pushes one of many bookshelves near his desk. The shelf reverses and a safe is on the other side. He pushes a code to unlock it, takes about fifteen thousand dollars' worth of cash, putting it into a nearby duffel bag. Akeem grabs a checkbook from one drawer in his desk and writes a check for thirty thousand dollars.

"This is the last time you will get any money from me. The cash is for your remaining wedding expenses and the check is for you to split with your mom. Spend it wisely."

"Eniola emailed you a contract requesting that you take full liability and ownership of the condo, and pay Tunde and I back our deposit within the next two years. We'll move out after you pay us off."

Akeem pulls out the signed document and gives it to Kofo.

"Thank you," she says.

"Just so you know, your credit won't be affected. I also emailed Eniola's document ensuring that I won't kick your mother out of the Long Island house."

"I hope all of this is worth it for you." Kofo takes the duffel bag from her father. "How do you have all of this money, anyway?"

"Through serial entrepreneurship. You should give it a shot and put your degree to use."

Kofo looks down at the bag, resenting that she desperately needs its contents.

"I hope you change your mind about coming back to New York."

"Kofo, I don't know when I'll be back! Stop asking me already!" Akeem slams the bookshelf into place after turning it around.

Kofo sniffles, holding the bag tight. It smells like her father's Acqua Di Gio Giorgio Armani cologne—she told Tunde to stop wearing it because it grosses her out when they are intimate and he shrugged it off, reserving it only for his working hours while he was away from home. Kofo will insist that he toss it out completely when they return to New York.

"Thank you. And thank you for the meal."

Kofo exits, leaving her father alone with his thoughts.

***

Kofo hangs her silk robe on the hook at her bedroom door in Akeem's house. It's quiet and close to midnight, but body won't rest. She feels a chill every time her feet touch the marble floor, and she hates it. She's eager to leave this house that feels like an icebox in an equatorial climate.

Kofo slides into the bed, mistaken on her assumption that Tunde is asleep. Tunde opens his closed eyes and then faces her. Kofo reciprocates, looking at her fiancé and reflecting on her father's "predictions" of Tunde. Tunde's lips curve into a smile.

"We should elope Tunde." Tunde's silence worries Kofo and she turns her body to the ceiling. "You're so lucky. Your parents are so nice," she whispers.

"I won't lie. They can't compete with this." They both snicker as Tunde leans in further, touching Kofo's face. "I'm proud of you for standing up to yours."

Kofo returns her face back to Tunde, giving a weak smile.

"I hope you know you are forming an alliance with the rudest member of our family."

"You mean the honest one."

Kofo's smile widens at Tunde's reassuring comment.

"I always used to say that I want my husband to be just like my dad. It looks like my father is actually the type of man I try to avoid. And everyone knew who he was, except for me."

Tunde strokes her, kissing her forehead. "He's basically cheating on your mom openly. He's just doing it the old school way."

Kofo sighs heavily and loudly. Tunde rubs her temples and pulls her in close before leaning in for a kiss. Kofo thought she wasn't in the mood, but once he makes contact with her lips, it delivers her remedy for the immense sadness weighing on her. Kofo surrenders as Tunde's kisses become more intense and she allows him to gently strip her naked. She senses that their lovemaking will resemble the beginning of their relationship. The connection that ebbed is now flowing again, and Kofo is on board.

***

The sound of rolling suitcases fills out the hollow foyer the next morning as Kofo and Tunde await their last moments in Akeem's house. Mr. Andrew—the same man who handled the luggage upon arrival—places his hand on the front door and Kofo taps his shoulder. She hands him a twenty-dollar bill.

"Sorry, I don't have any Naira, Mr. Andrew."

Mr. Andrew bows his full head of white at Kofo. "Thank you, ma," he musters before he opening the door to load their items in a car right outside. Tunde observes a hole in his trousers between his thighs and he presses his jaw. The sight brings flashbacks of London. A heavy cough from Akeem interrupts Tunde's annoyance as he approaches the couple.

"Make sure you treat her right," Akeem says to Tunde while extending his hand to Tunde.

Tunde prostrates by tipping his torso down briefly while holding Akeem's hand tight. He completes the handshake while staring into the eyes of a man that conjures up nothing but discomfort.

"I'm clear on how to do that, sir."

Kofo watches these two men battle their provision of her, knowing better not to intervene.

Akeem's lip curves into a slick smile. "You have to remain employed to do that, you know."

"I'm aware of what your daughter needs. That's why we're getting married. Thanks, Mr. Adebayo."

Tunde walks out and enters the car, leaving Kofo and Akeem alone.

"Take care of yourself, Kofo."

"I will." She looks down at his manicured, moisturized feet. "Are you coming to the wedding?"

"Only if my new family can join."

He is colder than yesterday. If she takes part in this conversation any longer, she will feel as empty as her father.

"Thank you. Bye Daddy."

Akeem leans in for a hug, but Kofo steps back and joins Tunde in the car.

CHAPTER 17

Akeem's driver waits in the car while Kofo and Tunde unload their belongings when they pull up to Uncle Bolaji's house. The icy goodbyes decline Tunde's mood and he kept silent the entire ride back when Kofo tried to engage him in conversation. Tunde saw the driver's eyes tracing them in the rare view mirror and the last thing he needs is for Akeem to know about any recent tensions between them. Their departing flight couldn't come soon enough.

They walk into Uncle Bolaji's house and find him reading the paper with a cup of fresh tea on the side table.

"Hi Uncle," they both mumble, wary of his reaction.

Uncle Bolaji doesn't respond, and the couple exchanges a worried look. Kofo steps forward to her uncle and sits on the couch next to him.

"Uncle, I'm really sorry for the way—"

Uncle Bolaji moves his newspaper down, rests it on his lap beneath his now folded hands, and reveals a disapproving facial expression. Kofo recoils in guilt while Tunde watches it all unfold, nervous.

"I don't want your apologies. I really don't."

"Uncle, I know I came off—"

Uncle Bolaji puts his hand up, stopping her.

"Go and beg your mother. Once you do that, we will be fine."

A long pause fills the room before Kofo nods in agreement.

Tunde puts one of his bags down and walks a few feet away from Uncle Bolaji before he prostrates. "Thank you Uncle, ma binu."

Uncle Bolaji side-eyes Tunde's demonstrative apology, unimpressed.

"You both are no longer welcome to stay here after this trip. There's been too much disruption since your arrival." Uncle Bolaji picks up his newspaper again as a barrier to reject any more apologies. Kofo and Tunde get the message and make their way upstairs.

***

Kofo and Tunde struggle with dragging their heavy suitcases up the stairs, drenching in sweat as Uncle Bolaji's house staff look on. They pass Morenike's room and the door is open. She and Eniola are reviewing piles of geles and look up at the couple. Both parties observe each other with caution as Kofo and Tunde walk by, unsure of what to say.

When they finally approach their door, Kofo stops.

"I'm gonna go to her now."

"Don't you want to cool down and rest?"

Kofo shakes her head, grabs the black duffle bag and walks into her mother's doorway.

"Hi Mommy. Hi Ennie."

"Hello," they both say in reluctant unison.

Kofo grabs a chair and positions it opposite their direction on the bed before sitting down.

"I'm really sorry about yesterday."

Eniola smiles with tight lips, but Morenike is a blank slate. Kofo expects chastising from her mother. Morenike's reflective stare complicates Kofo's ability to read her effectively.

"Never speak to me like that again. Or your sister. And Tunde."

Kofo sighs, relieved that her mother is back. Morenike plops the gele in her hand next to her on the bed and looks at her daughters with fierce intention.

"I grew up in an area of Lagos that is nothing like Lekki. We were a big family of nine children with very little resources. Your grandmother sent your Uncle Bolaji and me to beg for food and money after our school day. "

Kofo is thrown off guard again. She makes eye contact with Eniola, who is equally confused.

"I met your dad at a house party that introduced some of us 'area' folks to kids from more prominent families like your father's. When we started dating, he always bragged about how I was a slender woman with a big butt that knew how to cook. Not a woman from a less than fortunate family that was smart enough to get into prominent law schools all over the world. Not someone that passed three bar exams in the U.S. I helped your father map out his entire career. I'm telling you this because this is how your father views women."

Kofo leans into her chair. "Why didn't you ever practice law full time?"

"Well… I did for a year, but my hours didn't allow me to get home in time to prepare dinner for your father, so I had to stop."

Kofo frowns, sympathetic towards her mother's revelations.

Morenike leans in Kofo's direction. "Kofo… do you know why you are his favorite?"

Kofo hesitates, still uncomfortable with her mother's frank admissions. "Because I was a miracle baby after you tried so long, right?"

"No—you are spoiled. And you let him love you through money because that's all he knows, despite his complaints. That's why he was able to shield you from his ways for so many years."

Kofo resents this comment and contemplates if she should've left the duffle bag at her father's house. The money is a huge convenience, but it comes with unpleasant conditions. Kofo brushes off the thought and opens the duffle bag. Morenike and Eniola watch her sudden move.

"Well… I lived up to my reputation yesterday," Kofo says as she hands her mother the bag. Her mother's eyes widen with zeal as she looks at the piles of dollar bills inside.

"How did you get it from him?!"

Kofo shrugs. "I was just honest. And he's probably not coming to the wedding."

"He's going to be there. He always comes back Kofo. Always."

Morenike scours through the bag, more excited with her discovery of each stack of money. "Wow… good job, Kofo, I am very proud of you."

Kofo chuckles to herself, satisfied to make amends with her mother. "Why didn't you tell us we have two brothers, Mommy?" Kofo looks at Eniola again—she is eerily quiet.

Morenike closes the bag and looks up at Kofo. "If you would've listened to me before, I was trying to tell you we need to discuss this all as a family."

"You already know that he doesn't want to deal with any of us."

Eniola finally speaks. "What exactly did Daddy tell you, Kofo?"

"Nothing worth mentioning, Ennie."

Eniola rubs her shrinking belly. "How old are they?"

"Six and eleven. Ife and Jide. They knew about us and they even knew about the wedding."

Eniola shakes her head in disgust.

Morenike breaks the long-held silence between her daughters. "Let's talk about the wedding. But first…" Morenike rises and grabs Kofo's dust bag. "This is your missing jewelry and your shoes."

"Oh my God!" Kofo rummages through the bag after her mother hands it to her.

"You were right. Fisayo and a few others stole it. Your Uncle confronted them and asked them to show me their belongings. He wanted to fire them, but I just donated some money for new shoes to buy locally."

Kofo rolls her eyes at the extension of sympathy for thieves. "I gave that girl my last twenty dollars, trying to be nice." Kofo shakes her head, disappointed more in her own naivete.

Morenike understands where both Kofo and Fisayo are coming from. Her brother's hostility towards his house girls shocked her—it resembled the same vitriol Nigeria's wealthy exerted towards them when they used to do odd jobs and tasks after school. They swore to never speak to people like that, but Uncle Bolaji said that "being too nice is viewed as stupidity in Lagos." Morenike doesn't miss the stress connected to a life of extreme paranoia and distrust of others.

"They are poor Kofo. People are really struggling here."

Kofo drops her face at her mother's valid point.

As if Eniola could read Kofo's mind, she chimes in. "I'm sure you know not everyone in Nigeria or Lagos does things like that."

Kofo nods. "Yea… I know."

Morenike also nods. "It's just something you have to watch out for. You and Tunde will figure out what is the best approach in the future."

Kofo doesn't want to offend her mother or sister about her impressions of Nigeria after being away for so long. Maybe she'll stay at the Marriott in Ikeja that everyone is raving about on her next visit. The only issue with that idea is that she prefers to be on the island near Lekki. Preparing for a visit to Nigeria as a diasporan is a "thing" that natives downplay. Adjusting your mindset to operate in a society where there is no infrastructure, mounds of abject poverty, extreme levels of class disparity, outright extreme displays of toxic masculinity, high levels of Black people who bleach or "tone", corruption that pokes at everyone's attempts to maintain inner peace… Kofo fears that she cannot function in Nigeria without her mother's advisement over her every move. That picture in her mind is undesirable.

Morenike picks up the initial gele she tossed aside moments ago. "Okay, Kofo and Ennie. We have a lot of shopping to do."

***

Receiving the money shifts Morenike's behavior in a way that Kofo nor Eniola expect. At the florist stop, Morenike consults Kofo's opinion on various floral arrangements in a multitude of colors. When they arrive at the caterer, Morenike fights the chief cook about their refusal to provide jollof spaghetti for the foreigners with more sensitive pallets who cannot handle the spices of Yoruba cuisine.

After a full, exhausting day, they make it to their last stop at the wedding venue. Kafayat urged Morenike to arrange one meeting with all the vendors in one place, but she insisted that she wants to see their business locations before giving them any money. The caterer's visit alone was exhausting, and Morenike caved in. The photographer, videographer, limousine service, security and anyone else on the wedding planner's list show up, all seated at a large, rounded table.

"Good evening," Morenike says, proceeding to fan herself. The venue staff turned the air conditioners off to her dismay as she wipes a thick layer of foundation off of her face.

"Good evening, Ma," the chorus of vendors respond, eager for another round of business in Nigeria's lucrative wedding industry. Their voices echo through the sky-high ceilings of the building structure that resembles an empty warehouse underneath the current decor.

"Let's have everyone talk about their vision for my daughter's wedding. I want the makeup artists to start," Morenike points in their direction. Kofo sits next to her mother, debating her interest in this discussion that never included her from the onset. Eniola entertains herself alone chair near the door where a slight breeze passes through every couple of seconds.

Before the makeup artist begins, the wedding planner Blessing jumps up. "Hello, ma. I think we should actually do a walk through the venue step by step to make sure you're clear on how all the vendors fit into the vision for the event."

"No—I want us to sit down," Morenike says in a curt tone. "We have been running around all day and are tired."

"I know, but my concern is that you won't be clear on what—"

"I said no."

Blessing nods firmly in irritation at Morenike. Kofo doesn't want to hear her mother throwing orders around after such a great day of enjoying her company. Instead of filling her mind with anxious dread over Morenike, Kofo quietly makes her way around the venue.

The beautiful venue decorations shock Kofo. The left side has fuchsia and orange drapes hanging from the ceiling, and the right side has blue and orange drapes. Orange runners spill on both sides of on all white tables accompanied by white fabric chairs. The table setting is a fusion of blue and pink plates with gold details. Dramatic lighting cascades in tandem with the drapes throughout the ceiling and the center of the dancefloor is blue with gold text. Kofo does not know how Morenike pulled it off, but she effectively communicated a joint vision to the wedding planner. Standing in that room forces Kofo to admit her self-centeredness; it was the wake-up call she needed. Her family is indeed messy, but they will never leave her behind in their agenda to present the best image possible. The thought brought a smile across her face.

"Kofo," Eniola gets creeps up behind her. "Sorry, didn't mean to scare you."

"It's alright. What's up?"

"I know this wedding isn't exactly what you envisioned, but I hope you now have some perspective—"

"Oh my God, Ennie. Please."

"Hear me out."

"Why do you always do this?"

"I'm just trying to help you—"

"Can you just stop?!"

Kofo's raised voice startles everyone in the venue. Eniola moves in closer with a lowered voice.

"You constantly resist my advice. You just walked out of your meeting for your wedding. I'm checking on you for goodness sake."

"Maybe because I realized mommy has everything under control? What can I possibly contribute at this point?"

"A lot actually."

"I'm good. I don't need you to run after me to play backup to mommy. You don't know how to choose between being an auntie or my sister."

"Kofo… I just…"

"What is it?"

"I'm worried about you."

"How are you worried about me?"

"I'm worried about the mistakes you're making and what you're getting yourself into."

"Actually, I think that's bullshit. You believe you could be me in better form." Eniola rolls her eyes, shaking her head. "But I got this. I will figure my life out."

"No, you don't. If you did, we would be at your wedding in New York on your own dime. Tunde can't even take care of you right now."

That comment stings Kofo and she breaks eye contact. She wishes Eniola would just leave her alone to deal with her own thoughts. She wants to respond by saying, *you're gonna end up miserable like mommy if you don't mind your business*, but there are too many eyes and ears on them already. Kofo refrains from hitting below the belt.

"I love Tunde. That's enough for me for now. And what about you, Ennie? You don't have everything figured out either."

"Which is exactly why I'm all over you. I also know that you and Tunde love each other. I hope it's enough to keep you two together. Or you'll end up like me. Stressed, a failed engagement and a barely fertile single mother."

Kofo feels a pit in her stomach. Eniola's sulky nature drives her crazy. She is very good at playing small to win sympathy and it's working.

"I'm sorry Ennie. I hope you realize my situation is nothing to envy."

They stare at each other sympathetically for a long moment before Eniola puts her hand on her sister's shoulder.

"I'm sorry too, Kofo. I promise I will back off."

They embrace.

"Tunde is looking for work. The interviewing process was rough. He just started working with a recruiter that he's really excited about." Eniola raises her eyebrows, skeptical. "And you have a lot of support for your baby, myself included."

Eniola pauses. "I know. I spoke to mommy for a long time the same night that Tunde's parents visited. She agreed to go to therapy with me and we will raise Gbenga together."

Kofo squeezes her hand. "I'm thrilled to hear that."

Kofo and Eniola walk back to the meeting.

When they return, Morenike studies them both, breaking her rambling demands to the Master of Ceremony. "Are you two alright?"

They both nod and return to their seats while Morenike gets things done in a short amount of time, Lagos style.

CHAPTER 18

The next morning is a still morning—more still than usual. Tunde and Kofo drown out the sounds of okada bikes, the honks of cars stuck in traffic, and folks selling or haggling essential items during their previous mornings in Nigeria. The only audible sound is an enthusiastic rooster across the street.

Kofo lies on her back and stretches after hearing three rooster crows.

"Tunde." Tunde peels open his eyes. "It's time. We have to wake up."

He groans, ending a full night of sleep.

"Let's pray for a good wedding." Tunde dozes off and on as Kofo tugs at his arm. "Come on, babe."

Kofo slides off of the bed right onto the floor on her knees, resting on her forearms on the mattress. She opens her palms, inciting an Islamic prayer. Tunde follows suit, clasping his hands for a Christian prayer.

Tunde grins at his wife while she whispers a Kuli prayer in Arabic with her eyes closed. He does the same, listening as she conjures up the energy of God through her incantations.

"This is the first time I prayed in front of anyone outside of my family," Kofo says once she opens her eyes.

"Christ would be proud of your resurrection," Tunde says in a groggy voice.

They laugh and peck each other on the lips, resembling a married couple before a morning commute, or an arrival home for dinner.

Tunde begins his own version of a prayer in English, starting with Our Father.

***

Tunde dresses downstairs with his groomsmen and Kofo stays in her room upstairs to await the photographer and makeup artist. Fisayo straightened out her room and laid out her wedding attire on her bed while she got her makeup done. Uncle Bolaji's passive-aggressive olive branch through Fisayo satisfies her. Maybe he will welcome her back after all.

Eniola walks in with a royal blue dress holding Gbenga. Kunle tailored a matching baby agbada for her baby that draped his small body.

Kofo smiles at her adorable nephew, forcing the makeup artist to pause her elaborate contouring process. Kofo asked for correction on the foundation shade that is two shades too light for her skin tone, and gives Kofo's nose an unproportioned reduction. She initially looked unrecognizable and heavily masked, despite her insistence on a natural look.

Afropop music on Kofo's phone plays in the background while she charges its almost dead battery on her lap. Her WhatsApp goes off yet again, and she assumes it's another bridesmaid who running late, or on their way. It's actually from an unrecognizable number with a message that includes a video.

"Hi Sisi Kofo! Congratulations on your wedding today!" It's Jide and Ife in their fancy parlor making fancy videos for their half-sister. "We wish you long life, prosperity, and a happy married life. Please have a good morning and a wonderful wedding day. Bye-bye!" She hates how much they lower her defenses. If she were to have baby brothers, they fit perfectly. *How did they turn out so normal compared to her and Eniola? It feels unfair*, she reflects to herself.

Maybe that's why her father bailed. These thoughts rot her mood to the core—she didn't she get any acknowledgement of her wedding day from her father, likely because he probably won't show up on one of the biggest days of her life. Her vision of having her former hero walk her down the aisle, make a speech and do a reception dance is all dissolved. It's a sobering realization.

Eniola doesn't acknowledge the video and breaks her thoughts. "The bridesmaids are arriving. Do you want them to come in?" Eniola has a shaky relationship with self-confidence, but she is amazing at moving on with a show when backstage is in chaos.

"Have you heard from Daddy, Ennie?"

Her sister shakes her head no, making Kofo's face drop further.

"You can let the bridesmaids get dressed next door. Thank you, Ennie."

Eniola exits the room to fulfill Kofo's wish. Kofo watches the clip of her brothers again and frowns. The photographer fails at reading her vibe.

"I'm trying to capture you. Can you smile, please?"

Kofo puts down her phone and plasters an unconvincing smile. The picture will be a throwaway. Whatever photos preceded her brothers' message is her best bet.

She hears footsteps approaching her door and braces herself for more demonstrations of forced enthusiasm. Once she shifts in her seat to fully prepare, Mommy Bola and Sherifat from New York file in. They are in jewel-toned fuchsia traditional clothing with gold geles.

"Ayeee!!! Kofo!" they both scream, walking in circles around the bride.

"Hi," she responds, revealing her teeth.

"Fine, fine girl!" Sherifat walks over to Kofo's blue outfit. "Wait—is this a romper?!"

Kofo purposely hid it from these women to avoid this conversation. She wishes she remembered to tell Eniola to put it in an unoccupied room.

"Yes."

"Why would you want to wear pants on your wedding day?! That's like a bad omen for your marriage." Sherifat continues to inspect the train, oblivious to Kofo's disinterest in her opinion. The makeup artist finishes bringing her makeup back to something that resembles her face, and Kofo inspects it in the mirror, nodding.

"I love your makeup," Mommy Bola says.

"Thank you, Aunty Abidemi."

"I said you should call me Mommy Bola."

"I've been calling you Aunty for a long time, though."

Mommy Bola bends towards Kofo. "You know I am older than your mother, right?"

"I do, but what made you change your mind about how I should regard you?"

Mommy Bola leans back and shrugs, but her eyes look eager and show a desire to belong. She doesn't have any daughters, and took an aggressive level of interest in Kofo's wedding. Kofo will call her Mommy Bola if it's what she needs to feel recognized.

Sherifat breaks the ice between them. "Why are you down, Kofo? I saw you when you walked in. It's your wedding day!"

"I'm just tired."

"Pele, you'll get some sleep tonight."

Mommy Bola hums Ebenezer Obey's famous wedding day song, Eto Igbeyawo Medley, and breaks out into lyrics with the support of Sherifat.

Kofo spots Eniola walking in on them serenading her. It then dawns on Kofo that Uncle Bolaji made sure the air conditioner stays on in every room throughout the house. She prays he will allow her to pay his next electric bill as a token of gratitude.

Sherifat halts her singing. "I got you a gift, all the way from New York. Take it out so you can see."

Kofo pulls out a gold garter set with a sheer bra and thong. She snorts, breaking her static energy. This is the laugh she needed.

Sherifat leans in to share very obvious sexual tips. "Tunde will love this. Just make sure you twirl, then bend over so he can be fully ready for you. And make sure you wear stilettos to lift your bum so it's tight."

Kofo closes her eyes, chuckling. She wants to add to Sherifat's insights, but Mommy Bola might catch a stroke. "I probably should've opened this privately."

They all burst into laughter and Kofo leans in to give Sherifat a hug.

"Thank you."

Eniola is back on task. "Okay, Mommy and big sister… please, let's give Kofo some privacy. Sherifat, I need you to watch Gbenga for the day, I'll take you to the room where I have my pumped milk bottles—"

Mommy Bola wasn't having it. "No, wait! Let's do a prayer." She opens her palms and begins passionate incantations of Quranic prayers mixed in with Yoruba. After what feels like forever, Kofo opens her eyes to find Eniola. Her expression screams "help!"

"Okay, thank you very much, ma. Kofo is going to finish soon."

Mommy Bola is not done. "Let's see your shoes and your bags."

Kofo swallows and pauses while Mommy Bola and the other ladies seek her reply.

"Mommy Bola. I don't mean to be disrespectful, and I am happy to show it to you. But is there any way I can be alone after you view my shoes and my bag?"

Everyone in the room is taken aback, including the photographer and makeup artist.

Sherifat doesn't help by saying, "Kofo, you are being very rude."

Mommy Bola presses her mouth, letting out a quiet "humph," before she forms her next thought. "It's okay. I had my own wedding and I understand you. Show me your things and we'll leave."

Eniola grabs the dust bags with Kofo's requested items.

Mommy Bola blurts out, "Wait—where is Cedric?!"

Eniola tries her newfound courage again. "We broke up."

"Ah!!!" she yells, horrified. "What of your engagement Eniola?" Boundaries are not Mommy Bola's strong suit.

Kofo loves the discomfort her sister generates from her truth. Sherifat looks away at them all, avoiding any input.

"I am very excited to be an auntie soon."

Mommy Bola disregards Kofo, shaking her head in sympathy. "I'm so sorry Ennie."

"She has a mom and a sister that will help. Ennie will be fine." Kofo takes the dust bags from Eniola, revealing her luxurious accessories.

Sherifat catches on, helping them to ease up Mommy Bola's negative reaction to the news. "They are very nice, Kofo."

"Thank you," Kofo says in return.

***

Kofo's blue romper is fitted brilliantly with not a crease in sight on her silhouette. She shapes her natural twist out in a full-length mirror. Her massive eight-foot train releases an adornment of stones and gold detailing, cascading half of the room.

Morenike walks in, frenzied but immaculate in her jewel-toned fuchsia lace outfit. Kofo is glad that the makeup artist took notes from her session and applied Morenike's foundation properly.

"Ko-Fo! What are you doing?! Hurry up."

Kofo picks up and bunches her train, ignoring her mother, who refuses to breathe.

"I thought you were going to put the skirt I tailored for you over these pants?"

"I changed my mind."

"You need to change."

Kofo turns away from her mother. When faces the mirror, she finds her mother staring at her reflection. Kofo sees a jittery woman holding it together. She hates that for her mother, and Kofo fights her temptation to inherit those emotions. She fails. Her eyes water, unraveling the feelings they are stuffing down to outsiders with plastic smiles.

"Thank you for the suggestion, Mommy, but this is what I am wearing today."

A limo honks from Uncle Bolaji's driveway, interrupting their moment.

"I'll bring the skirt so you can change when we get to the venue."

"Have you heard from daddy?"

Morenike blinks, weary. "No, I haven't."

Kofo sniffles, worried that her makeup may bleed onto her dress.

"Your car is here. We need to go. Come on, Kofo."

"One second, I'm about to put on my shoes."

"Even Ennie is in the car, I don't understand—"

"Mommy. I said I'm coming."

Morenike invades Kofo's personal space to examine Kofo's puffy eyes while she completes putting on her shoes.

"What else do you have to carry? And you need Visine."

"That's the last thing I'm doing before I head out."

"Let me do it."

Morenike rummages through Kofo's cosmetics purse and applies the Visine. Kofo feels her mother's tense hands pressing her face.

Morenike creases her face at Kofo's hair. "Are they going to blow-dry that in the limo?"

"No."

Morenike rolls her eyes before Kofo leads the way out. She scurries behind her daughter, picking up the train when Kofo loses balance. They reach the stairs and Kofo reaches for her mother's hand. Morenike holds her tight and squeezes Kofo's palm. Kofo takes a deep breath in acknowledgement.

"Focus, Kofo. Focus," Morenike whispers to Kofo.

Kofo's limo SUV and Morenike's car were the only vehicles remaining on Uncle Bolaji's estate. They both hop inside of their respective rides. Kofo avoids looking at her mother one last time to prevent her need for another round of Visine.

"YAY KOFO!!!," all the bridesmaids scream, startling her as she climbs inside of the stretch limo. Multi-colored lights blind her, inspiring a club-like atmosphere.

Kofo removes her veil, giving the driest of smiles. For a flash of a second, she wishes Janelle was in that limo. Her professional skills would've soothed Kofo.

"Have you been crying?!" one drunk bridesmaid named Yemi, Maroof's younger sister, screams.

Kofo turns to face them, and they are all in shock at her puffy eyes. "My father isn't walking me down the aisle."

"Oh God no," Adebisi says and Abeni gapes her mouth open.

Yemi throws her hand up towards Eniola. "Ennie and your mom can do it!"

Eniola is next to Kofo and takes a softer, suggestive approach. "What do you think about that idea? You can lead us and we'll be behind you."

"I'll walk alone. Let me freshen up."

Eniola pulls out a cosmetics purse and peels off her high-heeled sandals.

"We gotta get you together right now." She cleans up Kofo's makeup.

***

They pull into the Central Lekki Mosque just in time. Kofo isn't one hundred percent, but she is in better shape. The bridesmaids get out first and swarm Kofo, ensuring that she looks her best and not a tear is in sight.

Guests file in with their best tailor-made lace designs. Daddies, Uncles and brothers present the best of Nigerian fashion with regal agbadas. Mommies, Aunties and sisters are wearing a mix of iro wrappers and buba blouses, or custom-made dresses. Kofo's family is a collective of fuchsia and Tunde's side is a sea of orange fabric.

Morenike stands by while she entertains an excited Busayo and Temitayo.

"Look at the beautiful bride!!!", they both exclaim once they spot Kofo.

"I love your pantsuit. It's so unique and elegant!" Busayo gushes with Temitayo nodding close by.

They rush Kofo with aggressive enthusiasm and Morenike watches in surprise at their reactions to Kofo's ensemble. She has the skirt from Kunle's shop inside of her car, but she decides she won't need it. When the mommies file inside, she charges Kofo, whispering in her ear.

"Ennie and I will walk with you."

"It's okay. I got it—"

"No. Let us walk with you."

"Ok...ok."

Kofo moves inside with her mom while Eniola holds the train.

***

The guests rise with some taking photos and videos as Kofo makes her way down the aisle. Her mother and sister interlock both of her arms. Kofo gazes towards Tunde at the altar and the Imam, who recites an acapella call to prayer that rings throughout the large mosque. His melodic voice soothes Kofo. She sees Tunde smiling as her steps progress in his direction. Morenike and Eniola swiftly move to their positions once she reaches Tunde.

Kofo spots Tunde's parents in her peripheral view and they exchange smiles. Morenike sits next to an empty chair over her fiancé's shoulder.

"As Salaam Alaykum, Adebayo and Bakare families," the Imam greets the crowd through a loud microphone.

"Wa-Alaykum-Salaam," the crowd choruses.

The Imam continues, but Kofo focuses on her mother trying to hold her head high, hoping her father slides into the seat next to her Morenike before the ceremony is over.

Halfway into the ceremony, Kofo's bowed head sees a pair of shoes at her father's seat. She looks through the corner of her eye and she can't raise her head suddenly, but the mystery is eating her. The shoes are Italian snakeskin leather with a patent finish. Not Akeem's style at all.

"Before we exchange the rings," the Imam continues, "let's have Pastor Folarin share some words with us."

The Italian shoes move in her direction. She looks up to confirm her excitement is a false alarm, and indeed it is.

By the time Pastor Folarin finishes, she hears Tunde's "in Jesus name, Amen" elicit a ruckus of laughter in the audience. An abrupt, passionate kiss from Tunde follows. It doesn't alter desire to see her father.

Kofo, get it together, she scolds to herself.

"I present to you, Mr. and Mrs. Bakare!" the Imam boasts, followed by cheers and loud whistles from the crowd.

***

The guests rush outside of the door to capture Tunde and Kofo filing out with the bridal party on their smartphones. The attention overwhelms her, making Kofo more self-conscious about her family's imperfections.

"Kofo! Look, this way!" Mommy Bola shouts.

"Smile!" Sherifat commands while flashing before Kofo could maintain a pose. Several other guests follow suit, their phones feeling like jabs when Kofo hears the snapping sound from their devices. She remains in place with Tunde as they capture the couple from every angle.

As Kofo steps into her limo, Sherifat creeps over to the door while holding a sleeping Gbenga.

"Where is Daddy?"

"He's coming."

"Do you want me to find out for you?"

"No, please. It's okay."

Sherifat nods with strange familiarity before walking off.

Kofo gives a loud, tired sigh once her bottom hits the limo cushion. Tunde studies her face for several moments.

"He's really not coming?"

"Tunde, I don't know."

"I'm sorry."

Kofo is quiet. There is nothing else to say.

"You are a beautiful bride."

"Thanks babe," she whispers.

Tunde takes her hand and squeezes it the same way her mother did earlier. Her shoulders sink as she melts into his torso.

"He could've at least showed up for the ceremony, Tunde."

"The day isn't over yet."

Tunde lifts her chin for a soft, comforting peck on her lips.

"Don't stress. Please."

"I'm trying," Kofo replies.

***

Tunde leans in for another kiss as they pull up to The Monarch Event Center, but a loud knock at the window interrupts him. He groans, his opportunity to calm Kofo down ruined. It's Sherifat again.

"Damn, what does she want?" Kofo murmurs before Tunde puts the window down.

"Kofo, you need to come out so you can walk in with your daddy," Sherifat orders.

"He's not here."

"Yes, he is. Look."

Sherifat points to the spectacle at the venue entrance about twenty feet away. Akeem, Yinka and their sons attempt to walk through the reception venue door. Yinka somehow gained access to the same pink fabric as the Adebayo mommies. Morenike blocks their path while others walk in. Indistinguishable Mommies try to ease her rage to no avail, including Mommy Bola.

"How is she wearing this fabric?!" Morenike shouts.

Mommy Bola gets in front of her. "Nike, that's enough."

"No!"

Akeem steps towards her as she guards the door. "Let me in, Nike."

"Get out!" she screams.

Kofo tries all she could to not feel her mother's pain and embarrassment. A pit in her stomach develops. Kofo is glad that Eniola decided to breastfeed Gbenga at a nearby hotel with the rest of the bridal party.

Tunde attempts to put up the window, but Kofo removes his hand from the button, stopping him. She needs more proof that Akeem is done with her family.

Morenike provides more insight. "How dare you bring this trash to your daughter's wedding?!"

"She is also my wife! You are saying this in front of our children!"

"If you didn't want them to know who you really are, you should've kept them at home!"

"I paid for this. I belong here!"

Yinka squares up and holds her children tight. "May we get in, please?"

Morenike pieces into her soul with a lethal glance. "Why are you talking? I should bash your head in two! Don't even look at me!" Yinka shrinks from the fury of Morenike. Morenike cannot sustain her anger—she has trouble breathing and Mommy Bola pulls her aside. Akeem and his family weasel through with some resistance. Murmurs circulate from everyone waiting outside and some guests indoors stretch their necks to inquire about what they just overheard.

Kofo closes the car window, slumping in her seat.

CHAPTER 19

The MC of the wedding is on a roll, building one joke after another.

"Before any of you in the crowd finds your next conquest tonight, let's bring in the wedding parties today, starting with the daddies led by Alhaji Akeem Sijuwola Adebayo, and Olumide Francis Bakare!"

The senior fathers in the family proceed down the reception aisle, with Akeem in the front alongside Tunde's father. They are tolerant of each other while grooving to Sunny Ade's record Appreciation. Tunde watches his dad demonstrate the maturity he hopes to develop over time from the car with Kofo.

"Now, the mommies, led by Alhaja Kadijat Morenike Adebayo and Adepeju Carol Bakare!"

Morenike is smug and proud as she whines her waist down the aisle to Sunny Ade's Merciful God with the other mommies backing her up. Yinka attempts to join, but she inspects Morenike look of disdain, and steps to the side as a spectating guest.

After the bridal parties do their processions, Tunde and Kofo hop out of the limo in traditional asoke and lace. It's flashy, glitzy and best of all, blue.

The MC doesn't skip a beat. "Mommies, Daddies, Ladies, gentlemen—please welcome the groom Babatunde Elijah Bakare and the bride Zeenat Kofoworola Adebayo-Bakare!"

Kofo and Tunde enter to a mix of various AfriPop songs with hundreds of guests ogling at the elaborate sequins, stones, and mesh webbing around their expensive fabric. Some attendees block the aisle for their second round of photos, prompting security to intervene.

The spotlight of this magnitude still overwhelms Kofo. The guests, who are mostly here on behalf of her family, care enough to spend money, dress up and watch a couple they barely know celebrate a pivotal moment in their relationship. She's been to weddings like this before, but never made the connection on how impersonal it feels. Kofo appreciates the support, but the scene she just witnessed from her parents makes it hard to accept her wedding with open arms. Most of the people in the venue believed in the myth of a cohesive Adebayo family unit until today.

She makes it to the elevated stage and drops into her high chair next to Tunde.

"Babe, let's eat." she grumbles.

***

Morenike eats a small plate of food to avoid spilling out of her dress and staying off guard with her husband turned arch-enemy sitting next to her. Yinka walks over to give Akeem a handkerchief while their house girl attends to the children.

"Sit." Akeem pats a chair next to him opposite Morenike and Yinka takes the seat.

The MC taps his microphone, preventing another outburst from Morenike or Akeem.

"We've completed all the dances. Thank you so much for showing us your skills! Let's begin the speeches," the MC yells into the microphone with enthusiasm.

The crowd half-listens as they inhale their traditional dishes.

"Mrs. Bakare declined to give a speech, so Mrs. Adebayo said she will speak on behalf of all parents. Are you ready Mrs. Adebayo?"

Morenike nods at the MC, rises, and takes the mic.

"As Salaam-Alaykum," she says in a steady tone to the crowd.

"Wa-Alaykum-Salaam," they say in return.

Kofo smiles as she watches Tunde's Christian parents take part in the Islamic greeting with the crowd.

"Thank you all for showing up to our family's wedding. I know we had a lot of changes throughout this entire process, but I am thankful to be a part of a community that is so understanding and accommodating."

The crowd eats up her compliments, responding with "Amin."

"My darling daughter Kofo… I'm so excited about your journey to marriage. I know you will rise to the challenge and adapt accordingly. Tunde—take care of my daughter. She will stand up to you if you don't."

One server hands Morenike a toasting glass of carbonated cider as she keeps her eye on Kofo. "When I first met Tunde, I observed him carefully, like I do with anyone that expresses an interest in my girls. But Kofo told me how much she finally felt appreciated by a man from our cultural background. I see how attentive and protective he is over your feelings, and he always does whatever is necessary to keep you happy. He helps to ease any conflicts or issues that you have and I like that. I know you both love each other dearly." Morenike raises her glass. "So, Kofo, Tunde… make sure you always remain committed to each other. I am excited to have our families become a unified front, and I am sure it will bear much fruit. And remember… I am your only mother on the Adebayo side. Call me if you need anything on our behalf."

Morenike inhales her drink while the crowd erupts in cheers, clicking glasses everywhere. Eniola stands up at the bridesmaid table, clapping in excitement at her mother with Gbenga in a carrier by her side.

After dropping her finished cup on another tray passing by, Morenike walks back to her table, staring with hostility at Akeem and Yinka.

"Wow… that is what you call a mic drop moment," the MC declares over the loud applause. Kofo nods as she eats a pile of party jollof rice.

Akeem nods at Yinka. She gets up from her seat.

"Oh—it looks like we have…," the MC takes a step back, aware of the tension.

Yinka makes her way next to him. "Another mommy to speak to the newlywed couple," Yinka gushes into the microphone.

"Well, what do you have for us? And what is your name?" he asks.

Before Yinka begins, Kofo creeps up on them, grabbing the mic from the MC. She turns to Yinka, drenched in sweat from the spices in the fish she gorged on moments ago.

"Hi." Kofo says with sarcasm to Yinka while giving a "fuck you" smile. Tunde watches his wife in horror, mixed with admiration.

"Yinka—thank you so much for attending my wedding today. Unfortunately, there is not much time in our program to accommodate any newly discovered, practically unknown, members of our family. Would you mind taking a seat so we can move to the next item on our program, please?" Kofo blinks to emphasize her rigid stance.

The MC attempts to ease their internal drama. "Um, it looks like the bride is a jokester like me, right?!"

Kofo gives him a high five while squinting at Yinka, channeling her nice-nasty energy she learned from Katie at work. The audience hushes to a standstill. Kofo nods, patting her face with a napkin from a server. Tunde keeps his eye on his wife while munching on ewedu vegetables, beef stew and amala swallow topped with gbegiri bean sauce.

This form of messiness from the Adebayos is a shock to many in the crowd. Uncle Bolaji smirks under his breath next to Kafayat. Mommy Bola shakes her head as though she just got news of a tragedy. Maroof and his mother exchange looks of surprise. Tunde's family members lower their heads, embarrassed for the Adebayos. Jide grins right next to the bar, nodding his head with pride.

Kofo saunters over to her mother and gives her a tight hug. "Thank you. Thank you so much," she says, taunting her father and Yinka. "Mommy—your beautiful speech moved me. I love you. Thank you all for coming today and I hope you have a great time." Kofo hands the mic to the MC and strolls back to her high chair.

Akeem and Yinka spend the remainder of the event in their seats with a few fans reassuring them of Kofo's disrespect. Morenike glows from the praise of her peers and Eniola curves questions about Cedric, encouraging wedding guests to admire her baby instead.

Kofo and Tunde finish their delicious meals and the crowd sprays them as they occupy the dance floor throughout the reception, refusing to engage in any family-related politics for the rest of the day.

CHAPTER 20

Kofo turns off her monitor after viewing an episode of "Insecure" in a business class aisle seat while Tunde sleeps next to her on their flight home. She's glad her mom and sister agreed to upgrade their seats from the economy. They can use the extra cash from Akeem for short-term comforts.

She turns to Eniola and her mother across the aisle on her opposite side.

"I'm gonna pee, Kofo. Can you watch Gbenga?" Eniola whispers.

She nods as Eniola carefully hands over her son to join the long line of flyers who avoided the airport bathrooms back in Nigeria.

Kofo slides into Eniola's seat.

Morenike sips on a cup of English Breakfast tea with biscuits. Kofo tried to get into her mother's British-inspired mid-day snack, but coffee is more aligned with her preference for hot drinks.

"Mommy," Kofo says. Morenike continues sipping her tea. "I'm sorry you had to go through everything in Nigeria. When we arrive back in New York, I want to start with a clean slate so our relationship can improve."

Morenike allows the tension to thicken further with her silence. "Okay," she says after a long pause.

"We need to act like an actual family."

"This is what it's like for many families."

Kofo lets her mother's comment sink in by looking down at both of their wedding rings.

"I want something different for Tunde and I."

"You will get it. But stop repeating my mistakes."

"What?"

"Make sure you have a secret account on the side in case."

Kofo lifts her eyebrows, unsure if she agrees with her mother's advice.

"I found out about Professor Schultz's sister."

"I'm surprised you didn't sooner." Morenike takes another small sip of her mocha-colored tea.

"It's the reason why I agreed to this trip."

"That makes sense."

Another pause passes.

"You can also keep my cut of the money. I'll figure something out when we have enough saved to move out of the condo."

Morenike takes her last sip. "Don't be stupid." She wipes crumbs and extra tea from her upper lip with a napkin. "Let's start a business."

Kofo giggles and waits for her mother to laugh out loud at what she believes is a joke.

"You want us to be business partners?"

"I suppose. We'll discuss it when we get settled back home. I'll handle all legal matters and contracts with Ennie, depending on what we decide to do. You can work your marketing skills to promote our business. We can help African women with their legal needs."

"Wow... I actually love that idea."

Morenike gives her a tired smile.

Kofo follows her gut instincts, still thrown off by her mother's proposition. "Uh... sure."

Morenike clears her throat to signal Eniola's return. She lifts her feet up with the reclining business class chair and closes her eyes.

"Great. I'm resting now."

Lande Yoosuf

ABOUT THE AUTHOR

Lande Yoosuf is a Nigerian-American novelist, Huffington Post blogger, screenwriter, filmmaker, and cofounder of the non-profit organization Black Film Space. She has 15 years of production, development, and casting experience in non-fiction programming, and has worked with several networks, including MTV, A&E Networks, NBC, WEtv, and Bravo. Her short film, "Privilege Unhinged", screened at the Martha's Vineyard African American Film Festival, Big Apple Film Festival, the DC Black Film Festival, aired on AMC's Shorts TV and was a finalist for "Insecure" star Jean Elie's short film contest under his company banner, Bassett House.

Yoosuf's second film, "Second Generation Wedding" screened at the Bronze Lens Film Festival, Black Girls Rock! Film Festival, and inspired the novel, "Ko-Foe." She has an affinity for telling stories that explore media influence, sociology, gender/race relations, pop culture and self-image themes. Lande is currently developing a mixed slate of feature films, documentaries and television pilots through her production company, One Scribe Media.

Yoosuf directed Antu Yacob's dramatic short film "Love in Submission", which screened at the Afrikana Film Festival,

Noire Film Festival, and the New York African Film Festival. The film was accepted into the "Emerging Black Filmmaker Film Collection", screened in over 60 theaters throughout the country, and was part of a diversity case study discussion about Hollywood at the 2021 Sundance Film Festival.

As Co-founder and Partnerships Director of Black Film Space, Lande works to contribute to expanded control, ownership, and media management for content creators of African descent across all cinematic formats and content platforms. She served as a host, workshop facilitator, speaker, and moderator for events with organizations like ARRAY, HBO, ABFF, BAM's New Voices in Black Cinema, The Root, and many others. Her speaking engagements received coverage from outlets such as The New York Times.

Lande earned a Bachelor of Arts from Brooklyn College in Television and Radio and honed her writing skills through classes taught by Jackson Taylor, the Associate Director at The New School's Graduate Writing Program. In her spare time, she loves to sing, read, travel, and spend time with her loved ones. She reps her Nigerian background proudly and holds down her hometown, the world-famous republic of Brooklyn, New York.

Stay In touch with Lande @LandeYoosuf and @OneScribeMedia on all social media platforms, or through her website www.onescribemedia.com.

Learn more about Lande's non-profit organization Black Film Space through the handle @Blackfilmspace, or at www.blackfilmspace.com.

Made in the USA
Middletown, DE
12 March 2023